A badman makes good when Butch Cassidy finds out one of his Wild Bunch stole the funds for a new school in **Barbara Barton**'s "The Outlaw and the School Marm."

In "Short Rope" by **T. L. Davis**, the hunter becomes the hunted when Jack Slade is condemned to execution by the Vigilance Committee he once rode with.

Shakespearean actor John Wilkes Booth is the second gunman in **Pat Decker Kines**'s intriguing story, "Who *Really* Killed President Lincoln?"

And eleven more tales of . . .

Black Hats

BLACK HATS

★

EDITED BY

ROBERT J. RANDISI

BERKLEY BOOKS, NEW YORK

This book is a work of fiction. Names, characters, places,
and incidents either are the product of the author's imagination or are
used fictitiously, and any resemblance to actual persons, living or dead,
business establishments, events, or locales is entirely coincidental.

BLACK HATS

A Berkley Book / published by arrangement with
the editor

PRINTING HISTORY
Berkley edition / April 2003

ISBN: 0-425-18708-X

BERKLEY®
Berkley Books are published by The Berkley Publishing Group,
a division of Penguin Putnam Inc.,
375 Hudson Street, New York, New York 10014.
BERKLEY and the "B" design
are trademarks belonging to Penguin Putnam Inc.

PRINTED IN THE UNITED STATES OF AMERICA

10 9 8 7 6 5 4 3 2 1

CONTENTS

★

INTRODUCTION

★

Any actor worth his salt will tell you it's more fun to play the bad guy. Just look at the fun Richard Boone had playing the villain in both *Big Jake* and *Hombre*, only to go on and be good guy Paladin in *Have Gun Will Travel* (although Paladin did wear a black hat—and everything else!) and later *Hec Ramsey*. And how about Gene Hackman in *Unforgiven* and *The Quick and the Dead*, chewin' up the scenery?

Well, I don't know if writers feel the same way. Is it more fun to write bad guys than good guys? I guess you'll have to ask them when you go to their book signings for this anthology. (You will support us by going to book signings, won't you? I thought so.)

In this second volume of Hats stories—following the success of *White Hats* (2001)—we have legends like Matt Braun and Donald Hamilton writing about the likes of Sam Bass and Wild Bill Longley. Novelists like Ed Gorman, Ken Hodgson, and—well—me, try our hands at some bad guys like Henry Starr, Harry Orchard, and Henry Plummer. And recent Spur winner Troy Smith spins a tale about Native American Black Hat Ned Christie.

There are fourteen stories in all, a good number of them written by authors you won't immediately know but will come to know if they keep writing stories this good. Also there are some Black Hats we can't identify for you ahead of time, because their identities are not immediately revealed in the stories. Makes it kind of fun when their names do pop up.

And you'll recognize Rod Miller and Lori Van Pelt from their appearances in *White Hats*. They are the only two authors to appear in both anthologies, the reasons for which are explained in the head notes of their stories.

It was a pleasure to put these two Hats collections together for you. I dealt with authors who knew their business, did their research, and produced stories of high quality. We have all benefited from this—some of us even got paid—and now you reap the final reward by getting to read these gems. Lucky you!

Robert J. Randisi
St. Louis, September 27, 2001

The Outlaw and the School Marm

BARBARA BARTON

Barbara Barton writes historical fiction for *True West Magazine* and the NOLA Magazine. She has also self published several books of regional history, *Ruckus Along the Rivers; Head 'Em Up, Move 'Em Out;* and *Den of Outlaws.* This is her first attempt at short fiction, with admirable results, I think. I won't reveal here who her Black Hat is. That would spoil part of the story. Enjoy.

★

Young Billy Trueblood's eyes nearly bugged out of their sockets as he watched Jim Barlow and his horse put on a one-man rodeo. Jim cut a bawling calf out of the herd with just the sway of his horse's body. Then that horse's ears pinned back on his head as he drove the calf away from the herd.

A few days earlier, Billy had watched an old outlaw cow pitch her tail toward the moon and streak toward the thick brush country. She was gone for sure, but Jim made a beeline toward the direction of her flight and soon unearthed the cantankerous bitty. Barlow had her plodding back to the herd in no time.

"How did you do that?" asked Billy one day as Jim separated a half-grown calf for the cook to butcher. He was a hefty steer with horns long enough to hang clothes on.

"Well, you watch that steer's beady eyes. Your horse is lined up with his head. If he jabs that way, you counter with a move the same way. Kind of wears the heart out of that Mr. T-bone after a while," Jim said with a careless shrug. Billy grinned because he knew it took a lot of hours astraddle a horse to make those moves.

Roundup in the spring of 1901 moved right along for the J Bar outfit in Montana. Greenhorns like Billy had the help of older, more experienced cowboys like Jim and his friends who showed these teenagers how to throw a rope and drag a cow out of a mud hole, or how to hold a calf while the branding irons scorched their hide.

Barlow and his four grizzled friends had just ridden up one day to the chuck wagon. None of the J Bar hands had ever laid eyes on them before. The new cowboys said they planned to sink some money in the nearby copper mines of Montana but needed a little stake before they tried their hand at the business. Being shorthanded and in the middle of roundup, the foreman hired all five right there on the spot.

Billy also noticed that Jim Barlow liked to entertain the cowhands with his trick horse. One time after a hard day of branding, the men were resting. Some stood by the coffeepot steaming over red coals, and others stretched out on the ground, resting, their saddles serving as pillows.

Jim sauntered toward the camp that afternoon, leading his white trick horse. He could flick his hat and the horse would bow, roll over, or paw his front foot as if he were counting. Young cowboys would dare Jim that the horse could not give the sum of two plus three. Jim proceeded to call out the two numbers, and the white pony pawed just the right number of times to show the sum.

Once, the herd was bedded near the town of Bluffdale. Jim decided to have some fun, so he persuaded his friends to go into town with him. Of course the white horse went also. At the Red Horn Saloon, Jim belted a few drinks and started a conversation with a man named Tom. He bet this cowboy that he could make his white horse roll over just by waving his hat.

Other cowboys shoved close to the bar and wanted to get into the action. Jim let young Billy keep track of the bets by taking their money. When everybody had a chance to bet for or against the trick horse, Jim proceeded out the saloon door and stood in front of the horse to give him a command. Just at the right moment, he motioned with his hat, and the horse rolled over. Most of the crowd clapped in praise, but a few men angrily grabbed Jim. "You're as bad as those men selling medicine," declared one man. "They said the stuff in the black bottle would cure what ailed you, but it didn't. You said this horse reacted to hat waving, but I saw that tiny wire you used to tickle the horse."

Jim Barlow shook his head in denial and turned toward the horse to do another trick. Instead of watching him, the crowd grew noisy. "Give me back my money," said another character.

"Leave Barlow alone. I want to see another trick, " said one young cowboy. Men began to shove each other, and tempers flared. Jim's friends quietly grabbed the money from Billy and mounted their horses. One angry man lowered his pistol at Jim. Just as Barlow swung into his saddle, he whirled around and shot the gun out of the man's hand.

"Let's head to the chuck wagon," cried Jim, and the cowboys left in a cloud of dust. They did not slow down until Bluffdale was out of their sight. Around the campfire that night, Barlow and his friends arranged their bedrolls so they could see anybody coming down the trail from Bluffdale, but no money-seeking strangers appeared that night in camp to reclaim their cash. Jim Barlow decided that trouble was over, but just to be on the safe side, he and his boys worked quietly and kept a watch toward the horizon.

All the cowboys drug out of their bedrolls the next few mornings with a grudge against the coming sunrise. The herd, stampeding after a lightning storm, kept all the cowboys occupied more than they wanted to be.

If Billy and his friend who were on watch the night of the storm had asked for help when they saw the first lead steer make a break, the stampede might have been smaller. However, the two young men thought they could handle the cows when they became excited over the flashes of lightning and began to mill about. By the time Billy woke up the whole camp, the herd was on their way toward the nearest mountains, five miles away.

The next days were spent collecting little bunches of three or four animal from where they had become isolated by the storm. Driving a few at a time back to the chuck wagon took most of two days. Billy felt he was the cause of the whole incident and was so dejected that he would hardly come to the campfire to eat until all the rest of the men finished scraping the last bite from their tin plates.

However, Barlow was one man who tried to talk to young Billy. He said, "The old cows would have taken off with their tails flying no matter who was on night call. Don't let this stampede worry you, 'cause you're gonna make a good cowhand." When the roundup ended, Barlow and his men drew their pay; Jim told Billy and the other cowhands good-bye, although Billy wanted to ride along the same trail as Barlow did.

Finally, Jim Barlow convinced the youn'un that he could not go with him. The real reason for his attitude was that Jim Barlow and his friends had other fish to fry. Fish that would be better fried without Billy and the other cowhands knowing their real identity. (By the way, their destination was not the Montana copper mines.)

BUTCH CASSIDY HAD his .45s aimed at the train engineer while his eyes flitted from the scared trainman to the action along the track. Will Carver and Ben Kilpatrick entered the mail car with dynamite in hand. A loud "boom" told everybody that one more train safe had lost its usefulness.

Butch Cassidy, alias Jim Barlow, and his gang were in action once more. The cowboy job at the J Bar Ranch was temporary employment for five men who normally made their living by more devious means. Harvey Logan and Flatnose moved from one seat to another of the train demanding valuables. The outlaws found that people released cash without too much pain, but wedding bands were harder to extract. Flatnose barked at one matronly lady, "Woman, hand over that purse," as he made a pass at it.

The well-dressed lady jerked it from his grasp and said, "Young man, mind your manners. This purse isn't yours."

Flatnose snarled, "Give it here!" She whammed him up the side of the head with the purse, but he reached out with his huge hand, closed it around her little wrist, and extracted the purse from her grasp. Her expression was that of defiance.

"Let's see what we have here," snarled Flatnose. As he dug into the purse he found an envelope filled with cash. "Whoopee, we've hit pay dirt," the outlaw yelled.

"Give that to me," she demanded. "Those funds are reserved to build a school in Wellington. I am the schoolteacher who will oversee the job." Flatnose chuckled as he threw the black shiny purse into the woman's lap but kept the money. Her anger and English accent made her words garbled to Flatnose. Laughing, he made his way down the aisle getting trinkets and money from the other passengers.

"Farewell, you good citizens," Flatnose mocked as he saluted and bounced out the train door. Butch jumped on his horse and motioned for the gang to leave the train. He headed straight in the night to the Hole-in-the-Wall. This was a remote hideout known to few people. The surrounding hills and rock formations made it an excellent place for Butch's men to hide themselves from the law. Butch Cassidy and four men on horseback slithered through this narrow opening in the red rock. On either side, steep cliffs towered over the outlaws as they passed into their sanctuary. Posses would look for them, but few lawmen would venture inside the sheer walls of this fortress. Lawmen knew that lookouts were posted on the rocks above them and would bombard anyone below with bullets.

When the outlaws reached their campground, the gang jumped off their horses and turned them into the pole corral. The stream bubbled through part of the enclosure and the lathered horses went for the water. They nuzzled the cool drink as the foamy sweat cooled and caked onto their sides.

Will Carver poked some sticks into the bed of coals. A

whip of his hat fanned the reddening sticks into a flickering flame. The coffeepot, black with soot, soon came to life as steam left the spout.

"Bring your saddlebags near the fire," ordered Butch. "We'll see what kind of haul we made." As the dawn slowly appeared over the canyon wall, Harvey Logan called out his take, followed by Butch, Flatnose, Will Carver, and Ben Kilpatrick. While the men counted their money, Flatnose relived his encounter with the School Marm.

"She said the money was for a school in Wellington," mimicked Flatnose in a squeaky, high voice.

"Maybe she was starting her own whorehouse," suggested Will. The men laughed at this. Each man related an incident where they had openly confronted a person on a train.

"I took money off a gambler once. We'd played against each other before. Didn't bother me a bit to take his cash when I remembered how much he'd won off of me," said Ben Kilpatrick. Butch listened to the banter back and forth.

He finally interrupted to ask Flatnose, "Did she say the money went to a school?"

"Yeah, that's what the English woman said."

Butch asked another question pointed to Flatnose. "And how much did you take from her?"

"Two thousand. What do you care?"

Butch's voice turned angry as he said, "Two thousand is what each of us made tonight. How about you giving your part back to her?"

"Not till hell freezes over," said Flatnose. "That's my money." He stomped off in the direction of his horse. Will moved quietly to intercept Flatnose, grabbed him by the shoulder, and popped him on the jaw with his tightened fist. Flatnose reeled backward. Six-foot Ben Kilpatrick took Flatnose's side of the argument and gave Will a punch to the stomach. Will was too short to outwit Ben, also known as the Tall Texan, but Harvey jumped in and defended Will. Fists were swinging right and left. Before long, more men were groaning on the ground than on their feet still swinging. Noses were bloody, shirts ripped, and moans sounded everywhere.

Butch looked on with disgust. He walked away but yelled over his shoulder, "You have just battled to a draw. I see that most of you would rather fight than help a little old School Marm." He saddled his dun and rode out of the hideout, never looking back.

Butch took the road to Wellington, knowing that the posse was on the lookout for him and his gang, the Wild Bunch. When the sun was beaming down from straight overhead, Butch was still riding. He turned in the saddle to look backward, and saw a cloud of dust. Cassidy angled his dun toward a clump of trees. The posse yelled out as they recognized his cream-colored horse. Butch cursed himself by thinking, *Why didn't I change mounts before I rode off in disgust?*

As the posse slapped leather, they strained to narrow the distance between themselves and the dun. Cassidy tried to get a little more speed out of his exhausted horse. Then he wondered why he had wanted to talk to the schoolteacher in the first place. *This riding on a mission for a school marm isn't such a good idea,* he decided.

Looking for a way out of his dilemma, Butch decided he must leave the road. The posse filled the air with lead. Cassidy heard a bullet fly by his head that nearly notched his ear. Suddenly the dun rounded a curve in the road and met several wagonloads of copper-mining tools, each wagon pulled by a team of eight mules. The dust was suffocating and blinded Cassidy. *Hey,* he thought. *Maybe the posse can't see either.*

Butch dove into a thicket of trees and hid himself in some thick underbrush. A rocky ledge concealed him on one side, and the bushy trees hid him on the other. He heard the posse yelling at each other. They milled about close enough he could have poked one with a tree limb. Cassidy was afraid to breathe and remained motionless in his hidden location.

For twenty minutes, he stayed in his hiding place. Finally Butch could no longer hear the lawmen, so he eased the nose of the dun out into the clearing. No whoops or gunfire ensued. He was safe. As crazy as it seemed, he spurred the horse toward Wellington, even though Butch knew the posse was ahead of him going to the same town. Wellington was where the schoolteacher lived, and Wellington was where he was going.

After riding a few more miles, Butch reined the dun in at a high point on a hill outside of town. He could see the main street from this location. Two saloons were situated across from each other. A mercantile was the first building on the right. *What can I do to find the schoolteacher?* he wondered. The posse knew his horse, so he hid the dun in a thicket of trees as near town as he dared.

As Butch looked closely down Main Street, he saw a bicycle propped against a backyard fence of a house at the edge of town. That was a vehicle he could navigate. While resting between robberies, he had previously enjoyed a bicycle in camp. Now he would use one for a good purpose; he wanted to find the School Marm. From his saddlebags, Butch pulled out his derby hat and dusted it off. In his mind's eye, he could see himself wearing this hat when

five members of his gang had joined him in making the famous Wild Bunch photo in Fort Worth a few months before. He had been dressed in a suit and white shirt then.
Now his riding clothes would have to do for a suit, but he
removed the chaps and holster. After stuffing his pistol into
his britches, he could look the part of a real tenderfoot as
he rode the bicycle with the black derby sitting smartly on
his head, provided he got the bicycle.

Butch sauntered along behind the houses, walking
slowly until he reached the bike. He hopped on it and rode
away quickly. A livery stable appeared on the left. He got
off the bike and walked along, holding the handlebars. As
he peered into the barn, he saw men unsaddling their
horses. They were the posse, no doubt. Butch withdrew
quickly from the barn, hopped on his bike, and circled to
the mercantile store. He parked the bike and went inside.

Butch asked directions to the school marm's house and
was told how to find the white house with red flower boxes
in the windows. After locating the structure, Butch parked
the bicycle nearby and politely knocked on the door. Margaret Donovan opened the door and had a puzzled look on
her face.

"Who are you, young man?" she said.

"I understand you had a bad turn of events happen yesterday on the train," Butch said.

"How do you know? Were you there?"

Butch shook his head "No," and threw up his hands in
defense and smiled. He said, "Let me just say I overheard
some men joking about how they took you to a cleaning on
the train. I'm so sorry that I want to make amends."

Margaret retorted, "How do you know so much? Are
you one of them?"

Calmly he replied, "No, Ma'am. I want to help you. How much did they take?"

"Two thousand," she replied. "That money was hard to come by."

Butch pulled his complete share of two thousand from his pocket, grabbed her hand with his other one, and placed the money into it.

"There's your cash. Build that school." He turned on his heels and walked out the door. As he moved quickly out the gate, he nearly bumped into Billy, whom he had ridden with at the J Bar.

"Is that you, Jim Barlow?" asked Billy.

"Yeah. How've you been?" answered Butch. He went on talking with the boy a minute and found that Margaret was the boy's aunt. Cassidy bid him a good day and left.

When Billy got into the house, he handed the *Laramie Weekly* to his aunt. They were both surprised to see the picture of the Wild Bunch on the front page.

Margaret said, as she excitedly pointed to the picture, "That man there is the one who gave me back my money. It says here his name is Butch Cassidy." Billy did not know how he was going to explain to his aunt that he had worked all spring with this crook. Before he tried to think this through, his aunt said, "Oh well, God works in mysterious ways. At least I got the school's money back." Billy decided that Cassidy was as good a crook as he was a cowboy, and that he never would tell his aunt the whole story of his spring in camp with Jim Barlow or whoever he was.

The Road to Hell

MATT BRAUN

If anyone in this book *doesn't* need an introduction to Western readers, it's Matt Braun. Already a legend in this business, he has recently added several new novels to his prolific career output, including *Hickok and Cody* and *Doc Holliday*, both from St. Martin's Press. Matt's books often feature historical figures of the West, both White Hats and Black Hats. This story is actually his only short story, and I'm pleased that it both fit our format perfectly, and that Matt allowed me to reprint it.

★

The sun dipped lower, splashing great ripples of gold across the water. Overhead a hawk veered slowly into the wind and settled high on a cottonwood beside the stream. The bird sat perfectly still, a feathered sculpture, flecked through with bronzed ebony in the deepening sunlight. Then it cocked its head in a fierce glare and looked down upon the intruders.

There were five men: lean and hard, weathered by wind and sun, all of them scorched the burnt mahogany of ancient saddle leather. Their faces glistened with sweat as they wrestled a stout log onto their shoulders, lifted it high, and jammed the butt end into the freshly dug hole. Small rocks and dirt were then tamped down solidly around the log until it stood anchored to the earth as if set in stone. This was the last in a rough circle of wooden pillars embedded in the flinty soil. The men stood back a moment, breathing hard, and inspected their handiwork with a critical eye.

One of them, somewhat older than the others, pulled out a filthy bandanna and mopped his brow. "Jest might hold 'em. If we get lucky."

The man next to him squirted a post with tobacco juice. "Who you funnin', Ben? A goddamn grizzle bear with dynamite in both fists couldn't move them logs."

"That a fact? You ever seen a bunch of mustangs when they was spooked?"

"What the sam hill's that got to do with anything? They're just critters. Only got four legs, same as a cow."

"Lord God A'mighty! Ain't you in for a surprise. A mustang ain't no critter, Turk. It's a freak o' nature. Like a blue norther, 'cept it's got legs."

"What a crock! A critter is a critter. Hoss or cow don't make no nevermind."

"Boys, we got about an hour of daylight left. Little less jabber and come dark we might just have ourselves a corral."

The men turned to look at the rawboned youngster who paid their wages. While they were older, and perhaps more experienced, everyone understood who was boss. There was a quiet undercurrent of authority to his words, and when his eyes settled on a man, they seemed to bore right through. It was uncanny, spooky in a weird sort of way—

as if he could read the other fellow's mind. Leave him stripped and vulnerable, his secrets a secret no longer.

They knew little or nothing of this youngster with the brush mustache and cold eyes. He was called Earl Stroud. So far as they could determine, he had neither family nor past. He volunteered nothing, and having looked him over, the men felt no great urge to ask questions. From his speech and manner of dress, they pegged him as a Texan; anything else was pure speculation, and best left that way. Yet there were many things they did know about him, bits and pieces gleaned from observation—a thinly sketched mosaic that told them not all, but perhaps as much as they wanted to know.

Earl Stroud had a seemingly inexhaustible supply of double eagles. After hiring them in Fort Worth, he had out-fitted them with extra horses, bought a wagonload of tools and gear, and laid in enough grub to feed a pack of wolves through the winter. He had asked few questions, satisfying himself that they were unmarried, in good health, and ac-quainted with the quarrelsome nature of cow ponies. In re-turn, he told them he was outfitting a crew to hunt mustangs. The pay was forty a month and food, which was generous, although not unusual, considering the hazards of the job.

But the oddest thing about Earl Stroud, and perhaps the most revealing, was that he evidenced not the slightest fear of being robbed. Not by them—though he had hired them out of saloons and knew nothing of their character—or by anyone else. Among themselves, when Stroud wasn't around, the men estimated his saddlebags contained up-ward of three thousand dollars. A handsome sum by any yardstick, more than most men earned in a decade of back-breaking toil. Yet his attitude was cool and collected, utterly devoid of concern, as if he couldn't imagine anyone foolish enough to try robbing him. That alone told them much about their boss. The cocksure manner, the pale gray eyes, and the care he lavished on his worn colt simply rounded out the tale.

Earl Stroud was a man who played for keeps.

All of the men had seen their share of hard cases. In Texas there was no scarcity of the breed. The young man who led them now was cast from a similar mold, and yet there was something different about him. If anything, more deadly. He never raised his voice, nor did he attempt to bully or browbeat, tactics commonly employed by self-styled bad men. Instead, there was an inner calm about him. That quiet, cocksure certainty was more menacing than a bald-faced threat. It was a warning sign, a simple statement of fact. He was one of those oddities of God's handiwork, a man who had purged himself of fear. Looking into his eyes, they knew that if he were aroused, he would kill. With icy detachment, like an executioner.

Still, as Earl Stroud led them west along the Brazos, they came to like and respect him. Though he was a hard taskmaster, he demanded less of the men then he did of himself. Moreover, he was damned fine company, stand-offish at first, but slowly warming as he got to know them. By the time their little column skirted Fort Griffin, which Stroud insisted be done at the crack of dawn, they discovered that he had a dry incisive wit and a natural flair for leadership. His orders were generally in the form of a request, stated in a tone that was at once pleasant and persistently firm. He chose good campsites, was constantly on the scout for Indians, and rotated the men on night watch without a hint of favoritism. Their respect increased mani-fold when it became apparent that he had permanently assigned himself to the dawn watch. Hostiles were partial to the early morning hours for surprise attack, and every man in the crew knew it to be the most dangerous time. It was still another clue to Stroud's character. But while the men's trust and regard steadily multiplied, they never lost sight of the fact that he was different.

West of Fort Griffin, where the Brazos split, Stroud led them along the Double Mountain Fork. This was virgin country, unknown to white men except for the military and buffalo hunters. These rolling plains were the ancient hunting grounds of the Comanche and Kiowa, abounding with wildlife; a vast, limitless land that swept westward in an emerald sea of grass. The party moved at a snail's pace, for the wagon slowed them considerably, and in a fortnight of travel they sighted not a single human being. In an eerie sort of way, it was as if they had entered another world, where man was the outsider, marching backward in time and space into a land where an older law prevailed. An atavistic law, founded on the most ancient expedient: survival.

Toward the end of July, near the headwaters of the Double Mountain Fork some hundred miles west of Fort Griffin, Earl Stroud found what he was looking for. A wide expanse of woodland, with cottonwoods along the river and a grove of live oaks stretching southward for a quarter mile. Bordering the shoreline was a natural clearing, with a rocky ford and stunted hills to the north, which would protect it from the chill winter blast of a plains blizzard. He called a halt and announced to the crew that their journey had ended.

Standing there, gazing around the clearing, he knew the spot was made to order. Somehow sensed the rightness of it. Perhaps of greater significance, though he was scarcely the superstitious type, he felt that time and place had joined hands to give him a sign. That morning Earl Stroud had turned twenty-six.

The ensuing month passed quickly, a time of sweat, excruciating labor, and immense progress. Stroud drove himself and the men at a furious pace, working from dawn to dusk, seven days a week. At the head of the list was a project that left the crew more puzzled than ever about this strange young man who had led them into the wilderness. He informed them that two buildings must be erected, a main house and bunkhouse. Again, the men asked no questions. They felled trees, snaked logs to the clearing, and worked like demons under his relentless urging. Both buildings were completed, including rough-hewn floors and stone fireplaces, within three weeks, although there still remained the moot question of who, besides Stroud, was to occupy the main house.

Afterward, erecting the corral was child's play. Stroud inscribed a circle on the ground, large enough to hold a hundred horses, and the men set about digging post holes. Once more, he drove them like a man possessed, never sharp or ill-tempered, but merely determined to see his vision a reality at last. For every drop of sweat they shed he shed double, and somewhere along the line a strange thing happened. He was still boss, and what he wanted was what he got, but curiously enough, the men came to feel that they were working not so much for him as with him. They had become a team.

Now, as dusk settled over the clearing, they stood back, weary and exhausted, and marveled on the fruit of their labors. Set off away from the river, shaded by tall cottonwoods, was a sturdy shake-roofed log cabin. It had three rooms with windows overlooking the stream and an oak

door four inches thick. Thinking back to the day they had
hung that massive slab in the entranceway, the men still
weren't sure if Stroud meant to keep somebody on the outside from getting in or somebody on the inside from getting out. With time, they had come to accept these little
mysteries as part of Stroud's character—simply another
riddle to be dusted off occasionally and inspected as a
child would scrutinize an old and treasured toy.

Across the clearing from the cabin, set flush with the
tree line, was the bunkhouse. It was large but compactly
built, with bunks on one side and the fireplace and a dining area on the other. Behind it, off in the woods, sat the
men's pride and joy: a spiffy two-holer. So far as they
knew, it was the first outhouse ever erected on the Double
Mountain Fork of the Brazos—an elegant, if somewhat
breezy, contribution to the advancement of civilization.

The corral sat squarely in the middle of the clearing, a
short distance from the river. The cross posts were springy
young logs, designed to absorb punishment from milling
horses without breaking. They had been lashed to the
ground posts with wet rawhide, and as the leather dried
and shrank, the corral was fused solid, as though girded
with steel bands. Looking at it now, the men agreed that
Turk Jordan might have been right after all. Nothing short
of a cyclone on wheels would bust out of there. Common
ordinary horseflesh wouldn't stand a chance.

Bunched in a loose knot, the five men stood there for a
long while, recalling a grueling month comprised of aches
and sprains and sweat-drenched days. They didn't say
much, just nodding and looking; none of them especially
felt the need for words. Their creation spoke eloquently for
itself. It wasn't fancy, but it was built to last.

Ben Hall finally grunted and flashed a mouthful of

brown teeth. "I got a notion Gawd never worked no harder buildin' the world. My bones feel like somebody beat me with a iron switch."

That got a chuckle, and heads bobbed in agreement. Not a man among them had energy left to work up a good spit. There was a moment of silence, as if everybody was waiting, and at last Earl Stroud cleared his throat.

"Gents, you done yourselves proud. I'm beholden."

Looking from one to another, he held each man's gaze for a second and smiled. Then he turned and walked toward the main house. They stared after him, and when he went through the door they still hadn't moved. None of them quite understood why, but his words had touched a nerve.

It was the finest compliment they'd ever been paid.

A week later they came to the escarpment that guarded *Llano Estacado*. Ben Hall was in the lead, for of the five men, he alone had seen the barren land that lay above. It was for this reason Earl Stroud had hired him back in Forth Worth. Twice before he had trapped wild horses on the Staked Plains and returned to tell the tale. Locked in his brain was a map of this uncharted wilderness, their key into and out of a deadly hostile land. Without Ben Hall, or someone like him, venturing onto the high plains was a hazard few men cared to risk.

Late that afternoon they emerged from the steep, winding trail onto the plateau above. They halted to give the horses a breather, and the men had their first look at *Llano Estacado*. Ben Hall had talked of little else since departing the Brazos, but nothing he'd said could have prepared them for the sight itself.

The plains stretched endlessly to the horizon, flat and featureless, evoking a sense of something lost forever. A

thick mat of mesquite grass covered the earth, but hardly a
tree or a bush was to be seen in the vast emptiness sweeping westward. It was a land of sun and solitude, a lonesome
land. As if nature had flung together earth and sky, mixed
with deafening silence, and then simply forgotten about it.
Nothing moved as far as the eye could see, almost as
though in some ancient age the plains had frozen motionless for all time. A gentle breeze, like the wispy breath of
a ghost, rippled over the curly mesquite, disturbing nothing. Perhaps more than anything else, it was this silence,
without movement or life, that left a man feeling puny and
insignificant. A mere speck on the sands of the universe.
The Staked Plains did that to men, for in an eerie sense, it
was like the solitude of God: distant, somehow unreal, yet
faintly ominous.

Farther west, the high plateau was broken by a lattice-
work of wooded canyons, and it was in this direction that
Ben Hall led Stroud and his crew. These rocky gorges were
all but invisible from a distance; a man sometimes found
himself standing on the edge of a sheer precipice where
moments before there had been nothing but solitary space.
Within these canyons was the breath of life—water—the
only known streams in *Llano Estacado*. The men rode
west not for water itself but because it served as a lure. A
bait of sorts. It was near these streams that the wild horses
roamed.

As they moved deeper into the trackless plains, Earl
Stroud had reason to feel pleased with himself. Back in
Fort Worth, rather than hiring men at random, he had taken
his time and selected with care. Every man in the crew had
been chosen for a purpose, and while his judgement was
hardly flawless, there was no deadwood among them. The
past six weeks had proved a stern test, one that would have

scattered lesser men by the wayside. Yet each of them had stuck, pulling his own weight, and by the sheer dint of hardships endured, they had dispelled any lingering doubt. These were tough men, determined and able, seared by wind and sun and time. They would stick to the last.

Ben Hall was perhaps the choice find of the lot. At the end of the war, he had drifted into ranch work and quite soon shown a remarkable gift for the ways of horses. Though lean, he appeared built of gristle and spring steel, and it was a rare bronc that could unseat him. Better still, he had a head on his shoulders and knew how to use it. He was smarter than he let on, and while he wasn't pushy, Stroud observed that he generally got things his own way. That he outfoxed the others without them knowing it made him a prize catch indeed. Horse sense and brains seldom came in the same package.

Clint Langham and Hank Blalock were two of a kind: not too bright, but long on savvy. They understood hooved creatures better than they did men, and most of their lives had been spent aboard a horse. Their legs looked warped; they were so bowlegged they tended to wobble when they walked. But when they stepped into a saddle, some change came over them. They sat tall and easy, taking on the grace of men who had found their niche astride a spirited cow pony. Moreover, they were magicians with a rope, and it was for this reason that Stroud had hired them. They could flatten a steer with loops that confounded the eye, and in another flick of the wrist have him hog-tied and begging for mercy. Savvy like theirs wasn't a gift so much as an art. It came only with time and unending practice.

The fourth member of the crew, Turk Jordan, was also a specialist of sorts. Short and chunky, built low to the ground, he had catlike reflexes and the strength of a young bull. There were few men his equal at wrestling steers or earing down a spooky horse. Aside from these more apparent traits, however, Jordan had been selected for yet another reason. Earl Stroud had a sixth sense for spotting men who could handle a gun; he suspected Jordan's quickness and sharp reflexes weren't limited to manhandling livestock. Off in the wilderness, where the odds were passable at best, having another fast gun along was something akin to an ace in the hole.

All in all, Stroud felt like a man who had drawn to an inside straight and caught the right card. Watching them, as the little party moved across the high plains, a surge of confidence came over him. He had four good men, each leading an extra mount loaded with supplies, and they were headed into a country where mustangs were thick as blueberries. Suddenly he wanted to laugh, jump up in the air, click his heels. For a man with a price on his head, he had the world on a downhill slide.

A fortnight later, the trap was ready. Stroud and his crew waited in a broad canyon, hidden against the sheer walls along both sides. Ben Hall was closest to the mouth of the canyon, the crucial position. The others were split into pairs and spaced at half-mile intervals across from one another farther down. All of the men had taken great care in concealing themselves behind rocks and in scrub-choked gullies, and now they stood fretful and anxious beside their fastest horses. This was the day, and if they had calculated right, all hell was about to break loose.

Their first herd of mustangs was due any minute now.

This was the hardest part—the waiting. Finding the canyon had been fairly simple, for the grassy floor and tree-studded creek was alive with hoofprints. After that it was a matter of Ben Hall bird-dogging the herd and determining from their movements the best place to construct a trap.

Less than a week was needed to sniff out the mustang's grazing habits. Tagging along behind them, he found that this herd was much like all bands of wild horses. They browsed over a wide expanse of the high plains, always drifting into the wind, and covered about twenty miles in four days. What made it interesting was that it was always the same twenty miles. The herd moved in a set pattern, roughly an elongated circle, which ultimately brought them back to their starting point. They stopped once a day to water, mostly at remote, pan-shaped basins on the plateau. But every fourth day, a couple of hours before sundown, they watered in the canyon. Warily, they then returned to the plains along about dusk and spent the night in the safety of open spaces.

Hall trailed them for six nights and five days before he was certain of the pattern. Then he rode back to camp with the news. Their grazing habits were regular as as clockwork, and just as predictable. With any luck at all, they could be trapped in the canyon like a herd of sheep.

Stroud listened, asked an endless stream of questions, and followed Hall's advice to the letter. The men worked three days out of four, avoiding the canyon completely on the day the herd came there to water. This was part of the plan laid out by Hall, and it was based in no small part on the cunning of the dun stallion that ruled the herd.

Sleek and barrel-chested, the stallion was heavily scarred from a lifetime of fighting wolves and doing battle with young studs who tried to steal his harem. It was a full-time job, for the herd contained close to thirty mares, half again as many colts, and several yearlings. But the stallion was equal to the task. His strength and ferocity in a fight were balanced by the wisdom of age and constant vigilance. He suspicioned anything that moved, and at the first sign of danger sent the herd flying with iron-jawed nips and whistling squeals of outrage. If the herd was to be captured, it was the stallion who must be outwitted. Under Ben Hall's directions, Stroud and his crew set about accomplishing that very thing.

The trap itself was simple affair, constructed along the lines of a funnel, but it was hellishly difficult to disguise. Since this was not a box canyon—the stallion would never water in a place that lacked an alternate means of escape— it was necessary to build two corrals where the sheer walls squeezed down to a narrow gorge. Built back to back, with a gate in between, the first was a catch corral, and the second was a larger holding pen to contain horses already caught. The next step was by far the hardest. After cutting posts, the men constructed a half-mile-long fence on either side of the canyon. The fence fanned out from the corral entrance in a V shape, with the broad mouth facing the upper end of the canyon floor. If it worked, the herd would be tricked into the open throat of the funnel, then hazed down the narrowing fence and driven into the corral.

With everything completed, the men came to the canyon before dawn on the eighth day and worked like demons cutting green junipers. These were used to hide the fences and corral, giving the trap a natural appearance. Once it was done, the men brushed their tracks from the canyon floor, erasing all human signs, and concealed themselves in the positions designated earlier by Ben Hall.

And now they waited. Deep shadows had already fallen over the canyon's westerly wall and sundown was but an hour away. The men began to sweat, despite a cool breeze, and their apprehension mounted as the fleeting sun dropped lower in the sky. Never before had the mustangs been this late. Unless they came to water soon, it meant they weren't coming at all. Not tonight. Perhaps never again.

Then, quite suddenly, the herd appeared. One moment the mouth of the canyon stood empty, and in the next, like some ghostly apparition, the mustangs simply material-ized. A barren old mare, the herd sentinel, was in the lead. She came on at a stiff-legged walk, ears cocked warily, eyeing the canyon for anything out of the ordinary. At last, satisfied, she broke into a trot and led the herd toward the creek.

These wild horses were a sturdy breed, high in the with-ers and long in the shoulders, with a wide forehead, small ears, and a tapered muzzle. They had the spirit of their noble ancestors, the Barbs, and from generations of bat-tling both the elements and predators, they possessed an al-most supernatural endurance. Honed by adversity to a single purpose—survival—they were the freest of all the earth's creatures. In motion, swallowing the wind, they could gallop to the edge of eternity and back again.

Behind the herd, the dun stallion came on at a prancing walk. Larger then the others, heavily muscled, he moved with the pride of power and lordship. Yet he was skittish as ever, nervously testing the wind, scanning the canyon floor with a fierce eye that missed not a rock or a blade of grass. He would water only at the very last, when the herd had taken its fill. Until then, protector as much as ruler, he would remain watchful and on guard, alert to any sign of danger.

Halfway between the canyon entrance and the creek, the stallion suddenly stiffened and whirled back. A vagrant breeze had shifted, and with it came the most dreaded scent of all. The man scent. Pawing at the earth, nostrils flared wide, he arched his neck to sound the whistling snort of alarm.

Ben Hall shot him at that exact instant.

As the stallion went down, fighting death as he had fought life, Hall charged the herd. Instinctively, they wheeled away from the creek, prepared for flight. But their leader was down, legs jerking in death, and this strange new creature barreled toward them. It uttered the blood-curdling scream of a cougar, and in its hand was an object that flashed fire and roared like thunder. Without their leader to command them, crazed with fright, the herd broke before Hall's charge and bolted down the canyon in a clattering lope.

The mustangs had gone only a short distance when other strange creatures came at them from either flank, screaming and firing guns. Their pace quickened, and tails streaming in the wind, the herd took off in headlong flight. Then, out of nowhere, two more riders appeared, forcing the herd straight down the middle of the canyon. Terrified, racing blindly in a thunderous wedge, the mustangs entered the juniper-lined funnel without breaking stride. The men on horseback stuck tightly to their flanks, hazing them onward with shouts and gunshots. Suddenly the funnel squeezed down to nothing, the only escape a narrow opening dead ahead.

Never faltering, the herd blasted through the corral entrance at a full gallop. The barren old mare and a yearling hit the far wall with a shuddering impact and toppled over backward, their necks broken. The rest of the herd slid to a dust-smothered halt, confused, then turned and started to retreat the way they had come. But the men were there, sliding long poles across the opening, and suddenly there was no escape. The mustangs milled about, wild-eyed and squealing, slamming against the corral at several spots. They tested the fence cautiously, though, with respect. For they had seen what happened to the old mare, and it was lesson enough. Slowly their panic faded and they huddled together in the center of the corral, trembling and frightened, staring watchfully at the creatures who had captured them.

The men were shouting and laughing and slapping one another across the back. Langham and Jordan even linked arms and danced a mad jig. But like the mustangs, their excitement slowly drained away. Instead, the hoots and laughter became a stilled amazement. Gathered before the corral gate, they just stood there, staring back at the horses. Somehow it wasn't yet believable, but what they saw was no mirage. They had actually done it: trapped themselves a herd of woolly-booger mustangs.

Ben Hall was flashing a wide grin, proud as a peacock, and he finally got around to shaking hands with the boss. "Lordy me, but ain't they a sight? Nothin' Gawd ever made that's prettier'n a wild horse."

"I guess not." Stroud smiled, but his eyes were thoughtful, somehow distant. "Sorry you had to kill that stallion. I was hopin' to get a good stud horse for breedin'."

"Weren't no other way." Hall met his gaze and held it. "The devil caught my scent, and he was fixin' to take 'em outta here lickety-split."

"You did what you had to. I know that, Ben. Guess I was just wishin' out loud."

A TANGLE OF arms and legs, breathing hard, they slowly came apart. Laura sat up, straightening her skirts, and patted a stray lock back in place. Then she came into his arms again, suddenly reluctant to have it end so quickly. They didn't say anything for a while, just sat there underneath the oak hugging and kissing, listening to the katydids serenade the night. But the stillness gradually fanned her curiosity, and when she could bear it no longer, she pushed him away.

"Now that's enough! You promised to tell me and so far you haven't done anything but muss me up something awful."

"I don't recollect you puttin' up much of a fight."

"Honestly, Sam—you're incorrigible! That's what you are. A wicked, naughty boy. Now, are you going to tell me or not?"

He smiled. "Well, first off, you've got the right fella but the wrong name. Figured if I was gonna have a new life I might as well have a new handle. Picked one out of a hat and came up with Earl Stroud."

"Earl Stroud?" Laura blurted the name, astonished and not a little mystified. Then she paused, repeating it several times to herself. At last, her cheeks dimpled in a smile and she gave his hand a big squeeze. "Oh, I like it! It's so dignified and—well, I don't know, almost like a banker's name."

"That's where I got it!" He let go a burst of laughter. "Off a bank window in Fort Worth."

"You didn't rob the bank!"

"Course not. I just borrowed the name."

"But I don't understand, Sam. Why did—"

"Just for openers, you better get used to callin' me Earl."

"Oh, fiddlesticks. Stop playing silly games and tell me where you've been for the last three months."

"I'm not playin' silly games. That's my name now. And where I've been is catchin' a bunch of wild horses."

She stared at him, thunderstruck, and repeated it in a tiny voice. "Wild horses. You mean real honest-to-goodness wild horses?"

"Yep. Hired myself a crew of men and went pretty near to the headwaters of the Brazos before I found the spot I was lookin' for." He hesitated and gave her an earnest look. "Built a humdinger of a cabin. Got a parlor with a fireplace, and a bedroom and a kitchen. Real fancy." Then before she had time to interrupt, he went on. "Anyway, me and the boys took a little sashay out to the Staked Plains and when we come back we had ourselves close to two hundred head of mustangs. You're lookin' at a man of means, case you didn't know it. All honest and above-board, too."

"But I still don't understand." Her face crinkled in an exasperated little frown. "What earthly good are wild horses?"

"Money, woman. Money!" He cupped her face between his hands. "We're gonna break them horses and teach 'em some manners, and come fall, I figure to make myself about four thousand dollars."

Laura was visibly startled. That was about as much as her father made in a year. And his was the most successful store in Denton.

"That's wonderful, Sam. But how long can you go on catching wild horses? I mean, it's dangerous work, and surely it couldn't be too steady."

"The name's Earl. And don't you worry your head about wild horses. I don't plan on being a mustanger much longer. Just till we can get a herd of brood mares built up and start ourselves a real ranch."

"You mean it? You're going to be a rancher?"

"God A'mighty, haven't you been listenin' to a word I said? Why do you think I went to the trouble of buildin' a cabin and a bunkhouse and a corral? And near busted my back catchin' all them horses?"

Suddenly Laura was listening, very intently, and she understood at last. She fluttered her eyelashes and prompted him with a coy smile. "Tell me—Mr. Stroud—why did you do all those things?"

" 'Cause I figured it was time I made an honest woman of you." He cocked one eyebrow in a mock scowl. "Unless you couldn't abide folks callin' you Mrs. Stroud."

She laughed and clapped her hands like an exuberant child. "Oh, I could! Honestly, I could. I just don't care anymore, Sam. Just so long as we're together."

"*Earl,* dammit! Honey, you gotta get used to that. The name's Earl."

"I'll remember, I promise." She threw her arms around his neck and embraced him fiercely. "I wouldn't care if your name was Judas Iscariot. Just so we can get married."

Oscar Belden hardly shared his daughter's sentiments. In fact, he was livid with rage. He had hoped that, with time, she would outgrow her infatuation. Failing that, he had every confidence the boy would get himself killed before too long. Either way, the Belden family would be shed of their own personal albatross, and his daughter would again return to her senses.

When the youngsters swept into the parlor with the news that they were to be married that very night, he was at first speechless. Then he went red as ox blood and began shouting. They stood there smiling at one another, arm in arm, as if he were some spoiled brat throwing a temper tantrum. Only by imposing an iron will was he able to calm himself. If anger wouldn't work, perhaps reason would. Facing them now, he took a grip on his rage and reversed tactics.

"Think for a minute, both of you. What kind of a life could you have together? Always running and hiding, never knowing when the law will kick down your door in the dead of night. That's not what you want for Laura, now is it, Sam?"

Laura countered with a fetching smile. "Mercy sakes alive, Daddy! You're just working yourself up for nothing. It's already settled. We have a ranch and a herd of horses and there won't be any more trouble with the law."

"But you can't know that for sure." The storekeeper was sweating freely now. "Why couldn't you wait a while? A year, even six months. Give yourselves a little time. If you really love each other, a few more months won't make any difference. Now will it?"

That was his best shot, the irrefutable logic used by fathers since Biblical times. But when he saw the look on their faces, Oscar Belden knew he was licked. His last-ditch effort had just shattered to smithereens against a stone wall.

"Daddy," Laura said sweetly, "will you call the preacher over, or do you want us to run off and live in sin?"

REVEREND VIRGIL PRYOR opened the good book and blinked sleep from his eyes. This whole affair seemed a trifle unorthodox, and he had a strong hunch the Belden girl was in a family way. If not, then he was going to be strongly indignant with Oscar Belden for rousing him at this ungodly hour. Barring a shotgun wedding or sudden illness, there was very little that couldn't await the light of day. The Lord hadn't said it just exactly that way, but Virgil Pryor felt sure He would agree.

Still, the youngsters did make a handsome couple. And from the looks of her folks, it was entirely possible the girl was in a family way. Oscar Belden looked mad enough to chew nails, and his wife had reduced her handkerchief to a sodden ball. The preacher sighed wearily and, in a resigned monotone, began the service.

"Dearly beloved, we are gathered together to join this man and this woman in holy wedlock—"

LANGHAM AND BLALOCK roped the horses selected by Ben Hall and dragged them fighting and kicking out of the corral. These were the mustangs the professor had picked to work on that particular day. Half of them were raw and untried, yet to feel a saddle or the weight of a man on their backs. The others were about half-broke, having been ridden and accustomed to a bridle, but they were still in school. As Hall had commented, they had a ways to go before earning a diploma from his bronc-bustin' academy.

The day's pupils were hauled down near the river and tethered to trees. Then the rest of the herd was driven from the corral and hazed through the ford to a lush grassland on the north side of the stream. There they could graze and water throughout the day, and toward sundown they would be driven back to the corral. Hank Blalock was left to keep an eye on them, just in case some hammerhead took a notion to quit the bunch and head back to the wide-open spaces.

There was only a slim chance of this happening, though. The mustangs had learned that a bunch quitter quickly came upon hard times. Shortly after being captured on the Staked Plains, each of the horses had been roped and thrown to the ground. When released, the horse discovered that one of its front feet had been tied to its tail with a piece of rope. It was a practical device that kept the mustangs from running, and after they had dumped themselves a couple of times, they simply gave up trying. The men drove them out of the canyon and trailed them for two days in this manner. Afterward, with the ropes removed, the mustangs behaved themselves. They could be herded any way the men wanted them to move, and few of them needed a second dose. Another day roped foot-to-tail convinced even the most stubborn of the lot that it was better to stick with the bunch.

With the herd grazing peacefully now, the workday began.

CLINT LANGHAM BROUGHT one of the tethered horses back from the river and released it in the corral. This was a raw bronc, a big rangy buckskin, and it looked to be a lively session. Langham hitched his own horse outside the corral and stepped down with a lariat in his hand. Stroud, along with Hall and Jordan, awaited him at the gate, and they all four entered the corral at once. This was a job they had been at steadily for the past three weeks, and there was little lost motion in their actions. Like a freshly oiled machine, with all the parts functioning properly, they worked well together.

The buckskin started racing around the far side of the corral as they fanned out and walked forward. Suddenly Langham's arm moved, and the lariat snaked out, catching the mustang's front legs in a loop just as its hooves left the ground. Langham hauled back, setting his weight into the rope, and the horse went down with a jarring thud. Working smoothly, every man to do his own job, the other three swarmed over the buckskin in a cloud of dust and flailing arms.

Jordan wrapped himself around the horse's neck, grabbing an ear in each hand, and jerked it back to earth just as it started to rise. Almost at the same instant, Stroud darted in with a length of braided rawhide and lashed the animal's back legs tight. While Jordan kept the horse eared down, Hall slipped a hackamore over its head, and Stroud clamped hobbles around its front legs. Pushing and tugging, sometimes rolling the horse up on its withers, Hall and Stroud then managed to cinch a center-fire saddle in place. As Hall jerked the latigo taut, Stroud eased forward and tied a blindfold around the mustang's eyes.

The entire operation had taken less than a minute.

Quickly, the ropes were removed from the buckskin's legs and it was allowed to regain its feet. Blinded and dazed, still winded from the fall, the horse stood absolutely motionless. The hobbles around its front legs kept it from rearing or jumping away, and the blindfold calmed it into a numbed stupor. However unwilling, the bronc was ready for its first lesson.

Langham and Stroud backed off and scrambled over the fence just as Laura walked down from the house. She couldn't bear to watch as the mustangs were thrown and tied—although she readily admitted that it was the most practical means of strapping a saddle on a wild horse—but she loved to watch the bucking. Langham touched his hat, grinning like a possum, and Laura gave him a winsome smile.

The sight of her was a constant source of agony to the men, for until Stroud showed up with his new bride, they hadn't seen a woman in close to four months. The dresses she wore were simple gingham affairs, not meant to be suggestive, but they fit snugly across her tightly rounded buttocks and her fruity breasts. There was considerable moaning in the bunkhouse late at night, but the men treated her like a fairy princess come to life. Though unspoken, there was general accord that it was better to look and not touch than to have nothing at all to look at. They suffered in quiet agony.

Standing between her husband and Langham, Laura felt her pulse quicken. Jordan had just handed the reins to Ben Hall and retreated back to the fence. Hall tugged his hat down tight and scrambled aboard the mustang. Whenever he mounted, no matter how many times Laura watched, she was always reminded of a monkey leaping nimbly to the back of a circus pony. One moment Hall was just standing there, and in the blink of an eye, as if springs had uncoiled in his legs, he was seated firmly in the saddle.

Leaning forward, Hall jerked the blindfold loose and let it fall to the ground. For perhaps ten seconds the buckskin remained perfectly still. The broncbuster sat loose and easy, just waiting, his lips skinned back in a faint smile. Then he moved his foot, and in the corral, the jinglebobs in his spurs gave off the thunderous chime of cathedral bells.

The buckskin exploded at both ends, like a firecracker bursting within itself. All four feet left the ground as the horse bowed its back and in the next instant came unglued in a bone-jarring snap. Then it swapped ends in midair and sunfished across the corral in a series of bounding, catlike leaps. Hall was all over the horse, bouncing from one side to the other, never twice in the same spot. Veering away from the fence, the bronc whirled and kicked, slamming the man front to rear in the saddle, and sent his hat spinning skyward in a lazy arc.

Hall gave a whooping shout and, in the middle of a jump, decided it was time they got down to serious business. Lifting his boots high, he raked hard across the shoulders with his spurs, and the spiked rowels whirred like a buzz saw. The buckskin roared a great squeal of outrage, and this time went off like a ton of dynamite with a short fuse.

Leaping straight up in the air, the bronc swallowed its head and humped its back, popping Hall's neck with the searing crack of a bullwhip. A moment later it hit on all four feet with a jolt that shook the earth. Then the horse went berserk. As if willing to commit suicide in order to kill the man, it erupted in a pounding beeline toward the corral fence. Hall saw it coming and effortlessly swung out of the saddle at the exact instant the mustang collided with the springy cross timbers. Staggered, the horse buckled at the knees and fell back on its rump. Like a drunk man, it just sat there for several moments, shaking its head and making pitiful little grunts.

Hall casually stepped back into the saddle as the mustang regained its feet, then he rammed his spurs clean up to the haft. This time there was less rage and less fight, ending in a series of stiff-legged crow hops that lacked punch. Hall hauled back on the hackamore for the first time, shutting off the horse's wind, and reined it around the corral in a simple turning maneuver. At last, he eased to a halt and climbed down out of the saddle. The buckskin stood where he left it, head bowed and sides heaving as it gasped for air.

Hall retrieved his hat and dusted it off. Jamming it on

his head, he walked toward the grinning foursome gathered outside the corral.

"That's gonna be a good hoss." He smiled and jerked his thumb back at the spent mustang. "Got plenty of starch."

"He don't look so starchy now," Turk Jordan cackled. "Looks like somebody twisted all the kinks out of his tail."

"Aw, he's jest restin'. Figgerin' what he's gonna do next time. Course, I'd bet a heap he don't run into that fence no more."

Earl Stroud laughed and squeezed Laura around the waist. She had never seen him in such good spirits. Nor had the men. They talked of it often in the bunkhouse. Since the lady had come to stay, and Ben Hall started busting broncs, the grim-eyed youngster was a changed man. Like night and day.

That evening the young couple came to sit on the front step of their cabin. The sweet coolness of night had fallen over the land, and they could hear the crickets warming up along the riverbank. There was a serenity about this place, something they both felt, almost as if there had never been another life except the one they shared here on the Brazos. Thinking about it now, Laura felt warm and giddy inside. These were the happiest days she had ever known. And she need look no farther for the reason than the man seated beside her.

"Keepin' secrets on me?"

"No, but your head might swell up and bust."

He chuckled and gave her a bearish squeeze. "Try me. Can't hardly be no worse'n it already is."

"I was just thinking how proud you made me. That it was you who built all this. The cabin and the horse herd and everything. Sometimes I have to pinch myself to make sure it's all real."

"Well, I had some help, y'know. It wasn't like I walked in here with an ax and a mouthful of nails and slapped it together all by myself."

"You're a paragon of modesty, Mr. Stroud." Her voice had a teasing lilt. "I wouldn't be surprised but what you're blushing."

"Nope, I clean forgot how. Been too busy buildin' empires."

"See, I told you. It went straight to your head."

"Judas Priest, can't a fella speak the truth in his own house?"

"Oh, you really are vain, Sam Ba—" She clamped a hand over her mouth and giggled softly. "I mean, Mr. Stroud. But it's still true. You're the vainest man I ever met."

"Caught you, didn't I? Any man that done that has got reason to be proud."

She laughed a deep, throaty laugh. "Maybe you don't catch me enough."

He considered it a moment and she could tell he was smiling. Then he chuckled. "I think you got somethin' there. What d'you say we hit the hay early tonight?"

"Mr. Stroud, I thought you'd never ask."

Since they were of a mind, there seemed no reason for further talk. They stood and he lifted her over the step and set her on the floor inside the cabin. As he swung the massive oak door closed and barred it, she crossed the parlor and blew out the lamp. Then she laughed that laugh again, and he heard the rustle of her skirts as she headed toward the bedroom.

Curiously, he had no trouble finding her in the dark.

★

Wise men and poets often remark that the road to hell is paved with good intentions. Perhaps it's true. A woman's love—even a ranch on the Brazos—sometimes isn't enough. Every man casts a shadow on his own personal road to hell; however far he runs, it's always there, a step behind, waiting for him to falter.

On July 19, 1878, a gang of bank robbers rode into a little town called Round Rock. Texas Rangers were waiting for them, and several men were killed in the ensuing shootout. The young outlaw leader, although mortally wounded, escaped on a fleet mustang gelding. He died two days later, July 21, his twenty-seventh birthday.

His name was Sam Bass.

The Man with a Charmed Life

MARGARET BZOVY

Born and educated in Southern California, Margaret Bzovy has been the host for the Western Writers Chat Group on AOL since 1997, writing articles for the newsletter as well as arranging guest appearances on the hour-long event that meets every Monday. She is a member of Western Writers of America, working with the membership committee under Chairman Larry Brown. She has also written various nonfiction historical stories for the online American West magazine, *Read the West* (www.readthewest.com), and numerous historical articles for the *Tumbleweed Newspaper* in Tombstone, Arizona. She lives with her husband, Ed, at the same home where they raised their eight children.

I believe this is her first published work of fiction. I'm glad she sent it to me.

★

The summer of 1880, Frank Leslie rode into Tombstone at the beginning of the wild years. His shoulder-length blonde hair under a wide-brimmed hat and the light deer-skin mountain-man clothes caused people to give him a second look as he rode into town, believing he was Buffalo

Bill Cody, the showman. Frank was known in other places as Buckskin Frank Leslie, hot tempered and quick on the draw. The Colt .44 at his waist had put a few men in their graves.

Tombstone was a silver- and gold-mining town in Arizona that pulled approximately forty million dollars in silver and three million in gold within a twenty-year period. Ed Scieffeln named the area Tombstone as a humorous retaliation at the U.S. Army, who had told Ed to keep out of the desolate Apache territory because the only thing he would find would be sure death and his own tombstone. Ed ignored their warning and headed into the section feeling sure there was a wealth of gold waiting for him. He was right. He found plenty of gold, and a town soon sprung up because of the many miners that staked their claims.

Tombstone was a rough, tough frontier town with saloons, gamblers, thieves, and loose women. Frank Leslie had heard about the wealth in Tombstone and headed out to get his share. He found the town had several streets with many businesses. Folks walked around town with guns under their coats in spite of the sign in the middle of town, which stated that guns were to be registered with the sheriff. Frank only grinned. This was the type of town where he could make a good living. He knew the only place to find out information would be at one of the saloons.

"What's your drink?" asked the bartender.

"Whiskey." Frank glanced into the mirror behind the bar to survey the room. There were several tables, and at one, three men played cards. The bartender placed a small glass in front of Frank and poured a yellow liquid.

"This your best stuff?" Frank asked.

"Cosmopolitan serves only the best. That'll be one dollar."

Frank knew the drink cost too much but remembered he was in a gold-mining town that would sell everything at sky-high prices. He dug into his pants pocket and shoved the coin across the bar.

"Come from far off?"

"Not far," Frank answered. "Know of any work around here?"

The bartender rubbed a cloth across the bar. "Matter of fact there's need of another bartender right here. The last man got killed."

Frank eyed the bartender and grinned. "I'm a very good bartender."

"Maybe so. The thing is, you'd have to get rid of them buckskins. Cut your hair and trim the mustache. We allow mustaches but they have to be neat."

Frank became the Cosmopolitan's new bartender. He felt strange with short hair, a fancy dress suit, and boots that cut into his feet. He couldn't resist buying a buckskin vest to preserve his nickname. His job was to serve drinks during the evening hours along with Mike Killen, the other bartender.

"This place really gets busy during the nights," Frank said.

"Everybody in town hits the Cosmopolitan," Mike replied.

Frank observed that there were guests that stayed on the upper floor. In the evening, well-dressed men strolled downstairs to gamble or socialize.

One evening, as Frank was cleaning glasses, his bright blue eyes caught the figure of a very charming woman. His heart raced as he watched her come toward the bar. "Who's the beautiful woman?" Frank asked.

"That's my wife. Don't get any ideas," Mike said.

Her name was May and she gave Frank a look he felt sure meant more than just a passing glance. Her smile chilled him to the bone. "I'm pleased to meet you, Mister Leslie." Her slender hand lingered near his on the bar. Frank glanced at Mike, then gave May a bright smile. Whenever she came around, Frank would offer to help her.

"I don't like you taking such notice of my wife, Leslie," Mike said.

"I'm only being kind, Mike. Don't take on so."

Frank had been working at the Cosmopolitan for several weeks and managed to take breaks out on the front porch. In the summertime it was cooler, and he enjoyed sitting on the hardback chairs watching the town lights and people ride by on horseback or in buggies. He could smell the desert sage as a warm breeze pressed against his face. He glanced around when the front door opened and beautiful May Killen strolled out onto the porch.

"Would you like to sit down?" Frank offered May the other chair.

"Why thank you, Mister Leslie. It's unbearable in my room."

"Please, call me Frank."

"You're such a nice gentleman, Frank."

It became a nightly occurrence with the two sitting on the front porch. Then they started to hold hands. Mike Killen began to wonder where his wife went while he was serving drinks, and he followed after her one night. As he stepped outside, the line of light from the opened door revealed May's hands in Frank's. "What the hell's going on out here?"

"We're just talking, Mike," Frank said as he pulled his hands from May.

"Holding hands don't make no talk," Mike yelled. He

pulled a gun from his waist and fired a shot at Frank. The bullet creased Frank's skull and in spite of the burning wound, Frank jumped at Mike and grabbed the gun. The two struggled into the hall. George Perrine, a guest, tried to pull them apart. Frank lunged at George and pistol-whipped him back, then continued the struggle with Mike. The two ended out on the porch with May screaming at them to stop. Frank shoved Mike back, raised the gun, and fired two shots. One bullet hit Mike in the face and the other in his chest. Mike was dead when he hit the porch.

The trial was not very long. The verdict was self-defense. Frank was acquitted, and he returned to work. He managed to court May throughout the trial and preparation of Mike's funeral. They were married soon after.

Perhaps the killing of Mike drove Frank to drink. He prowled the streets and started trouble in the other saloons. He staggered into Hafford's saloon and began shooting at the ceiling.

"What the hell you doing, Frank?"

"You've got sticky flies up there. I'm getting rid of them for you."

"Put that gun away, Frank."

Sheriff John Behan heard the gunfire at Hafford's saloon, and he rushed inside just in time to see Frank shoot a few holes in the ceiling.

"Get him out of here, Sheriff. He's costing me money."

"Put that gun away and get back to the Cosmopolitan," Behan yelled. "You show up one more time to shoot up a place, I'm putting you in jail."

Frank was known as an excellent shot. What he aimed at he hit. People got out of Frank's way when he was on a drunk.

May Killen Leslie was frightened out of her mind when

Frank came home wild and drunk. He forced her to stand against the wall while he outlined her body with bullets, just to prove he was alert and steady no matter how much he drank.

May was paralyzed against the wall, afraid to move. "Please, Frank, don't do this to me," May begged.

"Shut up and stand still," Frank yelled

"You're too drunk, please stop."

"I can shoot straight, drunk or sober."

"I'm leaving you, Frank. I won't put up with this."

By the time Frank finished his target practice, he was becoming more sober. He saw May with tears in her eyes and he felt humiliated.

"I'm sorry, May. I won't do it again. I'll quit drinking, you'll see. Don't leave me."

"I'm tired of it all, Frank. You come home drunk one more time and I'm leaving. I don't need to be used as a target just because you think you're so good with a gun."

"May, give me a chance."

"Only one more chance, Frank. You don't change, then I'm through with you."

"Listen, darling. I've an idea to buy in on a mine."

"What do you know about mining?"

"I've had some dealings with it. I can make some good money and then we can live high."

"I hope so, Frank. I won't abide how you are now."

Frank found a certain amount of gold at the mines in Cochise Pass, but he found it to be very hard labor. So hard he began to regret the whole thing. He sweated more than he pulled up in metal. His mining adventures found him without a job at the Cosmopolitan Hotel due to his absence. He soon quit the mining trade and looked for another bartending job. He found employment with Milt

Joyce and Wyatt Earp, owners of the Oriental saloon. Frank liked the two men right off. They accepted him as an equal. Wyatt arranged for Frank to have the power of arrest within the Oriental saloon, which gave Frank a new feeling of superiority.

"Just arrest those here in the Oriental that get out of hand," Wyatt told Frank. "Hold them from making any further trouble, then send word to me."

"I'll do that, Wyatt. I'll keep the order."

"Just stay away from the liquor," Wyatt warned. "We need straight heads around here. There's too much trouble going on these days."

"I'll watch for trouble," Frank said.

"Don't start the trouble," Wyatt warned. "Don't do like you did at the Soldiers' Hole saloon."

"What do you mean?"

"Remember when Russian Bill came into the saloon and you yelled at him if he had any money on him?"

Frank laughed. "You saw that, Wyatt? Well, he was a show-off."

"Maybe so, but it caused trouble," Wyatt pointed out.

"I only asked how much money he had on him," Frank explained. "He volunteered he had eighty dollars. I just told him slap it on the bar and he did so."

"Yes, then you offered drinks to the whole house on Russian Bill's money. That's what trouble is."

Frank grinned. "Well, he was paying too much attention to the pretty gal hired there I wanted to see him sweat."

"Don't be chasing the women, Frank. That's real trouble."

Frank took Earp's warnings to heart and stopped drinking. He found the days were going smoothly and without problems. He felt right at home with the Oriental saloon.

He had concern about the operations of the new saloon and directed his interest toward business. He believed he had to keep an eye on the other saloons to find out their whiskey prices and what else they served at the bar.

"What brings you in here, Frank?" Sheriff Behan asked.

Frank glanced around the Cosmopolitan and noted the dish of hardboiled eggs on the bar. That was something he could do at the Oriental.

"How much are you charging for eggs, Max?" Frank asked. He nodded at the men sitting near Behan. He knew who they were. The tallest man was Frank McLaury along with his brother Tom. He couldn't place the rangy looking kid.

"Eggs are free as long as a man drinks."

"Drinks more than two," put in the kid.

Frank picked up an egg and looked it over. "So, how much you charging for drinks these days, Max?"

"One buck just like you, Frank. Did you think we would be cheaper?"

"Who's your young friend, Tom?" Frank asked.

"This is Billy Claibourne," Tom McLaury said.

"I'm known as Billy the Kid, if you want to know."

Frank grinned at the egg in his hand. "Use to know a Billy the Kid," he said. "But he didn't look like you."

"I've plugged men for saying less about me."

"Don't rile Buckskin Frank, Billy," said Tom. "He'd shoot before you'd think about grabbing your gun."

Frank had met the men who hung around with Sheriff Behan. Men like Old Man Clanton, his two sons, Billy and Ike, William Claibourne, Tom and Frank McLaury. Men who did not like the Earp brothers and who let it be known. Frank understood the two factions in Tombstone that wanted control.

One afternoon Frank was working at the Oriental saloon when he heard that all hell had broken out on Freemont Street near the O.K. Corral. The hell included the three Earp brothers and their friend, Doc Holliday. It was a "war" against the Clantons, the McLaurys, and Billy Claibourne. Trouble had been brewing for months with all of those men. Frank didn't see the action, he only heard that the Earps killed Billy Clanton and both McLaury boys. It was said that Ike Clanton survived with a wound. Frank heard Ike Clanton yelling in the streets in a drunken fit that he was going to kill any Earp he saw, but Frank thought Clanton was all talk and no show. However, a gun battle ensued, one that was talked about for a long time. Every drink ordered was a message about the fight, and many opinions were voiced.

"Damned Earps as much as murdered those boys," one man said.

"Watch talk like that in here," Frank said. "This Oriental is half owned by Wyatt Earp. Keep a civil tongue or get out."

"Still a free country, Leslie."

"You're in Earp territory," someone warned.

"Better watch it, Frank'd as soon as pull his Colts on you as look at you."

"Hell with him and the hell with you. I'll drink at the Cosmopolitan."

"Done lost a customer, Frank."

"Worthless one to me. You see any of the action, Joe?"

"I was on Allen Street when I saw Wyatt and his brothers, Virgil and Morgan, walk toward Fourth Street. Doc Holliday joined them. They had guns drawn. Sheriff Behan told them to put their guns away, but they just walked right past him. I ran behind to see what was going to happen.

They met the cowboys on Fremont Street. Virgil told them to hand over their guns, but Billy Clanton pulled his and took a shot at Doc. Then all hell broke loose. After all the gun smoke cleared, the McLaury boys and Billy Clanton were down on the ground leaking blood."

"I'll tell you a fact," Frank said. "No Earp would deliberately gun down anyone. Wyatt doesn't usually carry a gun. He's too much with the law to just take off after those boys. Ike Clanton threatened Wyatt a number of times, and you know that man, he'd sell his own mother if he thought he would get something."

"I saw Old Man Clanton and Billy Claibourne run like rabbits into Fly's photography store," Joe continued. "Sheriff Behan was in there, and they watched the whole thing."

"I'd've liked to have been there."

"Well, where the hell were you?"

"Right here. Serving drinks and cleaning up. I heard all the ruckus of gunfire, but figured somebody was buying a new gun. Never thought there'd be that much going on or I'd have closed up and joined them.

"Whose side?" Joe asked with a grin.

"Do you need to ask?" Frank growled.

"I think Behan wanted the Earps killed, but it didn't happen that way."

SEVERAL WEEKS LATER, Frank was surprised to see Wyatt Earp walk into the Oriental saloon. Wyatt had been in jail, waiting for the big trial. The drinking customers craned their necks when he walked up to Frank.

"Haven't seen you in awhile, Wyatt," Frank said.

"Heard tell you've been associating with Ringo and Curly Bill," Wyatt said.

"Not to become friends, if that's what you mean," Frank said.

"I'm looking for Johnny Ringo. You seen him lately?"

"Haven't seen him," Frank said.

"Wells Fargo put up a large reward for Johnny Ringo, dead or alive. You hear about that?

"Heard something about that. Why?"

Wyatt gave Frank a long, hard stare, then turned around and left the saloon. Frank stood gazing after him.

THE LIFELESS BODY of Johnny Ringo was discovered near the trail against an old tree. He'd been shot in the forehead. Since no one believed anyone would try to shoot Ringo, it was considered a self-inflicted wound and therefore suicide.

Sam, the other bartender in the Oriental Saloon, took Frank aside. "Word is out that you shot and killed Johnny Ringo."

"Not me, Sam. Why would I do that?"

"Maybe for that five-hundred-dollar reward. Maybe it was about that woman Ringo took a fancy to."

"Got it wrong. I'm still married. Not looking for a new woman."

"Few saw you ride out after Ringo went out of town. They seem to believe you killed Ringo," Sam said.

"People see and say things that ain't always true."

"There's a big reward out on Ringo."

Frank only shrugged and rubbed the cloth around in circles on the bar top. Ringo had many friends who would avenge his death. Anyone claiming the reward would be a victim of that revenge.

Billy Claibourne's suspicions about who killed his friend Ringo could not be satisfied. He stormed into the Oriental Saloon and called Frank all kinds of offensive names. "You son of a bitch, you shot Johnny Ringo," Billy yelled.

"Billy, I got good folks in here. They don't want to hear language like that."

"To hell with them," Billy yelled. "I want to hear it from your own mouth."

"There's nothing to say, Billy. Now go cool off."

"Did you kill Ringo?"

"Look, Billy. There's time to talk and places to talk. You can't stop yelling, I'll have to ask you to leave."

"Damn you to hell, I'm going to kill you, Frank."

"Go cool off, Billy," Frank urged and walked Billy to the door and out onto the street. Billy crossed the street throwing curse words over his shoulder. Frank watched Claibourne stumble off, satisfied that the man would calm down.

"It don't look good, Frank," warned Sam. "Billy's coming across the street with a rifle."

"I'll take care of it, Sam," Frank said. "Billy's a stupid loco-head. Nobody can talk sense to him. He's all fired up about wrong things." Frank grabbed his Colt .44 from behind the bar and walked into the street, hollering, "Billy, don't shoot." Billy answered by triggering the Winchester rifle at Frank. The shot missed.

"Holy hell, Frank, watch out," Sam yelled.

"There's gonna be a shoot-out," someone yelled.

"Get out of the way. Leslie's got a gun."

Frank fired once and hit Billy in the chest. Billy was

still cussing as he dropped to the ground. People drew around him and one man said, "You were stupid to go after Leslie, Billy."

Billy's eyes found Frank and he gasped, "You did Ringo." It was his last statement.

"You killed Claibourne," Sam said. "Better watch your back. Somebody will want to kill you."

"I'll keep my watch," Frank said. "There'd better not be anyone stupid enough to come after me."

No man sought out Frank Leslie. The trials and the need to know what happened in the streets of Tombstone near the O.K. Corral were busy subjects, and soon men began to drift away. Conversations were guarded, and men left town quietly without looking back. Tombstone was beginning to look like a cemetery. Buckskin Frank Leslie saw the radical change come over Tombstone like a searing hot wind off the desert. He didn't like the change but knew it was inevitable. Time evolves around changes that make men older and create new beginnings.

The Earp brothers cleared out of Tombstone before their trials could come up. There was a big doubt they would have a fair trial. Morgan Earp had been shot in the back and killed. Virgil was shot in the arm while walking along Allen Street. The opposition was out to gun down the Earps. Sheriff Behan did nothing to calm the action. Virgil was sent to California to heal his wound and to accompany the coffin of his brother. Wyatt's wife, Josie, was secreted out of town. Wyatt rode north. Doc Holliday rode out of town. He was never seen again.

Sheriff John Slaughter replaced John Behan, the mines filled with water and dropped in their production. Even the violence subsided. The mean, cruel man had ridden off into the hills. Frank was the last of the old members of

Tombstone. He felt the warm breeze and knew Tombstone would never be the same.

Frank became nervous and quit the Oriental saloon. Too many strangers came into town, and it became a threat to him. He might get shot in the back while serving drinks. He accepted an Army job as a dispatch rider, then worked as a border customs inspector, but he soon quit. Frank decided his job would always be with the Oriental saloon, and he went back to work serving drinks. Milt Joyce sold out his interest in the Oriental and gave Frank the run of his Magnolia ranch.

"Going to California, Frank. Take over and watch the ranch for me," Milt said. "I've left Phelps on to help out. He's a good worker."

"Good luck, Milt," Frank called. "I'll manage the place for you."

About the same time, Frank received divorce papers from May claiming his many infidelities instead of his abuse. He wasn't too surprised as he hadn't seen May in some time. "Damn that woman. She thinks I should become a saint."

"You haven't seen your wife in some time, Frank," said Phelps.

"She stays to herself too much. Her looks have faded and she's nothing to me anymore."

"You sure know how to make the women come to you, Frank. You should give out lessons."

"What I know is for myself."

Frank went back to drinking and became friendly with Mollie Bradshaw, who was a favorite singer at the Birdcage Theater.

"Mollie, let me take you out of this theater and give you a real home life."

"I'm married, Frank. Do you expect me to just walk out?"

"You ain't happy with that husband of yours."

"So, I'd be happier with you?" Mollie asked.

"You and I get along real well, Mollie. I've got a ranch we can live at."

"Sounds too good to be true. I've worked here at the Birdcage for a long time. I don't know if I could manage just living at a ranch."

"You'd find it much easier than having a bunch of drunks all over you."

"I don't know. Getting a divorce takes so long."

"We can have a good life together, Mollie."

Henry Bradshaw was found dead in an alley one night. It was too convenient a death, but no attention was paid to it. He was simply put to rest in the cemetery, and any facts about how he got there were buried with him.

"Heard tell Bradshaw was shot in the head," Jim Simmons, the theater manager, commented to Frank.

"Nothing to me," Frank said.

Simmons grinned. "Some think you put him under since you've been seeing his wife."

"I've got better things to do than plug old Bradshaw. He's a no-account lazy buzzard. Mollie is well off without him."

Frank and Mollie moved in at the Magnolia ranch, and they tried to set up a good life. Frank worked at the Oriental saloon while Mollie fussed around the dusty house. Frank could tell life became a rather lonely vigil for Mollie. She wasn't used to keeping up a house. A room was plenty at the theater, and all she had to do was keep up her own appearance for the crowds. She could sleep all day and rehearse her songs during the afternoons, and by evening she was ready for the people to honor her with their praises. Frank knew she didn't get praises on the ranch. There was nothing to satisfy her with four dreary walls and too much empty land.

Frank couldn't handle the unhappiness that came between them. They never bothered to get married. He could not interest Mollie in being the ranch wife. He only assumed Mollie would take over and be the efficient woman. He saw the change come over her, and he began to drink in order not to have to face the issues. Then it all came to a hard confrontation when they began to quarrel.

"You think I'm nothing?" Frank yelled.

"I didn't tell you that," she said. "Now, stop waving that gun around."

"Miss Mollie, you're so high and mighty. What gives you cause to look down at me as if I ain't nothing?"

"Just the way you are. A braggart and a drunk."

"I don't brag about nothing I can't already do." Frank pointed the gun at Molly. His hand shook. He didn't like her face. Her makeup was smeared from sweating and crying. The black from her eyelashes ran into the red on her mouth and made a grotesque mask.

"You're a damned ugly woman," Frank yelled.

"You ain't nothing to speak of."

"Stay still, you ugly whore." Frank fired at what he thought was the wall closest to her shoulder; but the bullet hit her dead center in the heart.

The sound of gunfire attracted the hired man, and as Phelps walked into the living room, he saw Mollie on the floor. "Holy God, you shot her." Phelps kneeled next to Mollie. "She looks dead to me."

"Get away from her," Frank yelled, and he fired at Phelps. Phelps grabbed his side and crumpled to the floor.

Frank stumbled away from the two bodies and ran out of the house to saddle a horse. He knew if he was caught they'd hang him on the spot, and he wasn't going to wait around. He would get back to the Oriental and make them believe he had been there all the time. He had no idea his life was in a thick web with the strands closing in on him.

Someone informed the sheriff about gun shots at the Milt Joyce ranch. Two deputies investigated.

FRANK WATCHED DEPUTY Johnson enter the Oriental and stroll slowly toward the bar with his hand on the butt of his gun. "Evening, Frank."

"What's wrong, Johnson?"

"I've come to arrest you for the murder of Mollie Bradshaw."

"Any way for you to fix this for me, Johnson?"

"Not a chance, Frank. As much as I'd like. I'm afraid it's all over for you. Phelps already spilled his guts, and there's no way in hell I can fix that."

Phelps was a witness against Frank in a short trial. Frank was sentenced to twenty years in the Yuma, Arizona, prison.

The confinement of the prison was intolerable. Frank managed to break out. He didn't get far. The law brought him back and placed him in the confinement of a dark cell for two months.

"You'll be in the hole for a long time, Leslie," the warden said.

The prison guard moved behind Frank as he walked the distance to the cells of detention. "You ain't gonna like this one damned bit. You'll find going along with orders a lot better than this."

The dark, lonely cell changed Frank. When he was released he became a model prisoner, working as a pharmacist in the prison hospital. On his first day in the hospital, sick men were being brought in. A strange disease had attacked. Men filled the hospital beds, unable to care far themselves. Frank helped to save the lives of many of the prisoners.

"You've helped men get over their illness, Leslie," the doctor said. "You've worked long and hard. I'll put in a good word for you."

"I think we've got this sickness whipped," Frank said.

"You were sick. I thought I lost you, but you sure managed."

"I got working at it and didn't want to quit."

The *San Francisco Chronicle* ran an article along with a photograph about the model prisoner who saved lives in the Yuma prison. Frank received many letters from a woman admirer who saw his picture in the newspaper.

"Got another letter, Frank. Smells like woman to me."

"Don't be looking at my mail too close," Frank said.

"You're mighty lucky getting letters. She must think you're a hero." Frank smiled at the guard and took his letter to the corner of his cell. It was from Belle Stowell. She had recently been widowed and had read about him in the newspapers. She commended him for the good work he did in saving lives. Frank wrote back, and they began to know each other very well. He received a picture of her and he was very impressed with her loveliness. Frank felt the old rush of his heartbeat. He wrote things to her that he never thought he could write to another person, let alone a woman he'd never met. He became very attached to the letters she sent. Sometimes he read them over and over. He was sure he was in love.

"Good news, Frank," the warden said. "The governor is releasing you early on your good conduct. You did real good, Frank."

On November 6, 1896, Frank received a full pardon from Governor Franklin of Arizona, and he walked out the Yuma gates into the arms of his corresponding sweetheart, Belle Stowell.

"It's so good to hold you in my arms at last."

"You'll like San Francisco," Belle said, taking his arm and moving away from the prison gates. "I've a horse and carriage waiting. We can be on our way."

"I've heard San Francisco has big saloons."

"There's more saloons than you can count," Belle said.

They were married, and Buckskin Frank Leslie disappeared into another life. The name Buckskin was dropped, and he lost all association with Tombstone. He had lived among the most notorious men of the times, yet a charm of luck seemed to have guarded his every move. He lived quite happily in his new life, to the age of seventy.

Short Rope at Dawn

T. L. DAVIS

T. L. Davis wears many hats—novelist, screenwriter, play-wright, filmmaker, and ghostwriter. Here he adds to that list Western short story writer, with this tale of outlaw Jack Slade. He has written the novels *Shadow Soldier* and *Home to Texas*, as well as the full-length play *Chosen Realities*.

★

Jack Slade stood at the bar. His mind was just starting to clear as he surveyed the destruction he had wrought: shards of glass from shattered lanterns lay at his feet, broken whiskey bottles were swept into piles behind the bar, and there were bullet holes in the wall and ceiling. Shame descended, but only for a moment before being thrust from his mind by the comfort of defiance.

Miners and ranchers, who had gathered in the aftermath, stood just inside the door. Snow slid off their boots and began to melt at their feet. Their attention was focused on Slade: the terror of Virginia City.

Slade shot a glance over his shoulder. "Let 'em stare," he thought. There wasn't much else for the cowards to do anyway. They were store clerks and haberdashers; the type of men who knew the ease of society; men who relied on the certainty of law.

On the other end of the spectrum was Slade. He was a man who had stepped into the untamed West and brought order to the Overland Stage. He was a man who had lived far beyond civilization, where a man's strength and tenacity stood between life and death. Survival was power, and respect was earned. These new men, these latecomers, took power and placed it in stupid laws; they took respect and made it fear. They were hangers-on and usurpers and Slade didn't like them.

A cold wind blew across the frozen earth of Montana and up through the floorboards of the saloon. Slade didn't move. He was lost in thoughts of a different time. A time he better understood: the days of Julesburg.

"Julesburg," he muttered and rolled his eyes. "Damn Jules Beni for the arrogance to name a town for himself."

SLADE KNEW BENI as the biggest horse thief in Colorado Territory at least, and the most corrupt man on the payroll of the Overland Stage. He fingered the mummified ear dangling from his watch chain as his thoughts dwelled on Beni.

It was spring when Slade went to Julesburg Station to confront him. The fresh, thin air of Colorado was tinged by wood smoke coming from the chimney of Beni's small house. Slade rode up to the corral. It was apparent that Beni had been stealing Overland stock. He hadn't even bothered to alter the brands.

Slade shook his head in disbelief as he looked over the horses. Such an act showed downright contempt for the Overland, and for the owner, Ben Ficklin. It steeled Slade's desire to see Beni squirm. Slade gave orders to his men to cut the Overland's horses out of the corral and take them back to the station. The men were leading the stolen horses away when Slade crossed a broad prairie toward the house.

"Jules Beni, come on out here. Now!" Slade shouted. "We got business, you and me."

But Jules Beni was no man's fool, and he wasn't impressed with Ficklin's hired gun. Beni had been arguing with Slade for weeks over the operation of the Julesburg Station. The cards were falling against Beni, and he knew of only one way to stop it. He jerked a revolver from its holster and opened the door.

Several sharp cracks split the morning air. Magpies perched on the top rail of the corral took to flight. Slade heard the flapping of wings as he felt the first ball hit his shoulder. The second ripped into his side, knocking him to the ground. More shots were fired, and Slade lay taking ball after ball until, thankfully, he heard the dry click of the hammer on an empty chamber. Slade lifted his head to watch Beni walk back to the house.

"This is how I die?" he asked himself as he lay in the dust and a pool of his own blood. "Here, at the hands of a horse thief and a coward?"

Slade, despite his wounds, was outraged at the prospect of such an end. He spit. "By God, I won't," he declared, tensing the muscles in his jaw.

Everything was clear and sharp. Slade's senses were keen, probing outward as if to hold on to the world that was slipping away. Then he heard the creaking of leather hinges. Without the strength to raise his head, Slade peered from under his brow to find Beni approaching on stubby legs. Beni raised a shotgun to his shoulder and aimed it right at him.

"God, no!" whispered Slade.

Hot balls of shot splattered Slade. A large puff of smoke billowed out from the end of the gun and hung in the air. Beni was only a few yards away.

Slade's men, having heard the shots, approached at a gallop as Beni reloaded. They pulled up short when Beni swung the shotgun in their direction.

"When this man dies," Beni said, in a thick French accent, "you can stick him in a dry-goods box and ship him back to Ficklin!"

Enraged by the presumption of his death, Slade forced himself to speak loud enough for Beni to hear. "I'll live long enough to wear your ear on my watchguard!" he exclaimed.

Beni furrowed his brow for a second, then laughed. He gave a dismissive thrust of his jaw and backed toward the house with the shotgun held stiff against his shoulder.

SLADE RETREATED FROM the solitude of reverie. He stared at the whiskey and raised the glass a few inches. "Here's to ya, Jules. Even though you were a lowborn horse thief and a murderin' dog, you had more character than any of these here."

The saloon doors slapped open and two men stepped through. Jim Kiskadden and X. Biedler scanned the room and approached the bar. Jim grabbed hold of Slade's jacket as if to turn him around. Slade pulled free and narrowed his eyes.

"Get off me, Jim," he warned.

"For God's sake, let's go home, Jack," Jim pleaded.

"I ain't done havin' fun."

"The mood's against ya, Slade. Best listen to Jim and go on home," Biedler advised.

"I ain't thought much of you, X, but it seemed that at least you knew when to tend your own business," Slade said, goading Biedler. He was in the mood for some sort of resolution, and X. Biedler was just about the only man to show some sentiment against Slade and live.

"You've become my business, Slade," Biedler said, in that officious, denigrating tone he was so capable of producing. "I urge you to leave town immediately . . . for your own good, sir."

Slade slapped the bar with his hand, bouncing drinks farther down. He snorted a laugh, and with a dramatic, sweeping gaze, he took in the whole bar.

"My own good, is it? I've never known you to be so bold without the Vigilance Committee close at hand."

"Jack, please!" Jim begged, sure in his belief that time was running out.

Without acknowledging Jim's plea, Slade fixed his penetrating stare on Biedler. "Well?"

"You're to leave town immediately."

"Jack, you know Biedler speaks for the Committee," Jim urged. "Just go home."

"Hell, I believe the Committee's played out," Slade declared, staring into Biedler's tiny eyes.

"You have three hours," Biedler said, making a grandiose gesture of pointing at the clock. "Beyond that, I can not vouch for your safety."

With that, Biedler turned with a flourish of his long coat and walked out of the bar. Jim watched him go as if watching the last train of salvation pull out of the station.

"Jack, you know the men on the Committee. They're

serious. What you said to Judge Davis went too far. Hell, I went too far, too. Let's quit and go home."

"Let 'em do what they want. Ain't one of 'em going to stand up to me direct. Ain't one of 'em got the backbone of a lowborn horsethief. Nothing gave me more pleasure than hunting Beni down like a dog, nothing except him knowing I was comin'.'"

"I'm gonna go talk to 'em. I'll reason with 'em," Jim said, desperately searching for a way to divert fate, to resist the irresistible. On one hand there was the Vigilance Committee that had had enough of Jack Slade; on the other hand there was Jack Slade, who had had enough of vigilance committees and fake judges; a man who yearned for one last opportunity to have it his way.

AUTUMN WINDS WERE blowing cold as Jack Slade returned to the Overland. A long stretch of dusty trail and months of painful recuperation lay behind him by the time he stepped off the stage in Fort Laramie. Word had already gotten around to Jules Beni that Slade had miraculously recovered from his wounds and was back.

"By God, I'll finish the task!" Beni was reported to have said in front of everyone at the Cold Springs Station a few days earlier. It didn't take long for Slade to hear of it and set out for Wyoming.

Slade entered Fort Laramie administration headquarters and met with Major McFinney.

"You know Jules Beni tried to kill me," Slade began, his jaw thrust out. "He will do so again and in the same fashion, if I know the man."

"Yes," McFinney replied.

"He was never to return."

"He was given strict orders that he might live if he left for good," McFinney acknowledged.

"Well, return he has. That can only mean one thing in my mind. Therefore, I propose to hunt the man down and bring peace to the Overland," Slade boldly declared.

"The business you have with Beni is Overland business, not mine. I trust you'll take the proper course."

Slade nodded and left. A coach waited outside to take him to Cold Springs. The effects of the wounds were still obvious as Slade strode unevenly across the compound. He climbed up onto the box with the driver.

"Cold Springs!" Slade shouted.

Two men, Scott and Hodges, abandoned their protective positions at the corners of the stage and climbed in. Slade had come for Beni unprepared the first time; he wouldn't do so again.

Jules Beni had made some money trading horses and was in the process of getting drunk. Rarely a minute passed without his boastful arrogance shining through.

"My only mistake was in not getting closer," Beni said to an interested bartender. "Had it not been for six of his men bearing down on me, I would have walked right up to him and put the barrel to the back of his neck." Beni took a drink of whiskey. "As long as I'm here, you won't have trouble with Slade. I bet he won't get within ten miles of me. Not if he wants to live."

The fat bartender jiggled as he laughed. He dried his hands on a filthy gray apron and leaned on his elbow as he listened to Beni's stories.

X. BIEDLER CLOSED the door behind him and faced the others. Perhaps thirty men stared at him from under their hat brims, trying to get a sense of the outcome.

"He's having none of it," Biedler declared, and a quiet resolve spread from one man to the other. They knew what they had to do.

The men of the Vigilance Committee knew Slade. Often, Slade himself had sniffed out the murderers and thieves among the townsfolk. Many times, he had dispensed justice before the Committee could assemble. Other times, he had ridden with them and been at the forefront of their business. Now it was Slade they had to confront. Many of the men considered Slade a friend, and the vote was not tallied without hearing their dissents. But in the end the vote was unanimous. Even his allies recognized that he was out of control.

THUNDERING HOOVES BEAT against the frozen ground. An icy wind whipped across Slade's wide cheekbones as they neared Cold Springs Station. He saw, or thought he saw, a wisp of wood smoke on the horizon. Slade leaned forward in the seat and strained his eyes. His fists tightened around the stock of the rifle resting across his knees. He sniffed at the air.

Slade raised the rifle in the air and brought it down hard on the top of the stage.

"Yeah?" Hodges asked, leaning out of the window and holding onto his hat with a free hand.

"Up there it is." Slade pointed toward the low wooden structure rising slowly above the horizon as they neared. "Get around back as soon as you can."

"Yes sir!"

Slade nodded and turned his attention back to the station house. Inside was the man who had filled him with lead. Beni had taken his best shot and come up short. Slade felt invincible, above it, as if God had brought him through this terrible ordeal for the chance to watch Beni die.

The stagecoach rattled up to the station and stopped. The horses snorted and blew. Their muscles jumped beneath their skin. The side door swung open and Scott and Hodges jumped out to surround the building.

Inside, confusion flitted across the bartender's face. No stage was due in, not for a day, or two. He glanced at Beni, who remained frozen. Words no longer mattered. Judgment had come. But in his heart Beni was a coward, and he darted for the back of the station. He broke out a window and hefted his bulk up into the window frame. He looked one way, then the other. There was no easy way down, so he pushed himself through the window and to the ground. The pistol in his waistband fell free and clattered on the frozen earth.

It didn't take long for Scott and Hodges to appear around opposite corners of the building and hem Beni in. The pistol lay not far from Beni's hand. Scott saw Beni's predicament.

"You grab that hog leg and you're liable to get me in a jam," Scott said, knowing that killing Beni was something Slade wanted for himself.

Beni looked through long strands of greasy hair. An odd sense of giddiness came over him as he thought of defying Slade one last time. Beni chuckled. One lunge for the pistol would change everything. Above all, it would bring him a merciful death, something he could not otherwise count on. Long seconds passed.

"You could get us both out of this," Beni suggested. "You could let me go."

Scott snorted a reply. "Die now, if you want."

★

THE VIGILANCE COMMITTEE pushed out the door
and into the chilly Montana sunshine. They were a well-
disciplined mob, but a mob nonetheless. They thronged
through the streets carrying rifles and shotguns. Urgent
whispers rushed past them and through the town. As the
people of Virginia City became aware of the aim of the
Committee, others joined in. Some of the ranchers that had
stared at Jack Slade in the bar were now turning to follow
the Committee. Miners swelled out from nowhere to join
the fray, some carrying only clubs.

Slade felt something, an odd awareness that all was not
right. He narrowed his eyes. Even in a half-drunken stupor,
he could feel a reckoning coming. He hunched his shoulders against the cold wind that blew in from the north and
staggered down the sidewalk.

At the other end of the street, the Vigilance Committee
had swelled to over one hundred men. The sheer noise of
so many footsteps should have alerted Slade to his im-
pending doom. Perhaps it did and he simply no longer
cared.

"There he is!" someone shouted, sending the whole
herd of them into a jog toward the man in the long coat.
They engulfed Slade and swept him up into the maelstrom
of hate and fear that propelled them.

Slade was startled when he looked up to find so many
faces staring at him. He tried to shrug them off, but they
pinned his arms to his sides. They disarmed him and
shoved him back the way he'd come.

"I'm sorry, Jack," a voice said, close to his ear. When
Slade turned toward the voice, he found no ally.

"The Vigilance Committee has decided upon your execution," Captain Williams informed him, maintaining a

rigid gait and not bothering to turn toward Slade. "The Elephant Corral will be your end."

It was only then that Slade began to realize the depth of the trouble he was in. He searched each man's face for signs of sympathy and found only stiff, wind-chapped features and cold eyes.

"Get my wife! Someone has to get my wife!" he bellowed to the crowd. "I want to see her just once more before I die."

Jim Kiskadden trailed on the fringes of the crowd desperate for some way to help Slade. He whispered urgently to a boy standing on the sidewalk and begged him to ride to the Slade Ranch to get Virginia Slade. The wide-eyed boy was swept up into the excitement and, feeling very important, took off at a run to comply.

Slade could see the Elephant Corral looming ahead. As he neared, he noticed a dry-goods box beneath a corral pole and a noose dangling from the cross member. He recoiled from the sight and tried to break free, but these men had done this before. They knew the impulse to run would come, and they braced against Slade's reaction.

BENI APPEARED FROM around the corner of the shack a broken man. Behind him, Scott and Hodges had him covered with shotguns, periodically nudging him forward with the barrels.

Slade waited with a knife in one hand and a rope in the other. He pointed the knife at Beni.

"I told you I'd live long enough to wear your ear on my watchguard, and by God that day has come," Slade shouted over the wind.

Beni flinched against the thought and realized that

Slade's design for him was much darker than he had imagined when the pistol lay so close. What he would give for that chance again.

"Tie him up, boys," Slade said, tossing a rope to Hodges, who worked quickly to fashion a loop.

Beni allowed the proceedings to go along without a fight. He was numb, divorced from the horrible circumstances surrounding him. Yet, his mind searched desperately for some chink, some opening to plead his case. If it were anyone else, Beni felt sure he could cause a break in the momentum and maybe talk himself out of it; anyone but Jack Slade. Then the ropes pulled tight, securing him to a fence rail.

With his prey fastened to the fence, Slade took a more leisurely stance. There was no way for Beni to get out of it and no reason to hurry through a moment Slade had dreamt of. That image had been his inspiration for living.

"The only damn thing that pulled me through that awful time was the thought of seein' you like this, Jules Beni. When they washed my wounds out with whiskey, I thought of this very moment. God only knows what wretched hag bore you into this world, but I plan to take you out of it piece by piece."

With all of his hate intact, Slade drew down. The pistol jumped in his hand. Beni's shoulder exploded. The force of the bullet yanked Beni's body to the side. Slade fired again, this time at Beni's leg. Slade relished in the injuries for a while, but his enthusiasm slowly drained. Torturing Beni was not as satisfying as Slade had hoped it would be. It seemed then a pathetic brutality, and Slade did the merciful thing and pumped a round into Beni's head.

Slade approached the body of his enemy and studied it for signs of life. He calmly holstered the pistol and drew his skinning knife. A quick slash left Beni's ear in Slade's hand. Without comment, he pocketed the ear and walked back to the stage.

AND, THERE ON the Montana plain, Slade fingered the ear in his pocket and felt the noose close around his neck. So much had gone wrong in his life. It had been a long time since Slade had felt the sense of propriety he'd felt on the day he killed Beni. With the U.S. Army on his side and the whole of public opinion with him, he had killed a man most would call a "scourge." It was a justified killing and everyone knew it.

"This ain't right," he muttered as he looked out on the crowd of ranchers and miners.

As if on cue, Jim Kiskadden burst in to object. "What has Slade done? No one was killed last night, or the night before. What has Slade done to deserve such an end?"

Without answering him, the crowd descended and muffled his cries. They shoved him to the ground and beat him.

Captain Williams ignored the scuffle and proceeded to the box. He looked up at Slade and turned to address the crowd.

"Jack Slade is a public menace. We have all suffered at his hand in some way or other. Whether it be the fear we have for loved ones should a stray bullet from his pistol find its way to them as they walk innocently on the street, or in a more direct manner, we all know the danger he presents. For two straight days, this man has held the community hostage. Forty-eight hours and I submit that that was one hour too long." Captain Williams surveyed the crowd and turned slightly toward Slade. "Do your duty, men."

The dry goods box was yanked out from under Slade's feet, and he dropped two feet to his death. Nothing could have been more anticlimactic. Years of perseverance through hostile, deadly country, years of facing the worst men the West had spawned, ended with a short drop and a simple death.

The crowd, feeling a bit of relief but also a degree of guilt, turned reluctantly away from the dangling body. Something had ended: more than a man's life, but less than an era. And, just when they thought there was no price to be paid for the way it had been done, they were confronted with the image of Slade's wife riding hell-bent on a lathered horse toward them.

"What have you done?" she asked, jerking on the reins and staring down at the men. "You cowards! For what crime . . . ?" she asked, her voice faltering as sorrow overcame anger. "What have you done?"

A Stay for a Badman

Jim Etter is the author of *Ghost-Town Tales of Oklahoma—Unforgettable Stories of Nearly Forgotten Places* and other books about his home state. He has been a journalist in both Oklahoma and Texas, and is retired from *The Daily Oklahoman* newspaper.

★

Young Crawford Goldsby felt the noose being slipped over his head, and for an instant recalled something his mother once told him: "Boy, I pray and pray that someday you'll change. You got nothin' but hate all bunched up inside you."

He stood on the gallows, handcuffed and shackled, his arms and legs bound with ropes, his face covered, before one of the largest crowds at a Fort Smith execution. They were here to see the hanging of Indian Territory's most notorious outlaw, "Cherokee Bill."

Well, she was right. And he would keep hating right up to the end—if they expected him to cower and act remorseful, they could all go to hell. Following the reading of the death warrant and before the black hood was placed over his head, he had shunned the marshal's offer to say some last words. "I came here to die, not to make a speech!" he snapped.

Then he refused to listen to further words of the priest, Father Pius. He jerked his head away. "Let's get on with it."

Moments earlier, as he was accompanied to the scaffold by the party including his mother, Ellen Beck Lynch, and his colored "aunty," Amanda Foster, who helped raise him, he knew for certain his death sentence was final. An execution ordered by Isaac Charles Parker, U.S. judge for the Western District of Arkansas—the "Hanging Judge"—was rarely deferred in the final hour. But he, like all the condemned men in the crowded, stinking prison underneath the courthouse, had held onto faint hopes for a stay. While Cherokee Bill was known to be tough as iron, he was also human and would welcome a chance to keep living, even if only until a later execution date.

And now, despite his bluster, his hands, cuffed behind him, trembled as if by their own will. Sweat stung his eyes inside the hood, even in the sunny but mild March afternoon—to everyone else, a beautiful, tranquil day. Warm wetness trickled down one of his legs. Any second, the trap would spring.

"BUT, MAMA, DON'T you remember something else you told me one time? You said for me never to let nobody run over me," Crawford had responded to his mother that time. It was during one of his rare visits to her, more than five years after he left home. It was early morning before daylight, and they sat at the kitchen table of the small house in Fort Gibson, talking as they sipped coffee.

"And that's just what I done, Mama—I didn't let that man run over me. Leastwise, I didn't let 'im get away with it. And ain't nobody gonna run over me again. Not ever!" He tilted back his chair and reached the Winchester he had leaned against the wall a good yard behind him. He gave the rifle a loving pat, and grinned and winked.

At eighteen years, Crawford Goldsby had a smooth olive complexion and keen, handsome features, and the generally dark countenance and curly black hair that bespoke his mixed racial background. His build was solid and his movements agile, which gave him the character of full maturity and self-assurance.

But the incident he spoke of was his most bitter memory. It had been several weeks since the night of the dance, when he had taken the beating of his life, but he could still taste blood and feel the pain of a smashed nose—and deep humiliation. It was his happiest moment ever as he and pretty little Maggie Glass sat talking and sipping punch at the Fort Gibson social affair. But then he was forced to protect her from the drunken advances of Jake Lewis, an older man who was a known troublemaker and good with his fists, and they wound up outside. Crawford had been beaten, kicked, and left lying senseless in the mud.

A few days later he got hold of a six-shooter and went to where Lewis worked outside a livery barn and shot the man twice, and jumped on his horse and galloped off.

Lewis lived, though badly wounded, but from that moment on, Crawford had dodged the law and taken up with other wanted men who lived on the scout here and there within the Indian Nations.

"But, Crawford," his mother said, leaning toward him in her pleading way, "I didn't mean for you to go out and shoot somebody, and then start runnin' with bad people, and stealin' and mistreatin' decent folks—folks that never done you no harm. You was a good little boy at one time. And, Lord knows, I thought goin' to Indian school all that time would do you a world of good. But it seemed like overnight you just growed up and turned plumb mean."

"Them Indian schools wasn't that nice, Mama—leastwise, not for me. I got pushed around some there, because I wasn't very big then. And some of 'em called me names. They said I wasn't Indian—they called me bad names like 'nigger.' "

"I know, son, but what I mean is, you shouldn't have all that hate bunched up inside you. You don't have to hate every livin' soul around you. If you could only have a tender *feelin'* for somebody—repent, ask forgiveness of somebody you've done wrong. It's like the Good Book says, havin' the right feelin' will bring you salvation."

"I'll get my salvation with this, Mama," he said, slapping his Winchester again. With that he got up to leave. "I gotta be goin'—it's comin' daylight and there'll be folks in the streets. Besides that, it's about time for that man to finish up milkin' and sloppin' the hogs. Me and him don't have nothin' to talk about."

Crawford and his stepfather, William Lynch, had never gotten along. That was one reason Crawford had left home about a year after he got home from school, and gone up to near Nowata to live with his sister, Georgia, and her husband, Mose Brown.

Ellen Beck begged her son to stay for breakfast. But he didn't answer as he opened the door and cautiously looked out. The town was scattered around a stockade that until a few years before had been a busy Army post. Save for a few rooster crows, the community still lay quiet in the first rays of the sun. He quickly stepped to his horse, jammed the rifle into the saddle boot, mounted, and rode off, keeping the animal at a brisk but quiet walk.

It was a few days later when Crawford and his two partners, brothers Bill and Jim Cook, who were also part Cherokee, decided to collect their "Cherokee Strip" money. There would be payments issued to legitimate tribal members from the government's purchase from the tribe of the Cherokee Outlet. More than $6 million was to be paid to the Cherokees, with every tribal member listed as having sufficient Cherokee blood to receive slightly more than $265.

But to get theirs, Crawford and the Cooks would have to send someone for it, as they knew they would be arrested when seen in public by officers. So, along with two others, Jess Cochran and Jim French, they holed up for a few days at the Halfway House, a stage stop and road ranch of sorts between Tahlequah and Wagoner, two important locations in the Cherokee Nation.

The establishment, at the top of a slope a short piece up from the small stream of Fourteen Mile Creek, was also known as a den for whiskey smugglers and other wrongdoers. Effie Crittenden, the proprietor, a fiery little woman with somewhat of a tough reputation of her own, agreed to go to Tahlequah and get their money on the designated day.

Effie got back with the money, but a posse of lawmen would soon be on her trail.

Leaders of the Cherokee Lighthorse and other officers had gotten wind of the outlaws' whereabouts, and saw it as the opportunity to nab the two fugitives—Crawford Goldsby, wanted for shooting Lewis, and Jim Cook, charged with stealing a horse.

Shortly after noon on Sunday, June 17, 1894—the day after Effie Crittenden collected the money for Crawford and the Cook brothers—the posse, led by Ellis Rattling Gourd, chief of the Cherokee Lighthorse, rode out from the Cherokee National Capitol in Tahlequah. Riding with Rattling Gourd were Sequoyah Houston, a tribal deputy sheriff and a member of the Lighthorse; and brothers Dick and E. C. "Zeke" Crittenden, both known as gunfighters. Others in the party were Bill Bracket, Bill McKee, Isaac Grease, George Parris, Bob Woodall, and Nelson Hicks.

A few hours later at the Halfway House, Crawford and his partners had finished eating a leisurely meal and were sitting around smoking and discussing plans. They were getting too well-known in the Nations, they said, so might head down to Texas, or maybe west, all the way through Oklahoma Territory and into New Mexico.

But a shout from outside threw the room into a hush. "You in the house, we got you covered. Throw down your guns and come out, and with your hands up!" It sounded like Rattling Gourd. They all knew him.

In seconds, they were in defensive positions, both inside and outside the frame structure, all armed. Even Effie, though planning to stay out of the fight, had her pistol handy in case she needed it. Crawford, who by now was a crack shot with both six-shooter and his Winchester, stood outside and peered around the corner, the rifle cocked.

Nearly twenty minutes crept by in deafening silence. The men in and around the building couldn't see anyone, but reasoned the posse had to be across the clearing and in the blackjack timber where the rocky hill began sloping down toward the creek, the easiest and most logical approach to their location. It was a good distance, but within firing range. Sweating in the afternoon heat, and hearing only the occasional twitter of a mockingbird or the buzzing of a horsefly, the men waited, their Winchesters and pistols ready.

In a sudden surprise, one of the lawmen stood up from his brushy cover and called out, "Come on out, boys. Let's keep this peaceful"—and nearly in the same instant, Crawford caught the man in his rifle sights and fired. The lawman vanished as if by magic as the shot seemed to echo through the surrounding blackjacks and even the tall cottonwoods and sycamores down by the creek.

The fight was on. Guns popped and cracked both in the woods and in and around the frame building, the smoke at times so thick the woods were barely visible, and the air sharp with burning gunpowder. Lead slugs whined off rocks and whacked into the old wood of the Halfway House.

Crawford barely caught the words of one of the posse above the clatter of gunfire, "Sequoyah's been hit!" A pang of regret seized him, and a sickness welled from deep in his stomach. The man he shot was Sequoyah Houston! He remembered him from when he was small. The man was one of the few grown-ups to treat him well, sometimes playing his fiddle and telling funny stories for him and a few other youngsters. He also taught Crawford many things about the woods, like how to hunt and shoot, and how to make whistles out of hickory branches.

And Crawford had shot the man square in the chest. He knew he had most likely killed one of the few friends he ever had.

The fight raged. A few yards from Crawford, one of his partners screamed and dropped his rifle. It was Jim Cook. He stood bleeding, his face twisted in pain.

After a time, fewer shots were coming from the posse, which was a relief to Crawford and the others as the sun had lowered and was now blinding them with its glare. It looked like several of the posse had left. The best Crawford could tell, there were only two shooters remaining in the woods—he guessed the Crittenden brothers, who, eager gunfighters that they were, likely would be the last to quit fighting.

He also reasoned that most of the posse had left to take the injured Houston for help—most likely to the small store operated by Xerxes "Zack" Taylor, and wife, Jennie, not far from the creek.

Crawford hated what he had done but now could do nothing but fight back, along with the rest of his bunch, until they could manage to get to their horses in the barn behind them and scatter. The timber in that direction was thick and the hill steep and rocky, but it was their only chance. And now was their best time to go, before the other lawmen could return.

"If only I had known it was Sequoyah shooting at that house, I wouldn't have fired!" Bill said to himself and would later say over and over to his partners. But a bullet couldn't be taken back, and it did no good at all to keep thinking about it.

Before they could withdraw from the battle, Jim Cook yelled. He was hit again, this time, it seemed, in the shoulder, on the same side where he was shot the first time. He had been firing his pistol with his good hand as his other arm, soaked with blood, dangled, when he was hit again. But this time it apparently was with buckshot—which, at the distance, wouldn't do near as much damage as rifle or even pistol—so Crawford was hopeful he wouldn't slow them down in their retreat. He didn't aim to get caught.

One or two at a time, and with Jim Cook being helped along, all five finally got to their horses and rode down the rough hillside, the tangles of thick growth clawing at their faces and their mounts stumbling over rocks.

They soon scattered and all got clean away, except for the injured Jim Cook, who would be captured two days later where he lay wounded in a pasture near Fort Gibson.

And Crawford would soon learn that the gun battle had given him a nickname—one by which he would become famous. When officers questioned Effie Crittenden immediately after the shoot-out, she was asked if one of the men was Crawford Goldsby. And, while her answer was never explained, to Goldsby or anyone else, she answered, "No, it was 'Cherokee Bill.'"

Residents throughout both Indian and Oklahoma territories, as well as some elsewhere, would learn, from newspapers and other reports, much about the outlaw known as Cherokee Bill—who had a background not altogether typical of a desperado.

It was said he was born in Fort Concho, Texas, and was the son of George Goldsby, a "Buffalo soldier," who gained the rank of sergeant major before his military career was ruined by trouble involving a dispute between soldiers and civilians. His mother, as Ellen Beck, was born in Indian Territory and was the descendant of slaves.

Crawford Goldsby was believed to be part Sioux Indian and Cherokee Indian, with a background of Mexican as well as Negro. It was said he had a confused life as a boy, being sent to the two Indian schools, first at Cherokee, Kansas, for three years, then at the Carlisle Indian Industrial School in Pennsylvania for two years, followed by heated arguments with his stepfather.

Until he met Maggie Glass, his mother was the only person he loved, despite some bitterness he felt toward her for sending him away to school—although he had come to realize she had only done her best, as it was hard for her to care for him and his sister, Georgia, and two brothers, Clarence and Luther.

Cherokee Bill gained notoriety both on his own and as a member of the "Cook Gang" of outlaws, which soon after the Halfway House shoot-out went on a spree of robbing trains, stagecoaches, banks, and post offices throughout parts of both Indian and Oklahoma territories, and even getting chased out of Texas and New Mexico by lawmen.

Along with Bill Cook, Cherokee Bill, and Jim French, the gang was believed to have grown to include Sam McWilliams, also known as "the Verdigris Kid"; and at least three others: Lon Gordon, Henry Munson and Curtis Dayson.

The gang threw such panic across much of Indian Territory that, in addition to the posting of rewards for the capture of any or all the members, authorities wired the Office of Indian Affairs in Washington for help; and federal lawmen at Fort Smith acknowledged they didn't have enough funds or field deputies to corral the outlaws. Washington officials even threatened to abrogate the Indian treaties and establish a territorial government.

By his own deeds, Cherokee Bill was dubbed by writers as "the fiercest of the Cook Gang" and "the quickest man in the Territory with a gun."

He would eventually be blamed for killing three men, his brother-in-law Mose Brown, reportedly during a dispute over hogs; Ernest Melton, an innocent bystander during a store robbery by Bill and another gang member in Lenapah; and Lawrence Keating, a guard in the federal jail in Fort Smith. Bill shot the guard after managing to have a smuggled revolver in his cell.

Unofficially, Cherokee Bill was credited with a number

of murders that occurred during the Cook Gang's holdups and various scrapes. Some observers said he killed as many as fourteen men.

It was Cherokee Bill's love for Maggie Glass—along with the trickery of an acquaintance Ike Rogers, who also held a deputy marshal's commission—that brought about Bill's capture. With Bill, along with the unsuspecting Maggie, as a guest in Rogers's cabin near Nowata, Rogers and another man, after a hard struggle, managed to get Cherokee Bill into handcuffs.

Judge Parker would set the execution date for Crawford Goldsby as Tuesday, March 17, 1896. And that's when, after nearly a year behind bars during which Goldsby attempted a jailbreak and killed the guard, the outlaw known as Cherokee Bill would die on the gallows, at age twenty.

THE HANGING CEREMONY was taking longer than Crawford expected. Since he'd had almost a year to think, he realized there were only two men in the world he hated—Jake Lewis, whom he considered the cause of all his trouble, and Ike Rogers, who had betrayed him.

Which meant he had killed some that he didn't hate— didn't even dislike. Among them was the first man he killed, Sequoyah Houston, a kind man who had befriended him. He hadn't known he was shooting at Sequoyah that time at the Halfway House, but that didn't make him feel better.

There were others, too, like his sister's husband, Mose. He hadn't liked the man, but he wished he hadn't shot him down over a small disagreement. And Ernest Melton, who happened to be standing in the wrong place during the robbery in Lenapah. He had nothing against the prison guard, either, other than his being a lawman.

Why he had all those feelings now, he didn't know—it was like his many regrets, long kept hidden from even himself, now gushed out into the open.

His mother was wrong in thinking he had no sorrowful feelings about anything. Probably the worst of his regrets, in fact, was that it was too late to tell her how he really felt—to give her that one little bit of comfort before he died—especially since she was the only person still alive to whom all that would matter.

And now the only way he could do that—the only way he could *possibly* do that—was to say he was sorry. And to say it to his mother, if there was a way in Heaven's name he could!

He, *was* truly sorry for the many wrong things he had done, and would give anything if he could let her know that. He didn't mind dying at all—if only he could die knowing that at least his mother knew how he felt.

Crawford knew then that he *had* to tell her! He would die happily if he could only, somehow, send his last thought to her first.

Maybe if he wished strongly enough, he might communicate—maybe he could make his thoughts fly to where she stood in the crowded courthouse yard, weeping and telling him her silent good-bye. Maybe he could, if his last thoughts were and strong enough. Maybe . . .

"Mama, I'm sorry!" he actually heard himself call out, between sobs. "Please hear me. I love you, Mama!"

It was then that strange things began to happen.

The noose and hood were being removed, and Bill was jerked from his feverish thoughts by the brightness, and he was instantly back into what was going on at the moment.

He blinked against the sunlight, and the marshal, who was still holding the hood, smiled at him. He blinked again.

Somehow, there had been a stay. He was free! His mother was right! He had expressed his feelings, and it had brought his salvation.

Within minutes, he was riding away. He had never felt so uplifted. The day was bright and sunny, but there was no glare to hurt his eyes, and no sweaty heat. His horse went at a fast, easy gait, which raised no dust.

Strange as it seemed, he realized he was riding toward his boyhood home, where both Maggie and his mother were waiting for him. He would greet his mother first, and tell her what he wanted to say. He could hardly wait to see her, and to feel her hug him the way she did when he was small.

THE EXECUTIONER, THE physician, and two deputy marshals were astonished as the body was removed from underneath the gallows.

"He sure don't look like the mean one that he was, does he?" one of the deputies said.

"No, I never seen one of 'em look so peaceful," the other said. "Except for his broken neck, he looks like a sleepin' child."

A Good Start

ED GORMAN

Ed Gorman has written fiction in many different genres. His Western efforts have always garnered him great praise for novels, most recently for *Lawless* and *Ghost Town*, both recently published by Berkley Books. His short story "The Face" won him the ultimate Western prize, the WWA Spur Award for Best Short Story. It is with great pleasure that I present his newest effort, a story about Henry Starr, the first outlaw ever to use an automobile in a bank robbery.

★

"The last important outlaw in Oklahoma, Henry Starr, was the first bandit to use a car in a bank robbery."
— Jay Robert Nash, *Encyclopedia of Western Lawmen & Outlaws*

Sam Mines, the high sheriff of Pruett County, Oklahoma, was known to be exceptionally proud of three things—the forearm scar left over from a shoot-out with Tom Horn, from which both men had walked away; his 1914 Ford Model T; and his lovely seventeen-year-old daughter, Laurel, whom he'd raised alone for the past twelve years, following the death of his wife from cancer.

Pruett City, the county seat, was Mines's fiefdom. Like many towns of 15,000 at this point in the new century, Pruett City was caught between being a noisy old frontier settlement and a by-god real town with telephones, electricity, and a newspaper that came out three times a week.

Mines wasn't a mean man, but he was a tough one. If he caught you carrying a gun in his town, he'd run you in no matter who you were. A saloon fight would get you anywhere between three and five days in jail. And you'd pay for every penny of the damages you'd caused or you'd rot in jail. And if you, God forbid, ever struck a woman, be she your wife or not, you'd get the cell with the drunks, most of whom were eager for a fight. The lingering death of his wife had taught him about the strength and spiritual beauty and courage of womankind, and if you did anything to defile a woman—

On this particular night in early autumn, Mines slept the sleep of the just, a deep and nourishing sleep that would enable him to be the kind of military-style lawman he'd long been. Khaki uniform crisp and fresh. Campaign hat cocked just so on his bald head. His father's Colt in his holster.

A part of his mind was hoping for another spectral visit from his wife, Susan. He'd never told anybody, not even Laurel, that the ghost of his beloved wife appeared to him from time to time. He did not want amusement or pity to spoil the visits.

And then something woke him up.

Something he'd only imagined in the fancies of his dreams? Or something real? A lawman had enemies, and every five years or so—that seemed to be the cycle—

somebody would get paroled out of prison and come back to town to start discreetly harassing the man who'd sent him up. Garbage dumped on the front lawn. Dirty words painted on the shed door. Threatening letters clogging the mailbox. All these things had happened to Mines.

Moonlight painted the windows silver.

A barn owl somewhere; the wind soughing the autumn-crisped leaves that crackled like castanets; a horse in the barn next door, crying out suddenly, perhaps in its sleep, perhaps out of sheer loneliness. Town people kept just one horse these days, that for the family buggy that was rapidly being replaced by Tin Lizzies. Mines imagined that the animals got awfully lonesome being the only one of their kind, unlike the old days when every family had two or three horses.

A sound.

A kind of . . . ticking sound.

Almost like the sound large hail makes.

He grabbed his Colt from the holster on his bedpost, dangled his feet off the bed, straightened the nightshirt sleep had wound round him, pressed bare feet to the chilly wooden floor. And proceeded to find out just what the hell was going on.

As he left the bedroom, he glanced at the clock on the bureau. He'd just assumed it was the middle of the night. But it was barely ten o'clock. He'd been asleep less than an hour.

What the hell was going on, anyway?

SULLY DRISCOLL, AT nineteen, had done some pretty dumb things in his life. And this one, he realized as he heard the pebble striking Laurel's window, had to be just about the dumbest.

But he couldn't help himself. She hadn't spoken to him for three days, not since she'd seen him sitting on the town square park bench with Constance Daly—which he sure as heck shouldn't have been doing—and by now he was so desperate to speak to her, he'd resorted to this crazy idea.

He'd even scrubbed beneath his nails extra good tonight, just on the off chance that she'd hear the pebble against her glass and sneak down and see him. Sully worked at The Automobile Emporium, one of Pruett City's three gas stations and automobile repair shops. And also the best. Sully pumped gas because the owner made him. His real love was fixing cars. Second only to Laurel's beautiful, heart-shaped face, the sight of an engine in need of work was the most fetching thing Sully had ever seen. But a lad sure did get greasy and oily working in, around, and under a car. So he'd washed up extra good tonight.

Quiet street. Deep moonshadows. And the gink of a nineteen-year-old firing pebbles at a window. If her father ever caught him—

And that was when Sully saw the ghost.

Coming around the corner of the house. And moving faster than he'd ever heard of a ghost moving before. And Sully was something of a ghost expert, having practically memorized every single short story by Edgar Allen Poe.

But it wasn't a ghost, of course. It was big Sam Mines in his nightshirt. With his Colt out. Huge white feet slapping through the dewy grass like rabbits.

Sully's first inclination was to run.

Maybe Sam hadn't gotten a good look at him yet.

But, no. Nothing much ever got past Sam.

Sully said, "Evenin', Sam." Trying to sound as casual as possible.

There were times when Sam was a splutterer. You didn't see it very often—usually Sam was so cool, ice wouldn't melt on him—but every once in a while he'd confront a situation that exasperated him so much he'd start a-splutterin', spittle flying from his lips, eyes bugging out, the true deep red of rage discoloring his face.

But before he even had time to form a semi-coherent word, Laurel's window flew open—*Now* she opens it, Sully thought miserably—and Laurel leaned out and said, "What's going on down there, anyway?"

"IT WAS MY fault," Laurel said at breakfast the next morning.

"How was it your fault?" her father asked around a piece of fried potato.

"Because I wouldn't speak to him for three whole days and he was going crazy."

"That still doesn't give him any right to start throwing rocks in the middle of the night at your—"

"It was only ten o'clock. And they were pebbles, not rocks."

"Still."

"I shouldn't have gotten so jealous over Constance. He broke off with her before he started seeing me. And I've always been afraid that maybe he thinks he made a mistake."

"He's a grease monkey. He doesn't belong with a rich girl like Constance, anyway."

"Her father offered to set him up in his own garage."

Sam Mines glowered. "If he's not careful, I'll set him up in his own jail cell."

He took out his pipe and started filling the air with its wonderful aromas. This was the scent Laurel would always associate with her father. It was a breakfast and dinner smell, a meal finished, strapping Sam Mines leaning back in his chair and smoking his pipe, maybe a thumb hooked into a suspender, a curled charred stick match sitting on the saucer of his coffee cup.

But the light of this autumn morning was no friend to aging flesh, and as she looked at him, she saw that he was no longer "becoming" old (the way she'd preferred to think about it these last six or seven years). He'd arrived. He *was* old. Not by normal human being standards, perhaps. But certainly by lawman standards. Arthritis crimped his hands and knees and feet. And his blue eyes were somewhat vague when they looked at you. They weren't even as startlingly and deeply blue as they'd once been, as if age preferred to paint in pastels.

And Henry Starr was coming to town.

Everybody knew it but nobody said it.

Not to his face, anyway.

But down at the bank, where she worked as a teller, that was all anybody talked about or thought about.

Henry Starr, the first bank robber in the state to use a motorcar in his raids, was inexorably working his way toward Pruett City. You could follow his robberies with a southeast slanting line drawn on a map. Oh, he'd zig a little sometimes, and zag a little others, but the southeastern line didn't vary much. And someday soon, he'd be here. Mr. Foster, the bank's owner, had put on two extra shotgunned guards. He had a bad stomach, did our Mr. Foster, and he walked around these days popping pills and touching his stomach and grimacing.

And Dad would inevitably have a run-in with Henry

Starr, who was known to love shoot-outs, as well he
should, having won every darn one he'd ever been in.

She looked at her father now and fought back tears. He
looked old and somehow little-kid vulnerable. The liver
spots on his big hands resembled cancerous growths. His
arthritis-cramped hand gnarled itself around his pipe.

Henry Starr, who was not unintelligent it was said, had
likely sent a spy on ahead to look over Pruett City. And the
report back would be obvious: the sheriff's an old man;
he'll be easy pickin's.

Sam Mines consulted the railroad watch he always carried in his vest pocket. "Well, time for me to be—"

She smiled and took his hand. She wanted to jump up
and hold him to her and never let him go. But she knew
that such shilly-shallying would embarrass him. So she
simply finished his sentence for him "—time for you to be
pushin' off."

He smiled right back. "I sure wish you'd look around
for another beau, Laurel. That grease monkey's never
gonna amount to much, I'm afraid."

IT HAD BEEN funny with the whore last night. Usually,
he would have made love to her without any hesitation.
That's what whores were for, wasn't it?

But a certain thing he'd read in *The Police Gazette*
crossed his mind just as he'd begun to unbutton his
trousers—a thought so nagging that Henry Starr had but-
toned right back up again and kicked the whore out of his
hotel room.

The thought was this: a man named Max Bowen, whom
the magazine called "the most successful bank robber New
York City ever saw," attributed his astonishing run of fifty-

three bank robberies over eight years before being appre-
hended to the fact that the night before a robbery, he ab-
stained from both liquor and ladies. The way, said this Max
Bowen, that prizefighters did.

And so there Henry Starr had been, unbuttoning his
trousers, when the thought about abstinence struck him . . .
and he'd immediately ordered the whore out of the room.

This morning, as he cranked up his Model T and waited
for his lazy-ass gang to come tumbling down the hotel
steps so they could drive on to Pruett City and rob the bank
there, he wondered if he' d been stupid.

That whore sure was pretty. And sure did have a nice
pair of breasts.

Henry Starr, not a reflective man, gave a few moments
thought to how bank robbing had been not all that long
ago. Horses instead of cars. And no federal agents on your
ass unless you killed one of their own. And no telephones
to make tracking you down all that much easier.

The car, especially, was a mixed blessing.

Here it was, for example, a perfectly fine autumn day,
sixty degrees already at seven A.M., the engine should be
performing very well, and yet he still had to crank the
damned thing as if it was twenty below zero and the engine
block was covered with snow and ice.

Not to mention problems with tires, muddy roads, and
running out of gas.

The one nice thing was the speed.

You come bursting out of a bank with six or seven bags
of cash, hop into the car, and in a few minutes you're tear-
ing ass out of town at forty-five miles an hour—and God
help anybody who gets in the way.

That was where the Tin Lizzie beat the hell out of any
kind of horse you'd care to name.

The car finally kicked over.

And by that time his gang, yawning and toting huge mugs of steaming hot coffee, came hurrying down the stairs, knowing Henry was going to be damned mad about them sleeping in this way.

AS SOON AS Sully Driscoll opened the police station door, he knew he'd made another mistake. One just as dumb as last night's mistake of pelting Laurel's windows with pebbles.

"Help you?" said Clete Mulwray, one of Pruett City's twelve deputies. He sat behind a large desk, seemingly lost in a sinkhole of paperwork.

"I'd like to see the sheriff"

"Any reason in particular?"

"I guess I really should just talk to him."

Mulwray shrugged, stood up. "Wait here." He disappeared down a short hall.

He sure wasn't friendly. Sully wondered if the sheriff had told him about what Sully had done last night. No—if he had, the deputy would be smirking.

Mulwray came back. "First door on your left."

Sam Mines wore his familiar crisp khaki uniform. His campaign hat was angled from the top notch of a hat tree. With all the glassed-in law books, the office looked as if it belonged to a lawyer.

Sam said, "Help you with something?"

"I came to apologize."

"You apologized last night."

"Yeah, but I couldn't sleep much. All I did was think about how stupid I was. So I came to tell you again."

Sam leaned back in his chair. He didn't invite Sully to sit down. His eyes were even unfriendlier than Mulwray's.

"You ever think you might be better off with Constance Daly?" Sam said.

Sully swallowed hard. Was this Sam's way of saying he didn't want Sully to see Laurel anymore?

"No, sir. I—I love Laurel."

"Laurel can't give you your own auto shop."

"I know that."

"And Laurel can't give you a big house and a nice fat bank account."

"I know that, too. But I happen to love Laurel."

Job couldn't have sighed any more deeply than Sam Mines did at that moment. He leaned forward, elbows on his desk, and said, "Sully, I'm going to tell you something. And it's going to hurt your feelings. And I'm sorry for that in advance. You're kind of brash sometimes—and you're so crazy over motorcars you make people laugh at you—but you're a decent, hardworking lad, and I really don't mind you at all."

"Is that a compliment?"

Old Sam smiled. "Yeah, I guess it is."

"Then thank you."

"But."

"There's always a but, isn't there, Sam?" Sully said, hoping to keep the conversation light.

"Yes, I'm afraid there always is." Sam glanced away, as if preparing himself to say something he was reluctant to say. "Sully, you're a decent boy. And my daughter loves the hell out of you. But I want to ask you something, and I want you to answer me honestly."

"All right." Sully knew this was going to be terrible.

"Do you think you can make much of a living working at that garage?"

Sully felt sick. "You mean she could marry somebody with a better future?"

"That's a good way to say it, I guess."

"Well, I—"

"I want the best for Laurel, Sully. You can understand that, can't you?"

"Well, sure, but—"

"I wish you'd think about it, Sully. I know it's not the way young people like to think about their futures—once upon a time I was just as hot-blooded as you are—but just think about what Constance could do for you. And what somebody like Andrew Stillson could do for Laurel."

Andrew was a thirtyish bachelor, and a nice enough guy, who ran the local apothecary. Bu he wouldn't make a good husband for Laurel—

"I'll think about it, sir."

"That's all I ask, son. And about last night— Don't worry about it. I got too mad by half. Like I said, I was hot-blooded myself once." He smiled. "That's just how men are built, I guess."

THE NEWSPAPERS IN the state were after Henry Starr even more relentlessly than the lawmen.

And as he bumped and swayed along behind the wheel of his Model T, Starr thought of the lies they wrote about him and how they were purposely damaging his reputation.

There was a time when the Henry Starr name shone as brightly as that of Jesse James and the Dalton Brothers. Your first-class bank robber. A man that a lot of people secretly looked upon as a folk hero. The banks robbed peo-

ple, didn't they? Then what was so wrong about robbing
them right back? That was the attitude a lot of folks had.

Then came that damned robbery in Oklahoma City, and
people had never again felt the same quiet admiration for
Starr.

"Technically," Starr always said to his gang when he'd
been drinking—and Lord were they long tired of hearing
about it—"technically, I didn't shoot him in the back. I
shot him in the side."

This was in reference to one Horace P. Puckhaber, manager of the State Bank and Trust, who had been about to
throw a jar of ink through a side window so as to warn the
people on the street that a robbery was going on inside the
bank. Hopefully, the people would be smart enough to in-
form John Law.

At the exact moment he hurled the jar, Horace P. Puckhaber was standing with his hands held high, his back to
Starr. Starr had his Colt trained on the man. Starr hadn't
seen the plump little man earlier secret the jar into his
meaty fist. In order to throw the jar through the window,
though, Puckhaber had to turn sharply to his left. He would
then—this was the only way Starr could figure out such a
foolish but surprisingly brave act—pitch himself to the
floor and roll away behind a desk for cover.

Now, wouldn't *you* shoot such a man in such a situation? Of course you would. What choice would you have?
You had to stop him before that damned ink jar smashed
the window, didn't you?

So here's how it actually happened:

Puckhaber, his hands up, seemingly being as obedient
as a good dog, suddenly starts to turn to his left.

Starr sees the ink jar. Sees the window. Understands
what's going on.

He shouts, "Drop that jar!"

Then it gets confusing. Because at first—for just one second—Puckhaber starts to carry through with his plan. He keeps turning left.

At which point, by instinct, Starr fires his gun.

But all of a sudden, before the bullet tears into him, he turns away again, his back to Starr.

Well, he *almost* turns back.

Here's why Starr says that the press is lying about him: If you look carefully at the fatal wound, you'll see that it is actually on the side of the man. Very near his back, true— within an eighth of an inch— but still, technically, in the side.

Making Starr, at worst, a *side*-shooter.

Now, a man can live with a reputation as a side-shooter. But not as a back-shooter. Even though many legends have, in fact, been back-shooters—including Wild Bill and all four of the Earps—the people who read the newspapers and the dime novels don't know of it. They believe that their heroes are simon pure, just as white-hatted and blue-eyed and pearly-teethed as the hacks say they are.

Starr has shot and killed eight men. And all of them bankers, which is pretty much like killing Indians or coloreds, which is to say not much of an offense at all according to the general populace of this particular time and place.

Starrs is *proud* of murdering eight bankers.

Were these the same type of whore who'd foreclosed on his very own parents in 1881? Proud of being a front-shooter.

And not at all ashamed of being a side-shooter.

He just wishes that the newspaper bastards would lay off him about being a back-shooter. . . .

Such were the thoughts of Henry Starr as he rolled toward Pruett City in his Model-T.

★

WAS THERE ANY machine so wondrous as a Model T? A miraculous instrument of gasoline tanks, acetylene head-lights, inner-tube tires, and clutch, reverse, and brake. And was there any experience—excepting kissing Laurel—as much fun as spreading the innards out on a sheet and cleaning each one so that it performed to utter perfection?

That was how Sully spent the morning. George Adair, one of the wealthiest men in the area, had brought his son's car in for a quick clean-up. And had insisted that Sully do the work. More and more people asked for Sully person-ally. Hank Byers, the owner of the gas station–garage, was both flattered and hurt—flattered that he had the best garage man in town, and hurt that his own days as the reigning car expert had waned.

Usually, you could hear Sully whistling as he worked on cars. Who wouldn't whistle when he was doing—and doing well—exactly what God had put him on the earth to do?

But there was no music in his soul this sad day. Sam Mines had made it clear that he would not countenance a marriage between Laurel and Sully. And Sam was—whether or not she wanted to face up to it—in a position to discreetly undermine any wedding plans.

And Sully felt sure that was just what Sam would do.

LAUREL TAUGHT SCHOOL in the mornings. She was always home in time to fix her father his lunch.

Though today was sunny and perfumed with that most enchanting of scents—burning leaves and hazy hills—it was still nippy, so she fixed tomato soup, generous slices of cheddar cheese, and slabs of wheat bread. Food that would stick to the ribs and give you energy for this harbinger of winter.

Sam didn't mention last night until they were almost finished eating. "Sully stopped by to apologize again."

She smiled. "He wants you to like him, Dad. I want you to like him, too."

Sam frowned at his soup bowl.

"Something wrong, Dad?"

Sam sighed. "Well, I don't think *he* likes *me* very much right now."

She had been about to put the spoon to her mouth but stopped. Her father's demeanor had become troubling. She sensed that their comfortable little lunch hour was about to be spoiled. "Did you have an argument?"

"No, no argument."

"Well, what then?"

He leaned back in his chair. He looked nervous.

"You look as if you're afraid to tell me, Dad."

A kind of shame came into his expression. "Maybe I went a little too far."

She slammed her spoon down on the table. "Darn it, Dad. Tell me what you said to Sully. That's what we're talking about here, isn't it? Something you said to him rather than the other way around?"

The shame did not leave his handsome but age-wrinkled face. "I told him the truth was all, honey. The truth as I see it, anyway."

And then he told her what he'd said.

AT THE TIME the car pulled on to the drive, Sully was busy pounding nails into the leg of a wooden workbench that had gone all wobbly. He had a pocketful of nails and a hammer and was working fast as he could. He wanted to get back to his real calling: fixing engines.

He put the hammer down, wiped his hands on the bib overalls he wore to work in, and then proceeded out into the sunlight from the cool shadows of the garage.

Four men sat in a green Model T. There was a similarity of bulky body, of big-city suits, and of wide-brimmed dress hats that made him think of the covers of his favorite magazine, *Argosy*, whenever it ran a story about gangsters. The license plate read Oklahoma, all right, but that was the only thing local in the picture, which he was giving a quick study.

But that wasn't the only local thing, it turned out. When the burly driver spoke, it was with the familiar Okie twang that was Sully's own.

"Fill up the gas, kid."

Sully almost smiled. They were *imitating* the *Argosy* was what they were doing. Imitating the covers and the gangster silent pictures that were just starting to come into fashion.

Sully wondered if the driver had a crimp in his neck. The way he angled his head down, so that he hid virtually his entire face beneath the wide brim of his fedora— *No, not a crimp in the neck,* Sully realized. *The driver is hiding his face.*

"Yessir," Sully said.

And it was then that the driver seemed to forget himself. He raised his head just enough so that Sully could see his face and realize just who he was dealing with here.

Their eyes met, locked.

There was great, knowing rage in this man's gaze. The banality of his words had nothing to do with the hard anger of his brown eyes. "And check them tires, too."

Sully almost said, "Yessir, Mr. Starr."

But, thank God, he caught himself in time. If Starr knew that Sully had recognized him—

LAUREL WAS RAKING leaves when she realized what she *really* should be doing. Talking to Sully. Telephone was no good because it was a party line and saying anything confidential over the phone—well, you might as well be done with it and just put it in the newspaper.

She rushed to the garage and climbed aboard her bicycle with the outsize basket for carrying groceries, with the outsize light for riding at night, with the outsize horn for getting tykes, squirrels, dogs, kittens, and raccoons out of her way as she was rolling along.

Dad was speaking for himself, Sully. I love him and I know he means the best for me. But he's wrong about you. I know how much you love working on cars, and that's what I want you to do for the rest of your life—for the rest our lives. I don't want to go against my own father, Sully, but I will if I have to. One way or another, you and I are going to get married. I promise you that, Sully. On my sacred word.

And she would seal it—as did all the girls in the romance novels she wouldn't admit to reading or liking—with a kiss.

THE KID RECOGNIZED me, Henry Starr thought. No doubt about that.

With the all the Wanted posters everywhere, it was difficult to go anywhere without being recognized. That's why Starr had been thinking about leaving Oklahoma.

He'd heard Missouri was good pickings for bandits—he himself preferred the romantic sound of "bandit" to the drab word "robber"—and maybe it was time to give it a try.

As for the kid who was just now starting to put gasoline in the car . . .

One of the boys in the backseat leaned forward and whispered, "That kid recognized you."

"I know."

"Maybe we should kill him."

"We kill a kid like that, we'll have every lawman in the state down on us. You think it's bad now, wait till we do something like that. One more killing in this state and they'll probably sic the damn army on us."

"Then what you gonna do?"

"I'm gonna tie him up and gag him."

At which point Henry Starr opened the door and climbed out of the car.

LAUREL WAS RELIEVED to see only one car on the drive. Sometimes when she popped in to see Sully, he was so busy he could barely give her enough time for a simple hello.

Maybe he'd have at least a few minutes, if the repair work inside the garage wasn't too much.

She was no more than thirty feet from the garage, just about to sound her horn so Sully would know she was here and maybe wave to her, when she saw the big man take the gun from somewhere inside his suit coat, walk up to Sully, who was pumping gas, and shove the gun into Sully's back.

A robbery!

"Sully," she cried out.

The man turned and looked at her now. And half a second later another man in the car came lunging out onto the drive and started running for her, pistol drawn and gleaming in the autumn sunlight.

"Get out of here!" Sully shouted to her. "Fast!"

But her hesitation undid her. For such a bulky body, the second man could sure run fast. He closed on her, pointed the gun right at her face, and then escorted her to the gas station.

She and Sully were prisoners.

SAM MINES GOT the call just as he was leaving the sheriff's office.

A lawman to the east told him, "Hotel people think Starr and his boys stayed there last night. The night crew didn't pick up on it, but one of the morning people saw four men around a Model T this morning and was pretty sure that it was Starr and his boys. That means he's on a direct route to Pruett City."

"It sure does," Mines said. "Thanks."

THE LAST WORDS Sully said to Laurel—just before one of Starr's men gagged him—was, "I sure wish you wouldn't've come out here, Laurel."

"I had to, Sully. I wanted you to know that my Dad wasn't speaking for me when he said all those things."

"Aw," Starr laughed. "Listen to 'em. True love."

Once Laurel and Sully were both bound and gagged, Starr and his men left the station, got in their car, and pulled away.

SAM MINES ISSUED each of his three daytime deputies a shotgun. "I want two of you in front of the bank, out in plain sight where everybody can see you. And I want one of you on the back door. In plain sight."

"Shouldn't we try to ambush them?" one of his men said.

"Nope. Ambush would mean a shoot-out. A lot of people could get hurt. They won't see the two of you out front until they get close. And that's when I'll use my own car to pull up right behind them and order them to put their guns down."

"What if they start firing?"

"With three shotguns on them?" Sam said. "If they're that crazy, then so be it."

IT WAS SORT of funny, watching Laurel and Sully wiggle and waggle and wobble on their bottoms trying to extricate themselves from the ropes Starr's man had wound them up in.

Every once in a while, they'd try and talk around their gags. She was trying to tell Sully that she loved him. Sully was trying to tell her about the hopefully clever thing he'd done. He just hoped Sam could find out about it in time.

"THE CAR KINDA ridin' funny?" one of Starr's men said.

Starr sighed. It was always something with these guys. Someday he'd get himself a fine shiny new bunch of boys. Boys who weren't always complaining. Boys who weren't always second-guessing everything he said. Boys who were grateful to be in the presence of a man as notorious as Henry Starr. "The car is ridin' just fine. Now shut up."

He said this just after driving four blocks to the start of Pruett City's business district.

WHEN THE CAR came on the dusty drive, both Sully and Laurel looked up. If only the customer would come inside and find them—

This customer, whoever it was, was in a hurry.

Honked the horn not once, not twice, but three times.

He will come in and untie and ungag us, and Sully will grab the telephone and call Sam and tell him what he's done.

Hope gleamed in Laurel's lovely eyes.

They would be rescued at last.

She was sure of it.

And it was then, after a final frustrated honk, that the customer pulled away.

WITHIN A FEW MINUTES, Sam's men took their places in front of and behind the bank. Sam had quickly called in a couple of auxiliary men who'd do anything as long as they got to wear badges. These two men set about keeping the bank street clear, rerouting people so they'd be out of the way if any trouble started.

HENRY STARR HAD one of his few moments of peace. He liked Pruett City. There was something so pleasant about the tree-shaded streets and all the little white clapboard houses and cottages, the picket fences, the dogs and cats and tykes. He even cast an appreciative glance on the Lutheran church and its proud white spire that seemed to almost pierce the soft blue sky. Someday, when he retired . . .

"Hey, boss."

"Yeah?"

"You sure you don't feel nothin'?"

Starr did, but he didn't want to admit it. He was sick of their whining. Maybe he could *will* the obvious problem away by just not thinking about it.

He drove on.

THIS TIME THE customer, a middle-aged lady in a bonnet, goggles, and long driving gloves, came in and expeditiously freed Laurel and Sully from their bonds. Sully jumped up and ran to the phone. The operator put him through to Sam's office. The man left behind said that Sam was out. Sully told him what he'd done and told him to get the word to Sam immediately.

A FEW MINUTES LATER, Sam was in his own car with two of his deputies in the back, shotguns at the ready.

The scene was just as Sully had predicted. Henry Starr and his boys were in the process of pushing their car off to the side of the street where they could fix the flat tire Sully had given them.

Starr's gang was in no position to grab their weapons. Or even run. Not when they were being covered by three shotguns.

With Starr, it was another matter. With the speed and force of a much younger man, he grabbed a lawman and got him in a choke hold that turned the officer's face a dark sick red. The man was dying on the spot.

Starr relieved him of his gun and then stabbed the barrel of it against the man's temple.

"You," Starr snapped at Sam. "You drive that car of yours over here. We're goin' for a ride."

Everybody could see the resentment on Sam's face. What a way to wind down a career—helping a wanted killer escape.

But what choice did he have? The hostage was twenty-four years old and the father of three. Sam couldn't stand here and let him be sacrificed that way.

"Let him go," Sam said.

"Sure," Starr said. "That would make a lot of sense, wouldn't it? I let him go and you open fire. Now get your car."

Sam shook his head. He didn't have any choice. He would have to help this killer make his escape.

Or would he?

The shadows that had troubled Sam's eyes were gone suddenly. He walked almost jauntily to the car he'd kept running. Even if it meant that he had to give up his own life, he'd be damned is he'd help Starr escape.

He pulled the car up to Starr.

"Open the door," Starr said, meaning the passenger door.

Sam's jaw muscles bunched, and he muttered a lot of words the ladies wouldn't ever approve of. And then he pushed the door open.

Starr proved agile again. He flung the young deputy away from him and in the same motion, jumped in the passenger seat and jammed his gun against Sam's head.

"Drive," Starr said.

Sam drove. Boy, did he drive. And he knew just where he was driving to—at fifty-three miles per hour. Absolute top end.

"You ever seen what somebody looks like when the car

he's in runs into a tree at this speed?" he shouted at Starr above the roar of the engine.

"You crazy bastard! Slow down!"

"About a block from here's there's this old oak tree, Starr. It sits right on the corner. If you don't throw that gun of yours out the window, I'm going to drive us right into it."

"You won't kill yourself! Don't try and bluff me old man!"

"Won't I? Like you say, I'm an old man. I've had a good life. And I'll be damned if I'll help you escape."

Houses and trees and lawns began to sweep by as Sam kept the car at top speed. Buggies and carriages and bicycles all whipped out of his way, many of their occupants shaking fists at him after he'd passed.

"You got one block, Starr! Make up your mind. I'll be dead, but so will you." There wasn't any guarantee either of them would be dead—though there was a good probability they would be—but he didn't need to tell Starr that at the moment.

"Slow down!"

"It's comin' right up, Starr! Half a block!"

Starr saw the massive oak Sam was talking about. You could see him calculating his chances of surviving such a crash.

A quarter of a block now.

Sam gulped. Starr was a brave man in his way. Most men would've thrown their guns out a block ago.

Sam said a mental good-bye to his loved ones and began to angle the car toward the low curb so that the car would hit the tree at a solid angle. He wouldn't want to survive this kind of wreck anyway. It wouldn't be any kind of life being crippled or maybe without any mental faculties left.

And it was then that Starr screamed, "All right! All right! I'm throwing my gun out."

And just as Sam had been preparing to set his eyes on some angels—at least he hoped that was the general vicinity he was headed for—Starr flung his gun out the window.

And Sam, shaking, sweating, feeling a need to vomit, began the process of steering the car back onto the street and slowing down.

"SO WHERE DID you get the nail?" Sam asked Sully later that afternoon. Sully, Laurel, and Sam had gone to the ice cream parlor for sodas. Sam hadn't had to tell them about his cleverness and bravery. By now it was all over town.

"Had it in my pocket. I'd been fixing up that old workbench I use. Had a bunch of nails in my pocket, matter of fact."

"You just might've saved a lot of lives," Sam said. "I was afraid Starr and his boys might panic when they pulled up in front of the bank and saw my men. These days, bank robbers do some pretty crazy things."

They talked for another twenty minutes, and then Sam said he had to get back to the office. As he was leaving, he said, "I guess maybe I'd better think some things through, huh, son?"

Sully smiled. "I guess so."

After he was gone, Laurel said, "That doesn't mean he's changed his mind."

"I know."

"But it's a start." Then she took his hand and caressed it. "A good start."

The Guns of William Longley

DONALD HAMILTON

A publishing icon as the author of the famous Matt Helm series of espionage novels, Donald Hamilton wrote Westerns even before he brought life to his super-spy, including *Smoke Valley* (1954), *Mad River* (1956), and *Texas Fever* (1960). In 1967 he edited the Western anthology *Iron Men and Silver Stars*, which included this William Longley tale. He is presently living in Sweden, where I tracked him down for permission to reprint this story. When I received his letter, it was as if I was a young man again, finding the new Matt Helm on the bookshelves. It's a thrill to have him in my book.

★

We'd been up north delivering a herd for old man Butcher the summer I'm telling about. I was nineteen at the time. I was young and big, and I was plenty tough, or thought I was, which amounts to the same thing up to a point. Maybe I was making up for all the years of being that nice Anderson boy, back in Willow Fork, Texas. When your dad wears a badge, you're kind of obliged to behave yourself around home so as not to shame him. But Pop was dead now, and this wasn't Texas.

Anyway, I was tough enough that we had to leave Dodge City in something of a hurry after I got into an argument with a fellow who, it turned out, wasn't nearly as handy with a gun as he claimed to be. I'd never killed a man before. It made me fell kind of funny for a couple of days, but like I say, I was young and tough then, and I'd seen men I really cared for trampled in stampedes and drowned in rivers on the way north. I wasn't going to grieve long over one belligerent stranger.

It was on the long trail home that I first saw the guns one evening by the fire. We had a blanket spread on the ground, and we were playing cards for what was left of our pay—what we hadn't already spent on girls and liquor and general hell-raising. My luck was in, and one by one the others dropped out, all but Waco Smith, who got stubborn and went over to his bedroll and hauled out the guns.

"I got them in Dodge," he said. "Pretty, ain't they? Fellow I bought them from claimed they belonged to Bill Longley."

"Is that a fact?" I said, like I wasn't much impressed. "Who's Longley?"

I knew who Bill Longley was, all right, but a man's got a right to dicker a bit, and besides, I couldn't help deviling Waco now and then. I like him all right, but he was one of those cocky little fellows who ask for it. You know the kind. They always know everything.

I sat there while he told me about Bill Longley, the giant from Texas with thirty-two killings to his credit, the man who was hanged twice. A bunch of vigilantes strung him up once for horse-stealing he hadn't done, but the rope broke after they'd ridden off, and he dropped to the ground, kind of short of breath but alive and kicking.

Then he was tried and hanged for a murder he had done, some years later in Giddings, Texas. He was so big that the rope gave way again and he landed on his feet under the trap, making six-inch-deep footprints in the hard ground— they're still there in Giddings to be seen, Waco said, Bill Longley's footprints—but it broke his neck this time and they buried him nearby. At least a funeral service was held, but some say there's just an empty coffin in the grave.

I said, "This Longley gent can't have been so much, to let folks keep stringing him up that way."

That set Waco off again, while I toyed with the guns. They were pretty, all right, in a big carved belt with two carved holsters, but I wasn't much interested in leather-work. It was the weapons themselves that took my fancy. They'd been used, but someone had looked after them well. They were handsome pieces, smooth-working, and they had a good feel to them. You know how it is when a firearm feels just right. A fellow with hands the size of mine doesn't often find guns to fit him like that.

"How much do you figure they're worth?" I asked, when Waco stopped for breath.

"Well, now," he said, getting a sharp look on his face, and I came home to Willow Fork with the Longley guns strapped around me. If that's what they were.

I got a room and cleaned up at the hotel. I didn't much feel like riding clear out to the ranch and seeing what it looked like with Ma and Pa gone two years and nobody looking after things. Well, I'd put the place on its feet again one of these days, as soon as I'd had a little fun and saved a little money. I'd buckle right down to it, I told myself, as soon as Junellen set the date, which I'd been after her to do since before my folks died. She couldn't keep saying forever we were too young.

I got into my good clothes and went to see her. I won't say she'd been on my mind all the way up the trail and back again, because it wouldn't be true. A lot of the time I'd been too busy or tired for dreaming, and in Dodge City I'd done my best *not* to think of her, if you know what I mean. It did seem like a young fellow engaged to a beautiful girl like Junellen Barr could have behaved himself better up there, but it had been a long dusty drive and you know how it is.

But now I was home and it seemed like I'd been missing Junellen every minute since I left, and I couldn't wait to see her. I walked along the street in the hot sunshine feeling light and happy. Maybe my leaving my guns at the hotel had something to do with the light feeling, but the happiness was all for Junellen, and I ran up the steps to the house and knocked on the door. She'd have heard we were back and she'd be waiting to greet me, I was sure.

I knocked again and the door opened and I stepped forward eagerly. "Junellen—" I said, and stopped foolishly.

"Come in, Jim," said her father, a little turkey of a man who owned the drygoods store in town. He went on smoothly: "I understand you had quite an eventful journey. We are waiting to hear all about it."

He was being sarcastic, but that was his way, and I couldn't be bothered with trying to figure what he was driving at. I'd already stepped into the room, and there was Junellen with her mother standing close as if to protect her, which seemed kind of funny. There was a man in the room, too, Mr. Carmichael from the bank, who'd fought with Pa in the war. He was tall and handsome as always, a little heavy nowadays but still dressed like a fashion plate. I couldn't figure what he was doing there.

It wasn't going at all the way I'd hoped, my reunion with Junellen, and I stopped, looking at her.

"So you're back, Jim," she said. "I heard you had a real exciting time. Dodge City must be quite a place."

There was a funny hard note in her voice. She held herself very straight, standing there by her mother, in a blue-flowered dress that matched her eyes. She was a real little lady, Junellen. She made kind of a point of it, in fact, and Martha Butcher, old man Butcher's kid, used to say about Junellen Barr that butter wouldn't melt in her mouth, but that always seemed like a silly saying to me, and who was Martha Butcher anyway, just because her daddy owned a lot of cows?

Martha'd also remarked about girls who had to drive two front names in harness as if one wasn't good enough, and I'd told her it surely wasn't if it was a name like Martha, and she'd kicked me on the shin. But that was a long time ago when we were all kids.

Junellen's mother broke the silence, in her nervous way: "Dear, hadn't you better tell Jim the news?" She turned to Mr. Carmichael. "Howard, perhaps you should—"

Mr. Carmichael came forward and took Junellen's hand. "Miss Barr has done me the honor to promise to be my wife," he said.

I said, "But she can't. She's engaged to me."

Junellen's mother said quickly, "It was just a childish thing, not to be taken seriously."

I said, "Well, I took it seriously!"

Junellen looked up at me. "Did you, Jim? In Dodge city, did you?" I didn't say anything. She said breathlessly, "It doesn't matter. I suppose I could forgive. . . . But you have killed a man. I could never love a man who has taken a human life."

Anyway, she said something like that. I had a funny feeling in my stomach and a roaring sound in my ears. They talk about your heart breaking, but that's where it hit me, the stomach and the ears. So I can't tell you exactly what she said, but it was something like that.

I heard myself say, "Mr. Carmichael spent the war peppering Yanks with a peashooter, I take it."

"That's different—"

Mr. Carmichael spoke quickly. "What Miss Barr means is that there's a difference between a battle and a drunken brawl, Jim. I am glad your father did not live to see his son wearing two big guns and shooting men down in the street. He was a fine man and a good sheriff for this county. It was only for his memory's sake that I agreed to let Miss Barr break the news to you in person. From what we hear of your exploits up north, you have certainly forfeited all right to consideration from her."

There was something in what he said, but I couldn't see that it was his place to say it. "You agreed?" I said. "That was mighty kind of you, sir, I'm sure." I looked away from him. "Junellen—"

Mr. Carmichael interrupted. "I do not wish my fiancée to be distressed by a continuation of this painful scene. I must ask you to leave, Jim."

I ignored him. "Junellen," I said, "is this what you really—"

Mr. Carmichael took me by the arm. I turned my head to look at him again. I looked at the hand with which he was holding me. I waited. He didn't let go. I hit him and he went back across the room and kind of fell into a chair. The chair broke under him. Junellen's father ran over to help him up. Mr. Carmichael's mouth was bloody. He wiped it with a handkerchief.

I said, "You shouldn't have put your hand on me, sir."

"Note the pride," Mr. Carmichael said, dabbing at this cut lip. "Note the vicious, twisted pride. They all have it, all these young toughs. You are too big for me to box, Jim, and it is an undignified thing, anyway. I have worn a sidearm in my time. I will go to the bank and get it, while you arm yourself."

"I will meet you in front of the hotel, sir," I said, "if that is agreeable to you."

"It is agreeable," he said, and went out.

I followed him without looking back. I think Junellen was crying, and I know her parents were saying one thing and another in high, indignant voices, but the funny roaring was in my ears and I didn't pay too much attention. The sun was very bright outside. As I started for the hotel, somebody ran up to me.

"Here you are, Jim." It was Waco, holding out the Longley guns in their carved holsters. "I heard what happened. Don't take any chances with the old fool."

I looked down at him and asked, "How did Junellen and her folks learn about what happened in Dodge?"

He said, "It's a small town, Jim, and all the boys have been drinking and talking, glad to get home."

"Sure," I said, buckling on the guns. "Sure."

It didn't matter. It would have got around sooner or later, and I wouldn't have lied about it if asked. We walked slowly toward the hotel.

"Dutch LeBaron is hiding out back in the hills with a dozen men," Waco said. "I heard it from a man in a bar."

"Who's Dutch LeBaron?" I asked. I didn't care, but it was something to talk about as we walked.

"Dutch?" Waco said. "Why Dutch is wanted in five states and a couple of territories. Hell, the price on his head is so high now even Fenn is after him."

"Fenn?" I said. He sure knew a lot of names. "Who's Fenn?"

"You've heard of Old Joe Fenn, the bounty hunter. Well, if he comes after Dutch, he's asking for it. Dutch can take care of himself."

"Is that a fact?" I said, and then I saw Mr. Carmichael coming, but he was a ways off yet, and I said, "You sound like this Dutch fellow was a friend of yours—"

But Waco wasn't there anymore. I had the street to myself, except for Mr. Carmichael, who had a gun strapped on outside his fine coat. It was an army gun in a black army holster with a flap, worn cavalry style on the right side, butt forward. They wear them like that to make room for the saber on the left, but it makes a clumsy rig.

I walked forward to meet Mr. Carmichael, and I knew I would have to let him shoot once. He was a popular man and a rich man and he would have to draw first and shoot first or I would be in serious trouble. I figured it all out very coldly, as if I had been killing men all my life. We stopped, and Mr. Carmichael undid the flap of the army holster and pulled out the big cavalry pistol awkwardly and fired and missed, as I had known, somehow, that he would.

Then I drew the right-hand gun, and as I did so I realized that I didn't particularly want to kill Mr. Carmichael. I mean, he was brave man coming here with his old cap-and-ball pistol, knowing all the time that I could outdraw and outshoot him with my eyes closed. But I didn't want to be killed, either, and he had the piece cocked and was about to fire again. I tried to aim for a place that wouldn't kill him, or cripple him too badly, and the gun wouldn't do it.

I mean, it was a frightening thing. It was like I was fighting the Longley gun for Mr. Carmichael's life. The old army revolver fired once more and something rapped my left arm lightly. The Longley gun went off at last, and Mr. Carmichael spun around and fell on his face in the street. There was a cry, and Junellen came running and went to her knees beside him.

"You murderer!" she screamed at me. "You hateful murderer!"

It showed how she felt about him, that she would kneel in the dust like that in her blue-flowered dress. Junellen was always very careful of her pretty clothes. I punched out the empty and replaced it. Dr. Sims came up and examined Mr. Carmichael and said he was shot in the leg, which I already knew, being the one who had shot him there. Dr. Sims said he was going to be all right, God willing.

Having heard this, I went over to another part of town and tried to get drunk. I didn't have much luck at it, so I went into the place next to the hotel for a cup of coffee. There wasn't anybody in the place but a skinny girl with an apron on.

I said, "I'd like a cup of coffee, ma'am," and sat down.

She said, coming over, "Jim Anderson, you're drunk. At least you smell like it."

I looked up and saw that it was Martha Butcher. She set a cup down in front of me. I asked, "What are you doing here waiting tables?"

She said, "I had a fight with Dad about . . . well, never mind what it was about. Anyway, I told him I was old enough to run my own life and if he didn't stop trying to boss me around like I was one of the hands, I'd pack up and leave. And he laughed and asked what I'd do for money, away from home, and I said I'd earn it, so here I am."

It was just like Martha Butcher, and I saw no reason to make a fuss over it like she probably wanted me to.

"Seems like you are," I agree. "Do I get sugar, too, or does that cost extra?"

She laughed and set a bowl in front of me. "Did you have a good time in Dodge?" she asked.

"Fine," I said. "Good liquor. Fast games. Pretty girls. Real pretty girls."

"Fiddlesticks," she said. "I know what you think is pretty. Blonde and simpering. You big fool. If you'd killed him over her they'd have put you in jail, at the very least. And just what are you planning to use for an arm when that one gets rotten and falls off? Sit still."

She got some water and cloth and fixed up my arm where Mr. Carmichael's bullet had nicked it.

"Have you been out to your place yet?" she asked.

I shook my head. "Figure there can't be much out there by now. I'll get after it one of these days."

"One of these days!" she said. "You mean when you get tired of strutting around with those big guns and acting dangerous—" She stopped abruptly.

I looked around and got to my feet. Waco was there in the doorway, and with him was a big man, not as tall as I was, but wider. He was a real whiskery gent, with a mat of black beard you could have used for stuffing a mattress. He wore two gunbelts, crossed, kind of sagging low at the hips.

Waco said, "You're a fool to sit with your back to the

door, Jim. That's the mistake Hickok made, remember? If instead of us it had been somebody like Jack McCall—"

"Who's Jack McCall?" I asked innocently.

"Why, he's the fellow shot Wild Bill in the back. . . ." Waco's face reddened. "All right, all right. Always kidding me. Dutch, this big joker is my partner, Jim Anderson, Jim, Dutch LeBaron. He's got a proposition for us."

I tried to think back to where Waco and I had decided to become partners, and could't remember the occasion. Well, maybe it happens like that, but it seemed like I should have had some say in it.

"Your partner tells me you're pretty handy with those guns," LeBaron said after Martha'd moved off across the room. "I can use a man like that."

"For what?" I asked.

"For making some quick money over in New Mexico Territory," he said.

I didn't ask any fool questions, like whether the money was to be made legally or illegally. "I'll think about it," I said.

Waco caught my arm. "What's to think about? We'll be rich, Jim!"

I said, "I'll think about it, Waco."

LeBaron said, "What's the matter, sonny, are you scared?"

I turned to look at him. He was grinning at me, but his eyes weren't grinning, and his hands weren't too far from those low-slung guns.

I said, "Try me and see."

I waited a little. Nothing happened. I walked out of there and got my pony and rode out to the ranch, reaching the place about dawn. I opened the door and stood there, surprised. It looked just about the way it had when the folks were alive, and I half expected to hear Ma yelling at me to beat the dust off outside and not bring it into the house. Somebody had cleaned the place up for me, and I thought I knew who. Well, it certainly was neighborly of her, I told myself. It was nice to have somebody show a sign they were glad to have me home, even if it was only Martha Butcher.

I spent a couple of days out there, resting up and riding around. I didn't find much stock. It was going to take money to make a going ranch of it again, and I didn't figure my credit at Mr. Carmichael's bank was anything to count on. I couldn't help giving some thought to Waco and LeBaron and the proposition they'd put before me. It was funny, I'd think about it most when I had the guns on. I was out back practicing with them one day when the stranger rode up.

He was a little, dry, elderly man on a sad-looking white horse he must have hired at the livery stable for not very much, and he wore his gun in front of his left hip with the butt to the right for a cross draw. He didn't make any noise coming up. I'd fired a couple of times before I realized he was there.

"Not bad," he said when he saw me looking at him. "Do you know a man named LeBaron, son?"

"I've met him," I said.

"Is he here?"

"Why should he be here?"

"A bartender in town told me he'd heard you and your sidekick, Smith, had joined up with LeBaron, so I thought you might have given him the use of your place. It would be more comfortable for him than hiding out in the hills."

"He isn't here," I said. The stranger glanced toward the

house. I started to get mad, but shrugged instead. "Look around if you want to."

"In that case," he said, "I don't figure I want to." He glanced toward the target I'd been shooting at, and back to me. "Killed a man in Dodge, didn't you, son? And then stood real calm and let a fellow here in town fire three shots at you, after which you laughed and pinked him neatly in the leg."

"I don't recall laughing," I said. "And it was two shots, not three."

"It makes a good story, however," he said. "And it is spreading. You have a reputation already, did you know that, Anderson? I didn't come here just to look for LeBaron. I figured I'd like to have a look at you, too. I always like to look up fellows I might have business with later."

"Business?" I said, and then I saw that he'd taken a tarnished old badge out of his pocket and was pinning it on his shirt. "Have you a warrant, sir?" I asked.

"Not for you," he said. "Not yet."

He swung the old white horse around and rode off. When he was out of sight, I got my pony out of the corral. It was time I had a talk with Waco. Maybe I was going to join LeBaron and maybe I wasn't, but I didn't much like his spreading it around before it was true.

I didn't have to look for him in town. He came riding to meet me with three companions, all hard ones if I ever saw any.

"Did you see Fenn?" he shouted as he came up. "Did he come this way?"

"A little old fellow with some kind of a badge?" I said. "Was that Fenn? He headed back to town, about ten minutes ahead of me. He didn't look like much."

"Neither does the devil when he's on business," Waco said. "Come on, we'd better warn Dutch before he rides into town."

I rode along with them, and we tried to catch LeBaron on the trail, but he'd already passed with a couple of men. We saw their dust ahead and chased it, but they made it before us, and Fenn was waiting in front of the cantina that was LeBaron's hangout when he was in town.

We saw it all as we came pounding after LeBaron, who dismounted and started into the place, but Fenn came forward, looking small and inoffensive. He was saying something and holding out his hand. LeBaron stopped and shook hands with him, and the little man held onto LeBaron's hand, took a step to the side, and pulled his gun out of that cross-draw holster left-handed, with a kind of twisting motion.

Before LeBaron could do anything with his free hand, the little old man had brought the pistol barrel down across his head. It was as neat and coldblooded a thing as you'd care to see. In an instant, LeBaron was unconscious on the ground, and Old Joe Fenn was covering the two men who'd been riding with him.

Waco Smith, riding beside me, made a sort of moaning sound as if he'd been clubbed himself. "Get him!" he shouted, drawing his gun. "Get the dirty sneaking bounty hunter!"

I saw the little man throw a look over his shoulder, but there wasn't much he could do about us with those other two to handle. I guess he hadn't figured us for reinforcements riding in. Waco fired and missed. He never could shoot much, particularly from horseback. I reached out with one of the guns and hit him over the head before he could shoot again. He spilled from the saddle.

I didn't have it all figured out. Certainly it wasn't a very nice thing Mr. Fenn had done, first taking a man's hand in friendship and then knocking him unconscious. Still, I didn't figure LeBaron had ever been one for giving anybody a break; and there was something about the old fellow standing there with his tarnished old badge that reminded me of Pa, who'd died wearing a similar piece of tin on his chest. Anyway, there comes a time in a man's life when he's got to make a choice, and that's the way I made mine.

Waco and I had been riding ahead of the others. I turned my pony fast and covered them with the guns as they came charging up—as well as you can cover anybody from a plunging horse. One of them had his pistol aimed to shoot. The left-hand Longley gun went off, and he fell to the ground. I was kind of surprised. I'd never been much at shooting left-handed. The other two riders veered off and headed out of town.

By the time I got my pony quieted down from having that gun go off in his ear, everything was pretty much under control. Waco had disappeared, so I figured he couldn't be hurt much; and the new sheriff was there, old drunken Billy Bates who'd been elected after Pa's death by the gambling element in town, who hadn't liked the strict way Pa ran things.

"I suppose it's legal," Old Billy was saying grudgingly. "But I don't take it kindly, Marshal, your coming here to serve a warrant without letting me know."

"My apologies, Sheriff," Fenn said smoothly. "An oversight, I assure you. Now, I'd like a wagon. He's worth seven-hundred and fifty dollars over in New Mexico Territory.

"No decent person would want that kind of money," Old Billy said sourly, swaying on his feet.

"There's only one kind of money," Fenn said. "Just as there's only one kind of law, even though there's different kinds of men enforcing it." He looked at me as I came up. "Much obliged, son."

"Por nada," I said. "You get in certain habits when you've had a badge in the family. My daddy was sheriff here once."

"So? I didn't know that." Fenn looked at me sharply. "Don't look like you're making any plans to follow in his footsteps. That's hardly's a lawman's rig you're wearing."

I said, "Maybe, but I never yet beat a man over the head while I was shaking his hand, Marshal."

"Son," he said, "my job is to enforce the law and maybe make a small profit on the side, not to play games with fair and unfair." He looked at me for a moment longer. "Well, maybe we'll meet again. It depends."

"On what?" I asked.

"On the price," he said. "The price on your head."

"But I haven't got—"

"Not now," he said. "But you will, wearing those guns. I know the signs. I've seen them before, too many times. Don't count on having me under obligation to you, when your time comes. I never let personal feelings interfere with business. . . . Easy, now," he said, to a couple of fellows who were lifting LeBaron, bound hand and foot, into the wagon that somebody had driven up. "Easy. Don't damage the merchandise. I take pride in delivering them in good shape for standing trial, whenever possible."

I decided I needed a drink, and then I changed my mind in favor of a cup of coffee. As I walked down the street, leaving my pony at the rail back there, the wagon rolled past and went out of town ahead of me. I was still watching it, for no special reason, when Waco stepped from the alley behind me.

"Jim!" he said. "Turn around, Jim!"

I turned slowly. He was a little unsteady on his feet, standing there, maybe from my hitting him, maybe from drinking. I thought it was drinking. I hadn't hit him very hard. He'd had time for a couple of quick ones, and liquor always got to him fast.

"You sold us out, you damn traitor!" he cried. "You took sides with the law!"

"I never was against it," I said. "Not really."

"After everything I've done for you!" he said thickly. "I was going to make you a great man, Jim, greater than Longley or Hardin or Hickok or any of them. With my brains and your size and speed, nothing could have stopped us! But you turned on me! Do you think you can do it alone? Is that what you're figuring, to leave me behind now that I've built you up to be somebody?"

"Waco," I said, "I never had any ambitions to be—"

"You and your medicine guns!" he sneered. "Let me tell you something. Those old guns are just something I picked up in a pawnshop. I spun a good yarn about them to give you confidence. You were on the edge, you needed a push in the right direction, and I knew once you started wearing a flashy rig like that, with one killing under your belt already, somebody'd be bound to try you again, and we'd be on our way to fame. But as for their being Bill Longley's guns, don't make me laugh!"

I said, "Waco—"

"They's just metal and wood like any other guns!" he said. "And I'm going to prove it to you right now! I don't need you, Jim! I'm as good a man as you, even if you laugh at me and make jokes at my expense. . . . *Are you ready, Jim?"*

He was crouching, and I looked up at him, Waco Smith, with whom I'd ridden up the trail and back. I saw that he was no good and I saw that he was dead. It didn't matter whose guns I was wearing, and all he'd really said was that he didn't know whose guns they were. But it didn't matter, they were my guns now, and he was just a little runt who never could shoot for shucks, anyway. He was dead, and so were the others, the ones who'd come after him, because they'd come, I knew that.

I saw them come to try me, one after the other, and I saw them go down before the big black guns, all except the last, the one I couldn't quite make out. Maybe it was Fenn and maybe it wasn't. . . .

I said, "To hell with you, Waco. I've got nothing against you, and I'm not going to fight you. Tonight or any other time."

I turned and walked away. I heard the sound of his gun behind me an instant before the bullet hit me. Then I wasn't hearing anything for a while. When I came to, I was in bed, and Martha Butcher was there.

"Jim!" she breathed. "Oh, Jim . . . !"

She looked real worried, and kind of pretty, I thought, but of course I was half out of my head. She looked even prettier the day I asked her to marry me, some months later, but maybe I was a little out of my head that day, too. Old Man Butcher didn't like it a bit. It seems his fight with Martha had been about her cleaning up my place, and his ordering her to quit and stay away from that young troublemaker, as he'd called me after getting word of all the hell we'd raised up north after delivering his cattle.

He didn't like it, but he offered me a job, I suppose for

Martha's sake. I thanked him and told him I was much obliged but I'd accepted an appointment as Deputy U.S. Marshal. Seems like somebody had recommended me for the job, maybe Old Joe Fenn, maybe not. I got my old gun out of my bedroll and wore it tucked inside my belt when I thought I might need it. It was a funny thing how seldom I had any use for it, even wearing a badge. With that job, I was the first in the neighborhood to hear about Waco Smith. The news came from New Mexico Territory. Waco and a bunch had pulled a job over there, and a posse had trapped them in a box canyon and shot them to pieces.

I never wore the guns again. After we moved into the old place, I hung them on the wall. It was right after I'd run against Billy Bates for sheriff and won that I came home to find them gone. Martha looked surprised when I asked about them.

"Why," she said, "I gave them to your friend, Mr. Williams. He said you'd sold them to him. Here's the money."

I counted the money, and it was a fair enough price for a pair of second-hand guns and holsters, but I hadn't met any Mr. Williams.

I started to say so, but Martha was still talking. She said, "He certainly had an odd first name, didn't he? Who'd christen anybody Long Williams? Not that he wasn't big enough. I guess he'd be as tall as you, wouldn't he, if he didn't have that trouble with his neck?"

"His neck?" I said.

"Why, yes," she said. "Didn't you notice when you talked to him, the way he kept his head cocked to the side? Like this."

She showed me how Long Williams had kept his head cocked to one side. She looked real pretty doing it, and I couldn't figure how I'd ever thought her plain, but maybe she'd changed. Or maybe I had. I kissed her and gave her back the gun money to buy something for herself, and went outside to think. Long Williams, William Longley. A man with a wry neck and a man who was hanged twice. It was kind of strange, to be sure, but after a time I decided it was just a coincidence. Some drifter riding by just saw the guns through the window and took a fancy to them.

I mean, if it had really been Bill Longley, if he was alive and had his guns back, we'd surely have heard of him by now down at the sheriff's office, and we never have.

A Cold Day in Boise

KEN HODGSON

Ken Hodgson is the author of three novels, *The Hell Benders* (1999) and *Lone Survivor: A Novel Based on the True Story of Frontier Cannibal Alfred Packer* (2000), both from Kensington Books and *Hard Bounty* (2001), from Pinnacle. The Alfred Packer book certainly qualifies him to write about Black Hat Harry Orchard who, as the story opens in 1953, is in his eighties and a prisoner in the Idaho State Prison. It's a fascinating read.

★

December 1953

In Corliss Hawley's worst nightmare she had never envisaged herself inside such a frightful place as the Idaho State Prison. When the massive steel doors slammed shut behind her, she could not help but wince. The ominous sound reminded her of closing gates to a tomb.

"Don't let the noises upset you, ma'am," the burly yet friendly guard said. "After a while here, a person doesn't even notice."

"I don't intend to stay very long," Corliss said. Her throat felt dry.

"Yes ma'am, that's what I was told. This man you're here to see is our most famous prisoner, yet he hasn't had a single visitor since I came to work here."

"And how long ago was that, mister . . ." Corliss adjusted her glasses as she regarded him. Lately it seemed to be increasingly difficult for her to see anything clearly over a foot or two distant.

"Sam Elder, Missus Hawley." The guard pointed to a silver name tag pinned to his starched blue shirt. "I've been in charge of watching over visitors here for twenty-seven years." He grinned down at the slightly older woman who wore her gray hair pulled back into a tight bun. "I've never lost but a few, so far."

Corliss ignored the guard's attempt at humor and stared down the long shadowy concrete corridor ahead. A few small barred windows set deep into the thick ashen walls that showed it was snowing furiously outside. "Twenty-seven years without a visitor. I am surprised he agreed to see me. In my letters to him I only asked for a visit without divulging any reason."

"Harry Orchard's getting plenty old, and he's awful sick," Sam said as he began escorting her toward a distant steel door. "I'd say he's just lonely and mighty glad to have someone to talk to."

"The man is a murderer." Corliss was shocked by the hardness of her own voice.

"That's a fact. It's a well-known truth that if he hadn't gotten a solid case of religion and made a believer out of the parole board, he'd have gotten hung back in 1908. I hear tell that he's killed forty-one men. I'd reckon none of the famous old-time outlaws like Jesse James or Billy the Kid ever came close to that number. When preachers say there's help in the Bible, I'm sure most never figured on a an old-time outlaw like Orchard using it the way he did."

"If justice had been done, Mister Elder, that man would have been dust inside a coffin long before you were born."

"We don't judge them here, Missus Hawley, that's not our job. We simply make sure they stay put and don't cause harm to no one else."

"I may be addressed as 'Miss' Hawley, if you please. I have been a schoolteacher for over thirty years and never found time for marriage. Also, the correct phrase is, 'does not harm *anyone* else.' The usage of double negatives is easily avoided."

The guard nodded but said nothing as they approached the steel door with a small set of bars at eye level. He took the key ring attached to his belt and sifted through the assortment until he found the one he was looking for and inserted it into the lock.

"It's me, Marvin," Sam mumbled. "I've brought Harry's visitor."

The door opened without the expected squeak. A slender young guard stepped over to them without saying a word and held out his hand. Sam Elder unclipped the key ring from his belt and placed it in the young man's palm.

"There's no keys allowed past this point," he explained. "When the door closes behind us, Marvin or someone else has to let us out. This keeps the inmates from getting them by force and attempting to escape." The harsh slamming of the door when the young guard left added to her uneasiness.

"A wise tactic, no doubt." Corliss Hawley swallowed hard when she saw a skeletal old man sitting upright in a plain wooden chair at an oak table. A cup of coffee sending up wisps of steam was in front of him. A quick survey showed the table and chair were held fast to the bare concrete floor with heavy metal straps.

"Mister Harry Orchard, I presume?" Corliss found it difficult to control the hatred in her voice.

The bald-headed, pale old man stared at her and nodded. He was neither handcuffed nor chained as she had expected. Instead of a striped prison uniform he wore a tattered brown wool sweater and faded blue jeans. His expression was bland, unreadable.

"Here's a chair for you, miss," the guard said, sliding an oak straight-back to the table. "I'll have to stay in here while you two visit—it's the rules." He forced a smile. "Would you like something to drink? Coffee's all I can offer, but there's sugar and cream to go in it."

"Thank you, no." Corliss felt her heart thumping in her chest. "I am only here to ask this—this *man*, why he murdered my father!"

Sam Elder bolted close to the schoolteacher, raking his eyes for any weapon she might have hidden from the matron who was supposed to have searched her earlier. He saw nothing amiss.

"I'm sorry about this, Harry," the guard said. "I'll escort her out right away. I'd reckoned on her being a writer or some such."

Harry Orchard rolled rheumy blue eyes at his visitor, a thin smile formed on his lips. "That's all right, Sam. I can tell this lady has waited a long time to see me. She also appears to be as full of hate as my guts are of cancer. Tell me ma'am, just who your father was, and I'll do my best to remember if I killed him or not. . . . There were *so* many, and it was a half-century ago. I've been rotting in this place for forty-eight years."

Corliss took a few moments to steel herself, then took

the proffered chair, sat, and scooted up to the table across from Orchard. "I will not say that I am sorry you are dying, nor that you have been locked away here for such a long while. Not only did you kill my innocent father when you exploded that fiendish bomb planted beneath the train depot in Independence, Colorado, you murdered a dozen more!"

Harry Orchard cocked his head and focused his watery eyes on the snowflakes splattering against the barred windows. It was as if he were looking back through the years. "Ah yes, I set that bomb off personally using a pull wire. Two hundred pounds of Giant dynamite makes a tremendous explosion. I was only a hundred yards away when I yanked the wire. My ears rang for some time afterwards. I also distinctly remember a leg rolling past my hiding place. That device worked devilishly well, I must say."

Corliss swallowed. She had not really known what to expect from meeting the man she had hated with such intensity all of her adult life. Facing the man who had murdered her beloved father was something that she had known for years that she had to do. When word reached her that Harry Orchard was dying, the task could be put off no longer. What took her aback more than anything was the man's coldness. Here he was describing a man's severed leg flying past him with no more emotion than if he were describing the weather.

"Those men were simply waiting on the train to take them home. The date was the fifth of June, 1904. I was nine years old when my mother cried and told me father had been killed."

"A lot of good men died on both sides, Miss Hawley." Harry Orchard tented his hands; she noticed his fingernails were long and filthy. "That is unfortunately what happens in war. The great cause of the Western Federation of Miners was every bit a war. If you had been older, you might have understood at the time that your father was not a union member. This placed him squarely against those of us who were striving to raise the standards and safety for all of the miners and mill workers in this great country, and rescue them from the clutches of the robber barons that sapped their vitality and strength in return for a pittance."

Corliss was aghast. She had imagined Orchard sobbing an apology and praying for forgiveness. He had supposedly escaped the gallows by crying on the witness stand and confessing his guilt. Now that she was face-to-face with her father's murderer, the fiend was showing not the slightest remorse. "You are claiming that you killed all of those men in an act of *war*?"

"Oh yes. I was a paid soldier hired by none other than General Big Bill Haywood himself. All of this is a matter of record. Good men were dying by the droves in unsafe mines. The working conditions were abominable, no ventilation, no safety measures. Those poor miners were forced to work ten hours a day, six days a week, while being treated worse than cattle. I was proud to be a mercenary for their betterment. I am truly sorry that a few had to be sacrificed for the good of the whole, but I must add that this sad fact is not uncommon in harsh times."

"I see." She turned to Sam Elder. "I believe that I would like a cup of coffee. Black will be acceptable." Most of all Corliss needed a few moments to collect her thoughts. Harry Orchard's unexpected demeanor had throughly upset her.

While the guard rattled around the small room getting her coffee, she silently studied the old man's features. Harry Orchard's pale blue eyes were sunk deep into his skull, giving him the appearance of a corpse. His baldness and lack of eyebrows was likely the result of treatments he had been given for his cancer, she decided. The man was, after all, eighty-eight years old. It was long past time for the devil to take his foul soul. Corliss remembered that the years just before and after the turn of the twentieth century were marked by great labor unrest in the west. The man who murdered her father and so many others obviously looked on himself as a martyr. If she was to get any satisfaction from actually facing this man who she so desperately hated, it would be necessary to let him speak his mind.

"Black, strong, and very hot, miss," Sam Elder said, setting a steaming mug in front of Corliss. The room was cool, and white tendrils of fog drifted upward between her and Orchard. "Take care not to burn yourself."

The guard took a step back, then cocked his head in thought. "Most everyone knows that Harry here blew up the governor of Idaho. Aside from that I'd reckon none of us really know what all he's done." He hesitated. "Killing a governor ain't no small feat."

Harry Orchard bent over and blew on his coffee. Then he straightened and returned his attentions to Corliss. "The ex-governor's name was Frank Steunenberg. He was out of office in 1905 when I placed ten pounds of dynamite where it would be triggered when he opened his garden gate. He persisted in continuing to fight against labor reform, and I also held a personal grudge. My only regret is that I did not use more explosives. He was still alive when his wife and children found him. That man was tougher than I had thought, and he took a long time to die. I much prefer a clean kill."

Corliss met his gaze with her iron-gray eyes. "Perhaps

you would be kind enough to explain how you came to be such a *passionate* individual."

"Yes, that would be best." Orchard tented his hands again. "Education is pavement on the road to understanding."

"I do remember reading that you came here from Canada," Sam interjected.

Harry Orchard watched the snow falling on barred windows and began to speak. "That is true. I came to this country in 1896, when I was thirty years of age. How well do I remember the hope I felt back then. This was a country of grand opportunities, a place where any dream could be realized. I had only three dollars in my pocket when I took a job as a milkman in the bustling mining town of Wallace, in the northern part of this state.

"For nearly five years I diligently invested five dollars a month, that I gleaned from my salary of forty dollars for working hard ten to twelve hours a day, six days a week, into stock in the Hercules Mine. I thought this to be a good prospect, yet after putting over a thousand dollars into that mine with no returns, I understandably began to worry and voiced my concerns to my broker. He immediately referred me to a man who offered to buy my position—which by now was one-sixteenth ownership of the mine—for exactly what I had in it.

"Being naive in such matters, and trusting, I took him up on his offer. Less than two weeks later the Hercules Mine hit the mother lode and went on to produce millions. The investment I had been swindled out of made the man who bought my position of ownership very wealthy. A system that robs the working man as I had been robbed could not be allowed to endure. I quit my job and took a position with the Western Federation of Miners as a union organizer.

"This was in June of 1901. Needless to say I had become a very bitter man. Then, quite by chance, I happened to attend a lecture by the wonderful orator, statesman, and socialist, Eugene Debs. After listening to this man's brilliance, and to speeches by the illustrious Big Bill Haywood, George Pettibone, and Charles Moyer, I came to realize that through no fault of my own had I been swindled out of my fortune. A few robber barons controlled the entire system. The decks were always stacked against not only me, but all working men, long before they sat down to play the game."

Corliss took a sip of coffee and stared at the emaciated old man through white fog. Harry Orchard spoke with a practiced fanaticism that came from learning by rote. Even after a half century, his hatred against a system he perceived as having cheated him still burned with an unquenchable fire for vengeance.

"You had found a cause célèbre," she said.

"Far, far more than that, Miss Hawley. I had joined a brotherhood of the repressed who had banded together to fight for our rights as had the founders of this country. Many of them were miners skilled in the use of explosives. Under the urging of General Haywood, I began working as an apprentice union miner. I became quite proficient in the use of dynamite. It was the manufacture and deployment of delay detonators that was the difficult task to learn. Any idiot can light a fuse. It takes skill to be miles away, enjoying a whiskey in a saloon, when an explosion makes a significant impression on the system."

"Then William Haywood, who was defended by none other than Clarence Darrow and found not guilty of ordering and paying for the assassination of the ex-governor, actually was your mentor."

Harry Orchard's gaunt face become an emotionless mask. "I shall speak no more of that. The brave general's ashes now lay beneath the Kremlin Wall. I will continue my story if you wish, but do not ask me to besmirch my brothers. What I did, I alone take responsibility for."

"Go ahead, Mister Orchard," Corliss looked vainly for a saucer in which to set her cup. She remembered where she was and did not bother to ask the guard if one was available. "I am most interested in hearing more."

"Yes, for the sake of your understanding this will be necessary." Harry took a long drink from his cup. "The first operation I undertook in the war against tyranny was early in the spring of 1902. I was in Park City, Utah at the time when a boiler explosion at the Ontario Mine killed two men. Unfortunately that happening was labeled an accident. Afterwards, I made certain to leave no doubt that the Western Federation of Miners were sending unmistakable messages to the robber barons that their usurpation of the workers would be tolerated no longer."

"I wish to hear of your time in Colorado's Cripple Creek district."

"Yes, Corliss, I will get to the depot incident in good time." Harry Orchard seldom blinked and kept his watery eyes focused on the raging snowstorm outside. "Patience is a virtue, or so it is said.

"When I arrived in Cripple Creek, the war against oppression had already begun. This was in July of 1902, if I recall correctly. At first we merely tried to discourage the scabs by the use of brass knuckles and clubs. I must assure you that we tried our utmost to restrain from violence against those who attempted to foil our efforts by continuing to work and enrich the wealthy usurpers of the down-trodden."

Corliss snorted. "These scabs as you call them were innocent men who were only trying to feed their families."

Harry Orchard ignored her. "The violence began with the mine owners. Sherman Bell, who was a former Rough Rider and friend of President Roosevelt, is noted for saying, when he could not get juries to convict union men, 'Habeas corpus be damned, we'll give 'em post mortems.'

"And this he and others of his ilk did. Bell was paid five thousand dollars a year by the Mine Owners Association to make the union problem go away. The union was forced to fight or be routed. Members of the Western Federation of Miners were rounded up by the hundreds, loaded onto cattle cars, then taken to the Kansas border and tossed out on the prairie with nothing but the clothes on their backs. In the town of Victor, Bell shut down the newspaper and arrested the editor along with all employees for daring to champion our cause. So many union men were killed that the undertaker offered a discount to the mine owners if they would do their killings on a Saturday.

"It became necessary for us to resort to stern tactics. I set a small bomb on the skip of the Vindicator Mine with the intention of blowing up as many as twenty or thirty scabs. To my chagrin, the stupid mine superintendent and a lone shift boss triggered the mechanism, killing only themselves. A few weeks later, I and a few trusted accomplices managed to sabotage the elevator skip at the same mine. We wedged open the safety dogs and poured sulphuric acid on the hoist cable to weaken it. The combined weight of sixteen scabs were sufficient to cause that cable to snap and send all of those men plunging down that two-thousand-foot-deep shaft. I was informed the results were *most* impressive."

"I remember people talking about that horrible disaster. What I do not recall was your being associated with it," Corliss said, a fiery ache in her throat tormenting her efforts to speak.

"You are correct in that I was never charged with that . . . incident. Yet I was the freedom fighter who poured acid on that hoist cable. This is the first time I have spoken the truth of this matter." Harry Orchard shot a sickly grin of defiance at the guard and motioned with a bony finger to a barred window. "What are they going to do about it now? Put me in prison?"

Sam Elder snorted, shook his head, then turned to begin fidgeting with the coffee pot. This was one of the few prisoner interviews he had overseen that had become downright unnerving. Until now, Harry Orchard had simply been a number, an inmate who, many many years ago, had blown up a governor. Now that the frail-looking old man was boasting of killing others, Sam felt relief in the fact that Harry Orchard was feeble and ill. A younger, more muscular prisoner of his ilk could certainly be trouble. Big trouble.

Corliss took another sip of what she believed to be the worst coffee ever brewed, suppressed a frown, and said, "I suppose you did not know even one of those eighteen men, nor any of their names."

Harry Orchard sighed with resignation. "Miss Hawley, I can see that you are simply not grasping the point I have been endeavoring to make. No soldier in any war makes an effort to find out the names of those he kills in battle. The Western Federation of Miners was at war with the capitalistic Mine Owners Association. I do not waste one moment of my time, now nor ever, worrying aver dead scabs."

"You never allowed yourself to look back and ask in your mind if there could not have been another way?" Corliss asked.

Harry Orchard stroked his cheek with bony fingers. "Only once. This was in Denver, not long before the time I blew up the train depot in Independence—which is the incident that brought you here to visit with me on such a frightful day as this. I had received orders to assassinate the wife of Supreme Court Justice Luther Goddard. To accomplish this, I bought a woman's purse identical to the one I saw Mrs. Goddard carrying about and filled it with dynamite. For this particular device I used a mousetrap for a trip and rigged it to explode whenever she picked up the purse. Unfortunately a young girl of eight was visiting at the time, playing with Goddard's daughter. This child went to fetch the purse so they could have money to purchase ice cream. I felt badly when I learned of the girl's death, especially when I found out that her father was a staunch union member."

"Simply a sad casualty of war." Corliss was beginning to understand Harry Orchard's reasoning. This reality caused icy pin pricks of fear to play along her spine.

"Perhaps I have rushed to judgment, Corliss." Orchard leaned close and spoke; his breath smelled like rotting meat. "You are intuitive, as I first surmised. The famous alienist, Doctor Hugo Münsterberg—I believe most people today refer to them as psychiatrists—interviewed me at length when I was first arrested. His report stated that I had a keenly perceptive mind and an intellect that few Harvard graduates could equal. It is gratifying to," he glared at the guard, "to be in the presence of intelligence."

Sam Elder turned his head to look at the prisoner. "I go home at night to my family. You've been locked away in a cage since 1905. I reckon if I'm not as smart as you are, I can live with the fact just fine and dandy."

Harry Orchard gave a raspy cackle. "Have you ever noticed, Corliss, that lawmen are devoid of humor? Pity, it makes my life here so boring. I find my charges more interesting to be around than the guards."

Sam Elder spoke up. "Harry tends to chickens in the prison farm. He's done that for over forty years, since right after he got his hanging penalty reduced to life."

After a long moment of silence, Corliss said, "I came here wishing to ask the murderer of my father why he committed such a cold-blooded act. I did not know what to expect, but certainly not this."

"Ah yes," Harry Orchard cocked his head in thought. "I really cannot tell you more about that depot happening than you already know. After the bomb exploded, I felt it prudent to quickly depart Colorado. It was only later that I learned thirteen scabs had been killed.

"I know that you hate me for what I was forced to do, but I want you to understand I am a product of the times. And in those days, times were hard indeed. If the governor of Idaho had not been the man who swindled me out of my fortune, things might have turned out quite differently."

Corliss Hawley jumped up and glared down at Orchard. "Then *you* would have been a wealthy robber baron and no different from those you fought against with such vengeance." Her eyes narrowed. "His name was Miles."

"Huh?" Harry Orchard said.

"It was Miles. My father's name was Miles Hawley. He was thirty-seven years old when you took his life. I leave you to tend the chickens, Mister Orchard."

She turned her back to the old man and went to stand by the steel door. It took some time for the outside guard to open the door. All the while she waited for Harry Orchard to at least utter an apology. It never came.

Sam Elder escorted Corliss Hawley to the front gate. He helped the gray-haired lady put on her heavy coat, then watched as she walked outside to melt into the swirling whiteness of a raging blizzard. He would be glad when it was time to go home where he could be warm.

It was always cold inside those thick stone walls. Today, however, felt colder than most.

Who Really *Killed President Lincoln?*

PAT DECKER KINES

Most of Pat Kines's work have been nonfiction articles. She did, however, publish *A Life Within a Life* (1998), a book about Libbie Custer. Here she tackles the assassination of Abraham Lincoln as a "what if?" type of story. Naturally, her Black Hat is John Wilkes Booth . . . or is it?

★

The General felt the cold metal of the knife at his throat almost before he realized he'd been attacked. As he tried to reach for his pistol, the knife tightened. He felt a sharp prick of pain; a small trickle of blood ran down under the front of his shirt. He stopped moving.

"Stand still, dammit!" the stranger said, low and nervous. "I don't mean to cut yah less'n you make me."

As the General stopped struggling, the pressure on his throat eased. Though he wanted to reach up and stop the drips of blood coming from his throat, he resisted.

"You mought know what I'm here fer," the stranger said. "They call me the Collector." He pronounced his name *Ko-leck'-tuh*. He was obviously from the South. He was also obviously dangerous.

"I figger you know what I'm here to collect, don't ya?"

The General started to nod in assent, then realized this would not be a good move, so he managed a weak, "Yes, I know."

"You mought be lucky in war, Ginnel, but you ain't so lucky at cards," the Collector said, chuckling. "The Man sent me to git his money back. You run up quite a bill while you was at it."

The General sighed. "I don't have the money," he croaked.

"We know you ain't got the money *now*," the Collector continued, "but The Man, he's ready to make a deal. Mought you be interested in a deal?"

The General started to nod again, then cleared his throat and said, "Yes. I am interested in a deal."

"Good. The Man says he'll meet you at half-pas' eleven tonight, at the old church by Green's tavern. You know it?"

"Yes, I know it."

"Then be there. Otherwise, you gonna have another visit from the Collector, and it won't be as pleasant as this visit. You heah?"

Suddenly the pressure on the General's throat gave way and the stranger was gone, faded into the shadows as if he'd never been there. The General brought out his handkerchief and dabbed at his throat. His damned weakness had finally caught up with him. Well, he'd see what kind of deal "The Man" had in mind. If it was good enough, maybe he could erase his debts, once and for all. And after that, he'd never gamble again. As he made that vow, he had to smile. It was one he'd made many times before. "But this time I mean it," he muttered to himself.

The General arrived early at the church yard that night so he could check it over. He didn't want any surprises.

The night was as black as the hat on his head. The shifting clouds overhead moved like a magic lantern, allowing only a few stars to be visible. The headstones in the graveyard had a strange luminescence. He walked stealthily around the perimeter of the yard, checking for hidden gunmen. He felt his way around the walls of the old church, startling a few bats out of the bell tower. As his eyes adjusted to the dark, he neither saw nor sensed another human individual anywhere.

The stench from the nearby Potomac River made him wrinkle his nose in disgust. Now that the war was over, he hoped things would be cleaned up in Washington City. After all, it was the nation's capitol. It had really gone to ruin with the states warring over secession.

At eleven thirty on the dot, The Man appeared. The smell of his cigar preceded him. As he approached, the glow from the lighted end provided a focus for his figure, which appeared to be rather squat and spherical. Making no secret of his arrival, his footsteps crunched on the gravel of the drive.

The General waited for him, leaning against a large tombstone that was topped by an angel with raised wings. The angel looked down on him with prayerful hands and a stony indifference.

The Man walked up to him, taking out his cigar and crushing it beneath his foot.

"Ah see you are heah, General, suh," he began. "It's a wise move on your paht."

He was dressed in a wrinkled white suit that was easy to see even in the dark night. On his head he was wearing a spotless white Panama hat over his flowing gray hair. He clearly wanted to present the figure of a southern gentleman.

"We'll see how wise it is, after I hear you out," the General replied curtly. "And by the way, since the war ended, I'm not officially a general anymore. That was just a temporary title. I am now considered to be a brevet general. And I am one of many, I might add."

"Nevertheless, Ah like to think of you as a general," The Man said, a smile in his voice. "Ah don't care what your 'official' title is."

The General nodded in the dark. He, too, had always thought of himself as a general.

"As Ah said, it makes no difference to me. Ah'm here to give you a very generous offer, get those debts of yours paid off in *toto*. Maybe Ah'll even sweeten the pie with a little cash. What do you say to that, Suh?"

"Just speak your piece and be done," the General said brusquely.

The Man took a moment to pace among the headstones. When he came back to stand in front of the General, he lowered his voice.

"As you no doubt guessed, Ah'm from the South," he began. "We southerners don't like the way things are goin' up here in Washington."

"I'm not real happy about it myself," the General said. "Without a war, we soldiers do not have a whole lot to do. That's why I'm here in Washington—to find a job while waiting for the army to decide on its next campaign."

The Man drawled, "Maybe then we can do both of us a favor."

"Something tells me you'll get more out of this 'favor' than I will. What do you have in mind, southerner?"

"We want Lincoln out of the White House. Simple as that."

"And just how do you plan to do that without another election? Lincoln just won a second term, fair and square."

The Man pulled out another cigar and lit it, drawing in the smoke long and leisurely. When he blew it out, he looked up at the stone angel. "Funny," he commented, "you don't seem like a stupid man."

"Surely you don't expect me to kill the President." If this was the deal, it was *not* what he had been expecting. Indeed, in his wildest imaginings he had not bargained for anything this grim. A man who shot the President might as well shoot himself afterward. Otherwise, if caught, he'd be facing the hangman's noose.

"Now just what is it that surprises you about my proposition? That's what y'all do, isn't it? Y'all kill people. You, General, are a soldier, he is the enemy. Besides, from where Ah stand, you don't have a whole hell of a lot of choice. You owe me money—big money. Ah could wreck your career with just a few words. Ah could also wreck your marriage. Now, Ah *know* you don't want that."

The General gritted his teeth and tried not to show any emotion. Then he turned and pounded his fist against the angelic tombstone. He was trapped. He couldn't risk exposure of his debts. And he had no prospects of paying them off. His pay had just been dramatically cut. His only alternative was to do the job and make sure he didn't get caught afterward.

"Oh," The Man added, "Ah'll sweeten the pot a bit, so to speak. Ah'll throw in an extra thousand dollars. That should help you get back to where your sweet little wife is waitin' for you."

The General turned back to face The Man. He *could* use the money. "Let's say, for argument's sake, that I agree to your deal. Just how do you propose I execute this, this as-sassination?"

"Oh, that's entirely up to you," The Man answered breezily. "Ah trust you to find a way. You just have to do it within the month."

"What's the hurry?"

"Those are my terms. Take it or don't."

"How do I contact you, if I need to?"

"You'll either heah from me, if you're successful, or you'll hear from the Collector, if you're not. Then there's the police, the President's bodyguard. You'll have to find a way to avoid them. But nevertheless, it should be simple for a big war hero such as yourself. Now, Ah bid you a good evening." The Man turned away and sauntered back down the road the way he'd come, lighting up another cigar.

The General knew he had no choice if he wanted out from his burden of debt. He had to kill President Abraham Lincoln.

This proposition made him feel exceedingly sad. This was not an act of war. This was murder, and murder for hire. Had he really slipped so low?

He had nothing against the President. In fact, he rather admired him. Lincoln had handled himself well during the Civil War, and he as a general had fought for the Union, giving it his all. However, his gambling debts had accu-mulated until everything he earned was going directly into paying off the syndicate. They owned him now. He was sure they'd make good on their threats if he didn't do what they wanted. And he was adamant that his wife not know about his debts. He'd promised her that he'd given up his gambling, his drinking, his swearing. Well, he'd gotten rid of the last two. Two out of three was pretty good, he thought. But still, she expected him to honor his promises. Maybe she expected too much of him.

On the other hand, he adored his wife. She was his shining star, his anchor to reality. He always knew she'd be waiting for him at the end of each of his campaigns. She was everything he was not. She was refined and well educated, popular, sophisticated. She was also as good a rider as anybody he'd ever known, a good companion overall. He couldn't resist the offer by The Man to pay off all his debts and get an additional thousand dollars. He couldn't resist the chance to stay in his wife's good graces.

On his way back to his hotel, he strolled by the White House. Even at this time of night it was patrolled by security men, some in uniform, some not. But he knew that the President came and went pretty much as he wanted during the day. He wasn't always accompanied by his protectors, either. He often rode in open carriages, some he actually drove by himself. He gave speeches, attended public events. A clever man should be able to get close to him without much effort.

Several days went by and the General began to pay more attention to the President's daily activities. The Man had given him nearly a month, but that wasn't much time. The South was in turmoil and had been for months before the end of the war. Their former slaves were unruly and were running away. Since the Emancipation Proclamation in January of '63, they had been moving north by the thousands. Cotton and tobacco plantations were left in ruin, landowners were broke, unemployment was at outrageous percentages. Even the most basic commodities were in scarce supply.

He knew he had to complete his contract, and complete it soon, though personally he didn't see that getting rid of

Lincoln would bring any immediate relief to the South. Had The Man considered who would be in charge after Lincoln was gone? Andrew Johnson, the Vice President? He wasn't sure that man would be much of a leader, but maybe that's what the South was counting on, somebody to act as a puppet for a puppet government.

For over four years, the President had been receiving death threats. Since the day of his first election, the rebels had been determined to do away with him. Still, he'd managed to survive all this time. Not only had he survived, but he had just won another term.

Now that the Civil War was over, the army itself was diminished. The General himself had not only given up his generalship for a captaincy, but he had to give up his salary, too. His pay went from $8,000 a year to $3,000. He had depended on that full salary to support himself and his wife in the style they felt they deserved. They were so tight for money right now that they'd sold most of their horses and their furniture. His wife had gone home to stay with her family and friends and to wait for his return.

His men, those who had decided to remain in the army like himself, had commented on how edgy he had been lately. He had been staying by himself more and more frequently. He'd truly given up gambling, something he should have done long before. But he was still drawn to it. Whenever somebody invited him to a game of poker, he was tempted to give in, but each time he had declined. The men knew enough not to press the issue.

The last game he'd been in, he'd bet and lost everything, including his favorite saddle. He didn't think of himself as unlucky, yet he seemed to be totally unable to win consistently at cards. He'd been hailed as a hero in the war, everywhere he went. The newspapers fussed over him, prominent people entertained him. But his friends were falling away, one by one, now that he could no longer distinguish himself in battle.

His wife wrote him daily, anxious for him to return home and to make a decision about the army. She hoped that he would give up soldiering. It was too dangerous, she said, and she missed him too much when he was gone. He knew she was right about that. He missed her, too. But a streak of reckless abandon ran through his blood. He knew of no other experience that gave him such a rush as battle. To charge into the thick of things, saber held high, horse plunging beneath him, was a feeling like no other. Only gambling gave him a similar challenge.

For now, he guessed he needed to do something about completing the deal with The Man, and he needed to do it without much delay.

The newspaper the next day had an article about a popular play that was coming to Ford's Theatre. The article went on to say that the President and his wife were expected to attend the play the very next night. They had special box seats, open for viewing by the public. They would be coming and going in plain sight. The General saw that this was the break he'd been looking for. Who would expect anything to happen at the theater?

As he watched the White House, thinking about his plan, the President himself came out of the drive as a passenger in the Presidential carriage. As the carriage stopped at the end of the drive, ready to enter the street, the General got a good long look at the man who had been President for over four bloody years.

He was much aged since he'd taken office. His face, which always seemed long and unhappy, was much grieved. He had dark circles and heavy bags beneath his eyes, his beard and hair were unkempt. He was wearing his signature stove-top hat and his familiar black suit. He sat in the carriage with his head down, resting on his chest, as if he were already asleep, only fifteen minutes out of the White House door. He must be headed home.

The General had a moment of indecision. It didn't seem right to beat a man who seemed so beaten by life. He'd had a long fight with his torn country. Even the northerners weren't entirely behind him. How could a man survive without even a little positive support?

He'd heard that the President's wife, Mary Lincoln, was a shrew. She spent money faster than even the General did himself. And for what? Her house? Her person? Her entertaining? True, they'd suffered some losses within their own family. But every family suffered losses. Spending large sums of money wasn't the answer. The General knew that from experience.

Apparently the President's wife had expected a lot more out of the Presidency than what she got. To her credit, she had thrown off her southern sympathies, having come from Kentucky. Even her brother had fought for the South. But she should have known that, when her husband was elected at the beginning of a major crisis within the southern states, they would have a very tough life.

Indeed, the General thought, it was hard to imagine why anybody would want to be President of a country that was so ungrateful. And it was all for the release of a bunch of black people who didn't want to be in the country in the first place. Were those people grateful? He didn't know, but he supposed they must be. Slavery was a terrible thing. His entire family was church-going and religious. They'd always believed it was wrong to "own" people. But did it take a war to make them free?

After he watched the President ride on down the street, his head still on his chest, the General went back to his hotel.

When he picked up his room key, the desk clerk told him, "You owe for two weeks, sir."

"I know. You'll soon get your money." The General stomped up the stairs and into his room, where he fell on the bed.

"Where's the justice?" he moaned to himself.

The next day he studied the schedule for the play. He visited Ford's Theatre, examined the way it was laid out. The box seats were in the balcony. They were also expensive, but they were accessible to anyone. The President's box had a flag of the U.S. draped across the front. He would have to get tickets for a box seat, walk over to the President's box, pull the trigger . . . He couldn't go any further with the plan. He was facing an action that could get him executed, hanged. Then his gambling debts would be paid, but what good would it do him? He'd die in disgrace, but at least his wife wouldn't be forced to pay off his debts after his death.

To establish his alibi, he asked one of his friends to accompany him to the theater. He wanted to see the play, he said. As it happened, the friend had season tickets and was happy to invite him along. He was eager to see the President at the play, he said, as well as to see the play itself, *Our American Cousin*. Besides, a famous Shakespearean was acting there, a man named John W. Booth. This would be the opportunity of a lifetime. The General agreed.

The next day, April 14, Good Friday, as it happened, the General met his friend at the theater. They had box seats directly across from the President's. When they took their seats, the President was not yet in his box. The General's heart sank, and he mopped his brow. Had his hasty plans been made in vain? Was the President not coming after all?

Shortly after the play started, Lincoln arrived with his wife and another couple, who, his friend pointed out, were Clara Harris and Henry Rathbone. A security guard in plain clothes was stationed at the rear of the box. Before he sat down, the President leaned over the balcony to wave to the people in the audience, who were all watching his arrival instead of the play. They applauded politely.

After they had settled down again, the actors continued. The Shakespearean, John Booth, seemed especially miffed at the interruption of the performance.

After intermission, everybody again took their seats. The party who had been seated in the box beside the President had apparently left the theater at the break. Their box was empty. This was looking better and better.

Around 10:10, the General saw the security guard leave the President's box. He waited a few minutes, then made his excuses to his friend. He had to relieve himself, he whispered. The friend, entirely involved in the play, just nodded and waved without even looking up.

The General walked behind the box seats, which were curtained off from the balcony's hallway, until he was directly behind the President's box. Without hesitating, he drew back the curtain, aimed, and fired his pistol, ducking into the empty box next to the President's immediately after he pulled the trigger, and hid behind the curtain. He didn't wait to see whether his shot had hit the mark or not.

As the President's wife screamed, pandemonium broke out in the audience. Another shot rang out, but the crowd's panic covered the sound of the second shot. The General watched, amazed, while the actor—Booth—leapt from the

President's box to the stage some twelve feet below. As he landed, he slumped, his leg hurt, and all hell broke loose.

People were too stunned to react immediately. They watched in horror as Booth limped off the stage and disappeared. The curtain came down. Then the President's security guard was running after the perpetrator, and the General sidled back to his original seat.

"What's going on?" he asked his friend as he sat down.

"Somebody just shot the President," his friend said, excitedly, "and it looks like it was John Booth, the actor. He just leapt from the President's box onto the stage. I think he injured his leg while doing it. Wait till they catch him. They'll break more than his leg."

"Is the President dead?"

"There's no way to tell. We'll have to read the papers tomorrow. Somebody came and carried him out of his box, took him to a hospital, I suppose. His wife was shouting and screaming all the way." He lowered his voice. "That is one dramatic woman."

"Too bad I missed it," the General replied, trying to look regretful.

Sure enough, in the next day's newspapers, the President was declared dead. Andrew Johnson had assumed the presidency. The South was jubilant.

As for John Wilkes Booth, the newspapers declared that he'd been part of a conspiracy. Somebody in the theater was suspected of aiding and abetting his escape. A coconspirator, Lewis Paine, had stabbed Secretary of State William Seward in his home on the same night, but had only wounded him. He'd been captured immediately. It was assumed that Booth and other southern sympathizers wanted to throw the government into a state of chaos to give the South time to make a comeback.

The General had to smile as he read the newspaper. This Booth fellow was the one everybody was hunting. What a stroke of good fortune!

Twelve days later the papers reported Booth's capture. He'd ridden to a Dr. Mudd, who had set his broken leg, and federal authorities had found him and a man named David Herold, suspected to be part of the conspiracy, at a farm near Port Royal, Virginia. Booth was shot to death as he hid in a barn. His diary had been found, chronicling the conspiracy.

Late that night, in his hotel room, the General was wakened by a knock on the door.

"Who's there?" he called, getting up from bed and retrieving his pistol from the night stand.

The knocking continued.

The General slowly opened the door, holding his pistol behind him. As he had expected, The Man was standing there, a lighted cigar in his mouth.

"Come into the room," the General said softly. "I'm sure we don't want to talk in the hall."

As he stepped into the room, The Man pulled out the General's gambling IOUs and fanned them in front of his face. He then shuffled them together and tore them in half, then in half again. He laid the torn paper in an ashtray and touched his cigar to it. The paper burst into flames, and they watched it burn to ashes.

The Man pulled out his wallet then, extracting some large bills. "Here's the extra thousand dollars Ah promised," he said, handing over the money. "Ah feel that we actually got more than we paid for, with John Wilkes Booth being labeled as the killer, and who knows? Maybe he was the murderer. You've always been known as a poor shot. The end result is: We got what we wanted—no more

President Lincoln. Now let us see what the South is capable of."

As the General folded the money and put it away, The Man said, "Paid in full." Then he opened the door and left the room.

The General stirred the burned paper until he was sure nothing was left to be read. He grinned to himself as he went back to bed. He actually hoped he wasn't the killer. And he hoped the South was able to recover without the visionary President who had just been killed. Only time would tell.

A short while after the assassination of Lincoln, the General received a letter informing him that the army was going to travel to the Texas border to rid the state of some hold-out Southern Rebels, as well as trying to protect the border into the United States. This was a job he looked forward to, though his wife would have trouble with it. He would be back with the army and have a chance to be in action again. He had even been given a promotion from captain, along with a better salary.

He and his wife traveled to Louisiana. As she unpacked and settled them into their quarters, he looked up General Sheridan, to let him know they'd arrived.

He knocked on Sheridan's door and waited.

After the General opened the door, he said, "Lieutenant Colonel George Armstrong Custer, reporting for duty."

The People Versus Porter Rockwell

ROD MILLER

In putting *White Hats* and *Black Hats* together I made a concerted effort not to repeat writers. Rod Miller is one of only two authors who have stories in both books, but further, Rod managed to get into both books with the *same character*. Seems Porter Rockwell walked on both sides of the, uh, brim. The White Hats story was called "Separating the Wheat from the Tares, Being a True Account of the Death and Life of Orrin Porter Rockwell." This story differs in form and structure and, oh yeah, has a shorter title.

Rod has a book of Western humor, *You Ain't No Cowboy If . . .* , scheduled to be published in 2002.

★

Now comes V. Harmon Haight, District Attorney in the First District Court in and for the Territory of Utah, appearing for the People of the United States of America, Plaintiff, seeking from this duly summoned and sworn Grand Jury a True Bill against Orrin Porter Rockwell, Defendant.

"Thank you, Mr. Secretary. Gentlemen of the Jury, the oath you have taken requires you to evaluate the evidence

The People will present in this matter. Your duty is to determine whether or not probable cause exists to believe the accused committed a crime. If the evidence establishes such a probability, you must return a True Bill and, thus indicted, Porter Rockwell will stand trial to determine guilt or innocence. You may also, of course, refuse to indict— but after hearing the quantity of evidence The People will present before the Grand Jury, I doubt it.

"The crime for which Rockwell stands accused is murder. Now, gentlemen, this crime is not a recent one. The victim, one John Aiken, was last seen alive on the earth in October of 1857, just one month shy of twenty years ago. The details of the crime appear dim through the dust of passing years and the evidence obscured. And, even though you will hear from witnesses who place the defendant at or near the scene of the crime those many years ago, The People will not ask you to reach your decision in this matter on testimony of those long-ago events alone. No, gentlemen, you will be allowed to evaluate the man Porter Rockwell as a whole—to determine his role in this affair within the context of a life of bloodshed and carnage. But, since it is the murder of John Aiken for which the man stands accused, the evidence in that crime shall first be presented to the Grand Jury.

"GUY FOOTE, DO you understand the oath you have taken?"

"Yessir."

"Very well. Tell the jury, please, your place of residence in October of 1857."

"Nephi."

"And do you recall the events that are the subject of this inquiry?"

"Yessir. I'm told you're looking into what happened to them Aikens who came through there in chains."

"What did happen?"

"Well sir, as I said, they came through as prisoners, under the charge of Porter Rockwell and some other men. I didn't know them then, and I don't recall them now—"

"But you do recall Porter Rockwell. Why is that?"

"Oh, everyone knows Port. All us kids back then held him up as a hero."

"Do you still?"

"I can't rightly say as I do."

"What changed your mind, Mr. Foote?"

"It was this affair with them Aikens I'm trying to tell you about."

"Go on, then. I apologize for the interruption. Tell the jury the course of events."

"Port and his posse passed through town in the afternoon, and we all turned out to see. They rode on by and, I was told later, stopped a few hours farther on and camped by the river out there, the Sevier River.

"Late in the night I was woke up by some folks talking in the public room—my folks ran a sort of hotel, see, putting up boarders and travelers. I heard Porter Rockwell say, kind of mad-like, 'We made a bad job of it, boys—one of them got away.'"

"Did you *see* it was Rockwell?"

"No, sir. But it was his voice, kind of high and squeaky-like. Anyhow, they was gone when I woke up, and I didn't think much of it. Later on, though, one of them prisoners, Tom Aiken he was, came back to town afoot with a bloodied head and a bullet in his back. He hadn't his shoes nor

shirt, and was pretty thoroughly chilled. His story was that
the posse had fallen on them in the night, hollering about
an Indian attack, and whacking them over the heads. He
managed to get to his feet, he said, and run off but was shot
in the back—by Porter Rockwell, he believed, as he had
seen Port with a pistol in his hand—before he could make
his escape. But he managed to get away in the dark and the
willows, and hid out all night. Them others was killed and
dumped in the river, he says. Ma and Pa put him up in a
bed, and Doc fished a bullet out of his back.

"Along about evening, another one of them men
showed up—John Aiken this time—him, too, with a nasty
gash on his topknot and barely half dressed hisself. He
didn't remember nothing but waking up when he hit that
cold river, and managed to stay out of sight until he
thought it safe. He took to a bed at our hotel, too."

"Moving along, Mr. Foote, we understand from other
testimony that the local authorities opted to escort the two
'prisoners' back to Great Salt Lake City once they were
sufficiently recovered. You had a role in that?"

"Yessir. Me and Billy Skeen offered to make the trip.
There wasn't much on that time of year, and us being about
fourteen years old, thought it would make a fine adven-
ture."

"You weren't afraid?"

"Nah. Them two was pretty used up. They was barely
in shape to travel, so no one figured they'd try anything.
They was outfitted by folks in town—I remember Pa gave
John Aiken an old coat he had—and we set out. About
eight miles or so north of Nephi there's this place called
Willow Creek; nothing there but a spring and a sheep-
herder's cabin, but it's a convenient watering hole where
most folks stopped, as did we. While I saw to the team,

Billy and them others was stretching their legs. I heard that cabin door bust open and considerable gunfire and turned and saw both them Aikens fall, one of 'em near torn in two from shotgun balls. Someone in that shack hollers out for me and Billy to just climb in the wagon and get on home."

"Do you know who it was?"

"No, Mr. Haight, I can't say as I did then or do now."

"Could it have been Porter Rockwell?"

"He might of been in there, but it wasn't him hollering. I would of recognized his voice. So I guess I can't say he was there."

"How does the story end?"

"We lit out of there as ordered and went back to Nephi. Some folks went back out to Willow Creek after we said what happened, but nobody ever saw them Aiken fellas again, nor even their bodies. They figured whoever had shot them had dumped them in the springs.

"That evening, Rockwell and another man rode into town and spent the night at the hotel. A day or two later I found Pa's old coat hanging in a lean-to we had over the back door. It was stained with blood, and I counted eight holes in it. Billy Skeen saw it, too. I showed him."

"MR. SECRETARY AND gentlemen of the jury, I would like now, if you please, to read into the record a correspondence from one Albert D. Richardson of the *New York Tribune*, who visited Utah Territory in 1865 in the company of the eminent Schuyler Colfax, then Speaker of the House of Representatives in the United States Congress."

"What is your purpose in doing so, Mr. Haight?"

"Merely to show, Mr. Foreman, another aspect of Rockwell's character—to further establish a ready disposition toward violence, if you will."

"Go on, then."

"Thank you. This, from Richardson's published accounts in the *Tribune*:"

" 'While abroad on the streets of Great Salt Lake City yesterday I encountered the notorious Mormon assassin Porter Rockwell. The chance meeting was a frightful one, as Rockwell had me confused with Fitz Hugh Ludlow, another reporter, whom I am said to resemble, and who passed through Utah Territory some time earlier and had written in the *Atlantic Monthly* an unflattering description of Rockwell. He believed it was I who had characterized him as the murderer of one hundred and fifty men; and he significantly remarked that if I had said it, he believed he would make it one hundred and fifty one!' "

"STATE YOUR NAME and rank, please."

"Patrick Edward Connor, Colonel, Third Regiment, California Volunteers, Retired."

"Colonel, how did you come to know Orrin Porter Rockwell?"

"In 1862, I was ordered by the President and Commander in Chief to move seven companies of my command to Utah Territory to protect the Overland Mail route against Indian depredations. And, it was understood, to keep an eye on the Mormons, whose loyalty to the Union was suspect.

"I had heard of Rockwell. He enjoyed a certain notoriety throughout the West. I had even heard tales of his exploits in California in the gold rush years. But my first direct experience of the man came in the form of a report that he was riding through the streets of Great Salt Lake City as my command approached, offering any and all a five-hundred-dollar bet that my soldiers would never cross the Jordan River. We did, of course, and marched through the heart of the city with loaded rifles, fixed bayonets, and shotted cannon. We pitched our tents on benchland overlooking the city and established Fort Douglas among the Mormons."

"Fine, Colonel. Had you any direct dealings with Rockwell after that?"

"Considerable. If you have read your history, you know of the Battle of Bear River. I shall spare this assembly the details; suffice it to say that in the dead of winter, my California Volunteers located and attacked a camp of hostile Shoshone Indians in Cache Valley, killing more than two hundred, destroying their camp and supplies, and recovering property stolen from settlers.

"Rockwell was instrumental in this effort. He guided us to the savages and offered valuable strategic advice for overtaking the camp. He participated bravely in the fight, as well. But his greatest value came after the battle. I daresay that without his valiant service in obtaining teams and wagons to transport our wounded and unhorsed troops back to Fort Douglas, most of my command would have died in the cold and the storms."

"What is your opinion of the man?"

"Over time, I came to consider him a friend, Mr. Haight. One whom I admire greatly. I know of no better guide or frontiersman. He is, in my opinion, to use his own words in describing good things, 'all wheat.' "

"You say you became his friend, Colonel. Would you describe yourself, also, a confidant?"

"I suppose so. We have talked a good deal about his life.

Given all I had heard about him, I was curious about the facts of his history."

"You're aware, I'm sure, that Rockwell was accused of the attempted murder of Lilburn W. Boggs, governor, at the time of the assassination attempt, of Missouri."

"Yes. I questioned Rockwell closely about that incident one evening after we had shared a number of what he called 'squar whiskies.' "

"Would you relate to the members of the Grand Jury, please, his answer."

"He said, 'I shot through the window, and I thought I had killed him, but I had only wounded him; I was damned sorry I had not killed the son of a bitch.' "

"MADAM, WE SINCERELY appreciate your appearance before this Grand Jury to relate a difficult incident that must still grieve a mother's soul. If you will, state again your name for the members of the Grand Jury."

"I am Eliza Scott McRae."

"Mrs. McRae, I need not remind you that you are under oath. Relate, please, the events of your life in late July and early August of the year 1861 in which Porter Rockwell played a role."

"Well, Mr. Haight, my two sons, Kenneth and Alexander McRae, were accused at that time of robbing an emigrant. I don't know but what they might have done it—they were young men and full of themselves, and had been given to occasional mischief. But this crime was more serious, so I don't know.

"At any rate, Porter Rockwell and a police officer set out to track them down and, as it was told to me, they caught my boys a ways up Emigration Canyon."

"Were your sons then jailed and brought before the court?"

"No, sir. At an out-of-the-way place there in the canyon, they were gunned down with a double-barreled shotgun in the hands, I believe, of Porter Rockwell."

"Were there witnesses to this fact, Mrs. McRae?"

"None that could or would talk."

"Then why do you attribute the atrocious act to Rockwell?"

"On account of what happened next. Rockwell and that police officer rode up to my house with the boys toes up in the back of a buckboard. Port dumped the bodies into the dirt of my door yard. Then he spoke to me. He said, 'Mizz McRae, had you done your duty when raising these boys, I would not have been forced to do mine.' "

"GENTLEMEN OF THE jury, in my hand I hold reports from numerous investigations The People have conducted into the affairs of Mr. Rockwell. As you see, it is a stack of considerable thickness. I will not burden you nor the record of these proceedings with a full account. It is available for your perusal should you so choose. I must remind you, gentlemen, that Porter Rockwell stands accused—formally—only of the murder of John Aiken. We do not seek an indictment for all these crimes. But allow me, gentlemen, to read out to you a few of the more notorious incidents attributed to Rockwell. And recall the old saw, gentlemen: where there's smoke, there's fire.

"July 1850; Rockwell, upon orders from Mormon leaders, cured the sick old woman Alice Beardsley of the disease of 'apostasy' by slitting her throat.

"August 1850; an unidentified argonaut on the trail to

California was decapitated by Rockwell, Mr. Scott the sheriff, and another man, merely on the suspicion that he had been a member of the Illinois mob that killed Mormon leaders Joseph and Hyrum Smith in 1844.

"April 1851; Rockwell, leading a posse that captured four Ute Indians suspected of horse thievery, ordered the prisoners shot rather than returned for trial.

"October 1853; a government surveying party under the command of Captain John W. Gunnison is wiped out by a band of Indians led by Kanosh. It is believed that Rockwell inspired or participated in the atrocity.

"April 1856; the bullet-riddled bodies of Almon W. Babbit and his teamsters are found dead on the prairie near Fort Kearney, relieved of $20,000 in government funds en route to Utah for the construction of the Territorial Capitol. Papers belonging to Babbit and stock carrying his brand are found in the possession of Porter Rockwell days later at Fort Laramie.

"September 1857; Rockwell initiates aggression against troops of the United States Army marching to quell rebellion in Utah. Raiders, under Rockwell's command, burn forage, stampede livestock, destroy food and stores, thus endangering the lives of some 2,500 soldiers forced to winter on the high plains with insufficient supplies.

"February 1858; Henry Jones and his mother, accused of an incestuous relationship, are mutilated and murdered at their home in Payson. It is widely known that Rockwell was dispatched by authorities to dispense this 'justice.'

"September 1859; the sound of gunshots in downtown Great Salt Lake City led to the discovery of John Gheen, stretched out on the sidewalk with blood and brains oozing from two gunshot wounds to the head. Again, Porter Rockwell is widely believed to have been responsible for this 'apparent suicide' of a man troublesome to Church authorities.

"May 1860; two known outlaws, Joachim Johnston and Myron Brewer, staggering drunkenly from a saloon toward a boarding house, are gunned down on the street by an unseen assassin. Porter Rockwell is believed to have been responsible for saving the city the expense of a trial.

"December 1866; the body of a black man, Thomas Colbourn, also known as Thomas Coleman, was found with throat slit from ear to ear. Rockwell, in this instance, the leader of a group enforcing the laws against miscegenation.

"Gentlemen of the Grand Jury, I could continue. While much of the evidence is sketchy and covered up by those who have been in de facto authority in the Utah Territory these past thirty years, there is no doubt that this carnage occurred. And, I submit, there is little doubt that Orrin Porter Rockwell had a hand in these, and other, events attributed to his bloody hand. The most conservative estimate of the bodies in his wake runs to forty. Others place the tally much higher.

"The People ask you, as duly sworn members of this Grand Jury, to return a True Bill against this killer in one case and one case only—the murder of John Aiken. This indictment alone will be sufficient to bring Porter Rockwell to trial and justice; to rid our society of this scourge. Gentlemen, do your duty."

WE THE MEMBERS of the Grand Jury currently seated in the First District Court in and for the Territory of Utah, believe, according to the evidence laid before us, that sufficient cause exists to suppose that he did commit the crime and do herewith return a True Bill against Orrin Porter Rockwell and order that, thus indicted, he be tried in court to determine his guilt or innocence in the murder of John Aiken.

ADDENDUM: LET THE record show that on 29 September 1877 Orrin Porter Rockwell was arrested by the United States Marshal for the murder of John Aiken and delivered to the penitentiary for safekeeping.

ADDENDUM: ORRIN PORTER Rockwell did appear on 6 October 1877 before Associate Judge Phillip H. Emerson, where he was admitted to bail in the amount of $15,000, released from custody, and ordered to stand trial for murder during the October 1878 term of the First District Court.

ADDENDUM: 9 JUNE 1878; Orrin Porter Rockwell, awaiting trial for murder, died this day in his office at the Colorado Stables. Autopsy and inquest ordered.

ADDENDUM: 11 JUNE 1878; upon physician testimony and autopsy results, the Coroner's Jury investigating the demise of Orrin Porter Rockwell today brought a verdict of death by natural causes due to failure of the heart's action, finding no evidence of injury or poisoning. The body was released for burial.

On the Square

MARCUS PELEGRIMAS

Marcus Pelegrimas is a young writer trying to break into several genres at one time. It's an unenviable task, but he has managed to publish work in the mystery, horror, and Western genres already, and he's just turned thirty. He's recently appeared in the anthologies *Boot Hill* (Tor, 2002), *Desperados* (Berkley, 2001), and *Mystery Street* (Signet, 2001).

Here he shows how adept he is at Western writing with a story about former Billy the Kid gang member Dave Rudabaugh.

★

New Mexico, 1879

Nobody liked a rat.

Throughout history and in every culture, the one constant that bound the most virtuous man to the lowest criminal was the common hatred for that particular rodent. They were dirty. They were diseased. And they had no qualms about turning over their friends if the opportunity presented itself.

Sitting on the outer edge of the light given off by a sputtering campfire, Dave Rudabaugh shrugged off that last part of his analogy and took another pull from his whiskey-filled canteen. The fact of the matter was that he didn't know a whole lot about history. He didn't really know if rats even had any friends, but he knew well enough that he felt like a rat for what he'd done less than a day ago.

"Ain't you gonna eat anything?" asked Henry Rogers from the opposite side of the fire.

Henry was a bulky specimen with tree trunks for arms and a head full of sap to match. He might not have been too bright, but he was the kind of man that was most valuable in a fight. Too big to be scared and too dumb to get rattled. The scars he'd earned from countless scuffles made his face look like a map of the Union Pacific lines. Light blue eyes reflected just a hint of sentience, most of which was an illusion cast by the flames dancing in front of him.

Letting the fire water burn down his throat before looking up at the other man, Rudabaugh let out a deep breath and shook his head. "Edgar and the rest of 'em are probably eating off a tin plate in their jail cell right now. Kinda makes me lose my appetite."

"They knew what they was gettin' into when they robbed that train. Just like you did. They didn't think the law would track 'em down so quick."

It all played through Rudabaugh's head with perfect clarity. He and Edgar West had taken two other boys into Texas for what should have been an easy robbery. Hardly anyone had gotten hurt for a change, and they'd managed to ride off with enough cash to carry everyone over for a few months of the high life.

But in a matter of days it had all fallen apart when a posse led by Bat Masterson caught up with them near the state border. They'd split up and were supposed to meet at a small town fifty miles to the west. But then the law sprung out at Rudabaugh like monsters from a bad dream.

Rudabaugh could still feel the handle of his gun brushing the tips of his fingers when he'd tried to draw down on them, but that was as far as he'd gotten before he was staring down the wrong end of a rifle being held by John Joshua Webb. One of Masterson's men, Webb seemed to enjoy pressing the gun against Rudabaugh's skull.

After that, the information poured out of Dave's mouth like sour beer and stomach acid. He'd told the law everything he knew about Edgar and their meeting near the border. For his cooperation, he'd been allowed to leave.

"You think Bat will keep his word and let you be?" Henry asked.

Grunting while he shook himself out of his memories, Rudabaugh said, "It don't matter much. He won't be able to catch up with me again. Besides, he won't have any reason to come after me anyway."

"What do you mean?"

"I'm through with this bullshit of living on the run. I've had enough of being hunted by the law and getting shot at every other day. It's time for me to change my ways. Earn my living on the square."

When Henry laughed, it sounded like a bear coughing up a fur ball. The reaction shook his massive body as well as the ground beneath him as his voice rolled out through the night in every direction. "On the square? The hell, you say. You just feel bad about getting the rest of them landed in jail. Shake it off, Dave. You walked away from them law the only way you could. You survived."

Rudabaugh lifted the canteen to his lips and tilted it back, emptying the last of the whiskey into his mouth. The bottom of a bottle never burned as much as the top, but the same thing couldn't be said about the thoughts rolling around inside the outlaw's mind. In fact, the more he tried to digest them, the deeper they stung.

"Yeah," Rudabaugh said. "I survived."

If rats were good for anything, that was it. They survived.

DAVE RUDABAUGH HELD on to his good intentions for an entire year. He kept those intentions in the back of his mind every time he and Henry Rogers robbed a store or held up a stagecoach. By now, Rudabaugh's lean build and tumbleweed hair had taken on a more rugged appearance. His beady brown eyes weren't as cold as usual. Every once in a while, they even reflected some genuine emotion. Life on the square agreed with him nicely. At least, it did in the part of his brain that actually kept making plans to clean up his ways and those of the others who'd been thieving and killing right alongside of him.

Among those others was a man named John Allen. Possessing a build that allowed him to blend into nearly any crowd, Allen had the face of a mischievous boy half his age and was nearly as quick with the pistol as Rudabaugh. Having met up with Henry and Dave in Kansas several years ago, they bonded quickly and moved down to New Mexico to form the self-titled "Dodge City Gang." Allen got along famously with Rudabaugh and even started enjoying Dave's prolonged speeches about the joys of the quiet life.

But such diversions couldn't brighten his spirits in the fall of 1880 after the gang lost its main supporter and financial backer, a city marshal who'd decided to forsake his oath to the law for a twenty-percent cut of all the gang's

hauls. Such backing was the lifeblood of the Dodge City
Gang. And when it dried up, each of the surviving members felt it like a stake through the heart.

It was around this time that Rudabaugh thought back to
that night another lifetime ago when he'd been sitting with
Henry around that campfire. Mainly, it was the mention of
a particular name that struck a chord with him. A name
he'd been spitting into the air for the past hour.

"John Joshua Webb. *City Marshal* John Joshua Webb,
no less. Can somebody tell me how a goddamn City Marshal gets his ass planted in jail?"

Luckily, nobody in town seemed to care too much for
the Busted Flush Saloon. In fact, hardly anybody even
knew the shack was anything more than an old house or
condemned storefront. If only the place served beer that
didn't taste like horse piss, the Busted Flush would have
been a perfect base of operations.

Henry Rogers drained the rest of his beer and shrugged
amiably. "You never had a problem with Marshal Webb
before. Well . . . besides that business with Bat Masterson
last y—"

"Shut yer hole, Henry," Rudabaugh snapped. "I remember what happened last year. That's not what I'm talking about!"

Allen shook his head and ran his finger along the dented
edge of his mug. "I thought Webb had this whole town
working for him. Ain't that what he said?"

"Sure," Rudabaugh grunted. "He said that plenty of
times. And he managed to keep his end up for the percent-
age we gave him, but there ain't no connection good
enough to get him out of a murder charge that's already
held up in court. The damn fool just couldn't be happy

with what we had. He just *had* to kill that fella and just *had* to land in jail!"

Dave's words were followed by a short silence while he tried to keep himself from creating an even bigger scene. Just when he thought he'd managed to pull the reins on his temper, his anger was set off by the thorn that had been in his side for years.

"That jail part," Henry said quietly. "I don't think Marshal Webb wanted that to happen. That seemed like more of a mistake to me."

Glaring across the table, it was all Rudabaugh could do to keep from throwing himself at the bigger man and clamping his hands around that thick, muscular neck. But he managed to fight back the murderous impulse. And when he did, he felt an odd sense of calm descend over his entire body. Like a blanket that had been soaked in cool water, the feeling put out the fires inside the outlaw's soul and let him see everything that had happened in a new light.

"You know something?" Rudabaugh finally said. "You're absolutely right, Henry. Ol' Marshal Webb didn't mean to land in jail. He was just doing his part, just like when he and Bat Masterson cornered me in Texas. He was just doing his part then, and he's been doing his part ever since he threw in with us a couple months ago.

"When a man tries to do his part, he shouldn't get punished for it if he fails. Webb could'a sold us out, and he might have even been set free."

"Just like you did to Edgar after that train robbery," Henry pointed out.

"Yeah," Rudabaugh said, his teeth gnashing on the grit left behind by the swill he'd been drinking. "But he didn't hand us over."

"How do you know that?" Allen asked.

"Because if he did, the law would've been on us already."

Allen nodded and glanced furtively to either side. "That reminds me. Maybe we shouldn't stick around here too much longer, Dave. I mean, we'd be a hell of a lot safer somewhere else. Maybe we can pull together the Dodge City Gang somewhere else. But for now, it's probably best if we clear out while we can."

Rudabaugh turned in his chair as a smile crept onto his face. Resting his palms flat on the table, he began nodding as his thoughts flowed quickly through his alcohol-soaked mind. "I made a promise to myself long ago, John. It's something I've been trying to do for awhile now. . ."

"Christ almighty," Henry muttered. "Not this again."

Ignoring the bigger man's comments, Rudabaugh kept nodding and went on unaffected. ". . . but I just didn't know how to go about living like an honest man. Making my money on the square. I get wrapped up in thieving and killing because I do it so damn good. But maybe I should be doing something else. Something different."

"Oh really?" Allen mused. "Like how different? You want to chuck your gun and open a restaurant? Maybe plow a field?"

"No," Rudabaugh said through clenched teeth. "I'm talking about something else. You've been saying we need to run, and normally I would agree with you. But it's time to stand up and do the right thing. That's how a man starts to change. He steps up and does the right thing."

Allen regarded Rudabaugh with no small amount of amusement. "And after that, it's living on the square, I suppose?"

One last nod, and Rudabaugh figured his point had been

made. "Exactly. On the square. Just like I've been saying this whole time."

"And how do we step up and do the right thing?" Allen asked. "Because if you want to turn yourself in, you can damn well do that on your own."

"We need to do something to prove that we ain't just murderous rats. We need to prove that we stick by our own when all hell breaks loose. We need to help them that's been helping us." After leaning in closer to the middle of the table, Rudabaugh said, "We need to break City Marshal Webb out of jail."

THE ALCOHOL WAS still flowing through the bodies of all three men as they skittered through the darkness like a trio of rodents darting from knothole to knothole along a rotten baseboard. In fact, Rudabaugh felt as though his feet hadn't moved faster in his life as when they'd carried him someplace he never thought he'd be going: *toward* a jail.

As for the others, Allen and Henry weren't certain if they were actually taking part in Rudabaugh's plan or if it was just some delusion fueled by all the foul liquor they'd been pouring down their throats. Either way, they both knew it was too late to head back once they'd crept up to the side of the jailhouse and drawn their guns.

Actually, they passed the point of no return once Henry reached out and caved in the skull of a deputy who'd been keeping watch on the side of the building. The young lawman's body hit the dirt like a sack of flour, leaving a trail of blood as he was dragged across the ground to be stashed beneath the porch of the marshal's office.

"How the hell did I let you talk me into this?" Allen hissed as he crouched in the shadows.

"It's the right thing to do, John," Rudabaugh whispered.

"No. The right thing to do is get out of here, which is exactly what—"

Allen's words were cut off as Rudabaugh slammed the palm of his hand against his mouth. Greasy wisps of hair poked out at odd angles from a dented hat, giving Rudabaugh an even wilder appearance than normal. His eyes glittered like a wolf who's just spotted its prey, and his teeth flashed in the moonlight when he spoke.

"We're gonna do this," Rudabaugh snarled. "We're busting Webb out, and we're leaving town together. And do yourself a favor . . . don't kill any of them lawmen or they'll put a price on your head too big for anyone to resist." Turning around to look at Henry who'd just sidled up behind him, Rudabaugh added, "You got that? No killing."

Henry looked back to where he'd stashed the body and nodded. Rudabaugh held his pistol tightly and took a long, sobering breath. It was a ritual he used every time he was moments away from a fight, and so far it hadn't failed him yet. Despite the fact that he'd run over the hastily constructed plan several times with his partners, Rudabaugh could only hope that they would all remember their parts.

And it was with this sense of hopeful confidence that Rudabaugh motioned for the first stage of the plan to commence. He was relieved to see Henry rush away from them to circle around the jailhouse just as they'd discussed.

The big man wasn't anywhere close to graceful as he shuffled with his back hunched over from shadow to shadow. But he did a good enough job of keeping quiet until he was far enough away from the others.

Turning to Allen, Rudabaugh plastered on the steely expression that was his mask through most of his robberies.

It was the face of a true killer who wasn't about to be diverted from his goal. It told the entire world that he meant business. It told Allen that the only way out of this now was either with Marshal Webb in tow or all of them inside pine boxes.

"You there," came a voice from the front of the jailhouse. "Where do you think you're going?"

The guard couldn't have been more than nineteen or twenty years old and was too wet behind the ears to notice the fact that one of his companions had disappeared in the last few minutes. Gripping a Spencer rifle in trembling hands, the kid straightened his back and planted both feet on the ground. Even so, the fear leaked out of him like water from a cracked barrel. It rode on the chilled night air, a sweet scent playing in the nostrils of all three outlaws who'd come to know that odor all too well.

Henry held his hands easily out to either side and sauntered a few steps closer to the young lawman. "Just out for a stroll," he said, emphasizing his drunkenness. "I heard you got yourself a marshal in there."

Doing his damnedest to sound forceful, the deputy said, "Get on home before I call out some more men to take you there."

Rudabaugh led Allen around the other side of the jailhouse. Both men came to a stop when they could see the back of the young guard talking to Henry. The kid's fear hung heavily in the breeze, bringing a twitch to the outlaws' trigger fingers.

Rudabaugh stepped forward with his eyes locked on the back of the guard's skull. Every step he took, he thought about how easy it would be to kill this kid and walk inside the jail.

Just as Rudabaugh was about to swing for the back of

the guard's head with the handle of his gun, he spotted something out of the corner of his eye. It was no more than a flicker of movement, but it was enough to allow the outlaw's basic instincts to take over.

"What the hell's goin' on here?" shouted the second guard as he made his way toward the jailhouse.

For a second, Rudabaugh froze. His mind raced with a stream of notions on how he could not only accomplish what he'd come there to do, but also get out of there alive. If he'd had a few minutes, he might have come up with something. But since all he had was a fraction of a second, Rudabaugh twisted on his heels and acted the way his instincts dictated.

Like the calm that came before a twister dropped down from the sky to level a town, the momentary quiet seemed to slow the whole world to a crawl. In that time, Rudabaugh knew his life depended on the next thing he would do. And with that much at stake, he knew better than to go against the very grain of his being.

In one fluid motion, Rudabaugh brought the pistol up, snapped the hammer back and pulled the trigger, sending a piece of lead through the air and into its target.

The second lawman still had his hand on his weapon when Rudabaugh's bullet slammed into his shoulder and knocked him flat onto his back. Impacting on the ground with a solid thump, he wheezed once as all the air was driven from his lungs and a wave of pain washed through his upper body. The wound stung like all hell, but it was in his shoulder and nowhere near anything vital enough to threaten his life.

"Take them down, Cal," the wounded man grunted. "Behind you!"

The first deputy was already spinning around to face

Rudabaugh, raising the rifle in his hands high enough for him to sight down its barrel after levering a round into the chamber. Rudabaugh was so close that the end of the rifle brushed against his skin as the deputy's finger tightened around the trigger.

Blinking once to fight back the moment of doubt that hovered in his mind, the young lawman gritted his teeth and tried not to think about what he was about to do. Suddenly, his ears were filled with a loud, although muffled explosion. For a moment, he was certain he'd made his first kill, but then he started to wonder why his own head hurt so damn much.

Then he realized his finger was no longer on the trigger. The rifle was sliding from his hands and a veil of black was spreading over his eyes until he couldn't even see the porch as it rushed up to pound against his face.

Henry could still feel the rattle in his arm after bashing the butt of his pistol into the guard's skull. The kid had dropped so fast that Henry had to jump back to avoid getting his boots trapped beneath the unconscious kid's body. Still thinking about the plan, the big man turned toward the front of the jaiihouse and smashed down the door with one well-placed boot.

The door slammed against the inner wall, breaking its top hinge in the process. Henry was already inside, walking down the short row of cells while looking for the disgraced Marshal Webb.

Outside, Rudabaugh hopped down from the porch and ducked around the building. Allen was right beside him, his breath coming in ragged bursts while he nervously scanned the night around them.

"Shit, Dave, all the law in this town will be headed this way."

"Actually, it looks like they're already here."

Rudabaugh's words hung in the air like a dark specter. Both outlaws squinted into the shadows while trying to staunch their loud, racing breaths. Once they were able to quiet themselves a bit, they could hear the sound of boots crunching against the soil in a quick, almost frantic pace. That was soon followed by voices which spread out to cover the area surrounding the jailhouse.

"They're still there, boys," one of the approaching voices said. "Take your time and fire when you get a clear shot. There ain't nowhere for them to go."

Allen looked up at Rudabaugh with rage burning like twin coals behind his eyes. His teeth ground together with such force that Allen was unable to speak right away. "What now," he snarled when he could manage it. "You wanna tell them about your plan to live on the square? Maybe they'll feel sorry for you and only put a few bullets in our hides."

Gunshots started popping in the distance, sending chunks of lead into the side of the jailhouse to form a pattern which closed tighter around Rudabaugh and Allen as more of the approaching deputies got close enough to make them out in the dark. From inside the building, there were also explosions of gunfire as well as the thumping of heavy boots against the floor.

Rudabaugh could only imagine what was going on inside. And though he wasn't too happy about going into a jailhouse that was probably filled with lawmen, he liked the idea of staying outside and playing the part of clay pigeon even less. "All right," he said to Allen while tightening his grip on his gun. "Let's get what we came for."

Without waiting for a response, Rudabaugh bolted from his shadow and rushed toward the front of the jailhouse. A primal battle cry welled up in the back of his throat and tore through the air along with the increasing gunfire. The moment his boots touched upon the jailhouse's porch, Rudabaugh was firing into the ranks of the lawmen closing in around the building, dropping a few of them to their knees and one or two onto their backs.

In the space of a few heartbeats, he was inside the jailhouse and kicking the broken door closed behind him. Hanging precariously on its single hinge, the door managed to stay in place despite the bullets which punched the occasional hole through the flimsy wood.

"You find him, Henry?" Rudabaugh asked in a haggard yell.

Before his eyes could take in the sight before him, Rudabaugh's senses were overpowered by the blast of a shotgun roaring through the enclosed space. He could see the large shape of Henry Rogers standing in front of one of the cells at the end of the row, but couldn't quite make out the bigger man's face.

"Henry!"

Turning toward him, Henry had one of his hamlike fists wrapped around the bars of a cell. He looked at Rudabaugh for a moment, blinked, and then pitched face-first onto the floor. It wasn't until he was sprawled out on the boards that the wound in his back could be seen.

Rudabaugh's eyes widened at the sight of his partner's shoulder blades protruding from the gaping crimson hole. If Henry hadn't been so big, the shotgun blast might very well have torn him in half. Once Henry was out of the way, Rudabaugh could see the man who'd killed him.

Deputy Sheriff Lino Valdez held the smoking shotgun in both hands, shifting his stance slightly to aim at Rudabaugh. A fine mist of Henry's blood had spattered across the front of his shirt and face, giving the lawman a grisly, monstrous quality that struck a chord deep in Rudabaugh's soul.

For a moment, the outlaw stared across at the shotgun's second barrel . . . the one that had yet to be fired . . . the one that had his name on it.

Rudabaugh's first impulse was to throw himself to the side. Although he wasn't the praying sort, his mind was focused on a message to the Almighty as he pushed off with both feet and twisted himself in midair so that his back pounded against the wall.

All Rudabaugh could feel at first was the impact of his back against the place where the wall met up with the bars of the first cell. Dull, throbbing pain rippled up and down his spine like the fingers of a devil intent on plucking out his bones one at a time. By the time his ass finally landed upon the floor, Rudabaugh was firing again, desperately trying to focus enough to take aim.

But his bullet sparked against the bars of Marshal Webb's cell, causing the corrupt official to drop to his belly and cover his head with both hands.

The shotgun in Valdez's hands went off a second time, emptying the second barrel in a spray of lead, fire, and smoke which filled the narrow hall in a cloud of expanding doom.

Knowing that he only had one more bullet in his cylinder, Rudabaugh struggled to think of a way he could use that to get out of this building with his life and Webb intact. His thoughts were cut short when he saw Valdez toss the empty shotgun to the ground and go for the pistol strapped to his side.

Rudabaugh took a deep breath, lifted his pistol . . . and fired.

In his mind, he'd been picturing that single shot flying

fast and true, destroying the lock on Webb's cell and allowing his partner to escape. But Rudabaugh's actions weren't quite up to his expectations and instead the outlaw sent his last round to the one place he knew would be his safest bet: right through Valdez's face and out the other side.

The deputy sheriff stood on wobbly legs for a second or two as Rudabaugh charged down the hall. Finally, like a puppet whose strings had been cut, Valdez dropped to the floor in an awkward heap. Outside, the gunshots had been tapering off, but drawing closer with every second that passed.

"That one's got the keys," Webb said from the floor of his cell. Jabbing his finger between the steel posts, he pointed to Valdez's belt. "There! Right *there!*"

Rudabaugh rushed to the still-twitching body and plucked the ring from its loop on the deputy's side. "John's outside," he said while working key after key into the lock. Once he found the right one, he twisted it in the mechanism and pushed open the door. "Now take off out the back and head for our normal spot. We'll meet up with you later."

Before Rudabaugh could say another word, he was nearly bowled over by the retreating form of Joshua Webb. He followed in the crooked lawman's steps, bolting out the back door and coming face to face with a pair of startled lawmen.

Rudabaugh's fist flashed toward the knife strapped to his leg and lashed out with the blade as he continued to run. He wasn't sure if he hit anything and he didn't care. All that concerned him was that he continued to put that jailhouse behind him. And he didn't stop running until his lungs refused to pull in another breath.

Parral, Mexico, 1886

"Now this," Rudabaugh said to himself as he sat down to enjoy another drink, "is more like it."

A lot of things had happened after that night in New Mexico. Among them, Dave Rudabaugh had ridden with Billy the Kid and been chased down by the seemingly tireless Pat Garrett. After that, he'd wound up in a Las Vegas prison where he was reacquainted with his old friends Webb and Allen.

The trio broke out of there through a hole in the wall and once again parted ways. Since then, Rudabaugh had been getting his taste back for the old dream of finding a life where he was less likely to die in a hail of gunfire.

Starting off simply, he'd made his way across the border where he at least wouldn't have to worry about the law hounding his every move. It felt great to be in Mexico. The warm air was like an inviting hand across his face, and the constant feeling of danger was removed from the back of his mind. In its place was a sense of relief.

A sense of victory.

The cantina was a sorry excuse for a building. Its walls seemed to be merely leaning in on each other without the benefit of any such luxury as nails or mortar. Inside, the locals sat around their rickety tables, singing songs, telling jokes, and playing cards.

Merely seeing the card game made Rudabaugh feel more at home, so he headed to an empty seat at one of the tables and bought himself some chips. Just over an hour later, Rudabaugh's sense of calm was blown to hell.

"Give my money back, *vendejo*," grunted a dark-skinned man sitting directly across from the outlaw.

Rudabaugh put on a well-practiced look of innocence and looked around in disbelief. "Excuse me?"

"You heard me, gringo. You cheated, so you hand back the money."

Shaking his head, Rudabaugh tossed his cards onto the

table in a fit. On top of trying to maintain his facade of self-righteous anger, he tried even harder to keep the Jacks he'd palmed from fluttering into view. "All I want is a friendly game. So keep your mouth shut and that's all we'll have."

The Mexican pushed away from the table and jumped to his feet. Instinctively, Rudabaugh did the same.

For a moment, both men looked across at each other as the entire cantina fell silent. Even as he watched the other man's gun hand, Rudabaugh wondered why, of all the people in the world, this kind of thing had to keep happening to him.

"Take back what you said," Rudabaugh warned. "And we can both get back to our game."

"You're a cheating dog, gringo. I won't take back shit."

Rudabaugh's temper spiked as his vision became tinged with red. Before he could think about what he was doing, his hand was already flashing toward his gun.

Seeing this, the Mexican went to arm himself. His muscles twitched once as the shot blasted through the air, and kept right on twitching as Rudabaugh's bullet tore through his skull.

The player to Rudabaugh's left cursed in Spanish and leapt back a step, his eyes wide with fright. The moment his hand went for his pistol, he saw Rudabaugh turn toward him. The rest was a haze of smoke and burning pain as a chunk of hot lead dug a tunnel through his heart.

"Jesus Christ," Rudabaugh grunted as he looked around inside the cantina. "A man can't go anywhere for a square deal anymore. Not below the border . . . not anywhere."

He muttered about the injustices of his life as he stormed from the cantina. His words stopped short when he realized that his horse was no longer tied to the post where he'd left it less than an hour ago.

"Son of a bitch!" he roared. "Thieving goddamn Mexicans!"

Whipping around on the balls of his feet, Rudabaugh charged back toward the cantina and kicked open the door. He was several steps inside when he realized that the entire room was shrouded in darkness.

"What the hell?" he grunted as hands clamped onto his arms and neck from all directions.

Rudabaugh felt his gun belt get torn from his waist and fist after fist pound into his ribs and jaw. All the while, he was being shoved across the floor to a spot near the back of the cantina. So many thoughts were rushing through the outlaw's mind that Rudabaugh couldn't make sense of them all. It was as though his brain had unleashed a flood between his ears that roared with a wild, deafening power.

Finally, a single lantern came to life over his head. Before he could get a look at it, however, Rudabaugh was slammed up against a wall where he was cornered by a huge Mexican bristling with sweat and rage.

"We don't want your kind here," he said through a thick accent and a spray of spittle. "You killers come to our country and stink it up like pigs."

"Wh . . . what?" Rudabaugh stammered. "I don't . . . I don't know what . . ."

The Mexican produced a large, rusted machete from a scabbard hanging from his belt. Holding the chipped blade up to the outlaw's face, he grinned and said, "After what happens to you, no more of you pigs will want to come here again."

"But . . . I just . . . but I just wanted to start over! I wanted to make my living—"

"On the square!" the Mexican said.

And just as Rudabaugh was wondering about the other man's choice of words, he was shoved further back into the cantina and kicked savagely in the balls. When he doubled over, spewing his lunch onto his boots, he was pushed down until his chest slammed against a small table made of a single thick block of wood.

Although he couldn't see it, Rudabaugh could feel the edges of the square pressing against his ribs and gut.

"Hold this pig down on that square," the Mexican shouted to a few members of the crowd that had gathered around the outlaw. "Stretch him out good."

Rudabaugh wondered if the path of the straight and narrow had ever truly been open to him. He wondered this as the Mexican raised that old machete high over his neck. He kept wondering as the chipped blade chewed through his flesh.

And he even wondered it for a few seconds as his decapitated head was held up for all the locals to see.

Living on the square.

Perhaps . . . it was enough . . .

. . . to die on the square.

The Bloody Years

ROBERT J. RANDISI

Miracle of the Jacal (Leisure, 2001) is the most recent Randisi Western novel. It's the story of the legend of Elfego Baca. Also published recently were the anthologies *White Hats* (Berkley, 2002) and *Boot Hill* (Forge, 2002). Here's a story about the "bloody years" of Henry Plummer and his gang of "Innocents."

★

1

It was January 10, 1864. Sheriff Henry Plummer finished his breakfast, sat back, and patted his full stomach. It was the best breakfast, and possibly the best meal, he'd ever had. He stood up, walked to the window, and looked out at the gallows. The hanging would take place later in the day, when he'd make that long walk from the jail to the gallows. He'd made it before, but today it would be different.

He turned as U.S. Deputy Marshal John X. Biedler fitted the key into the lock of the cell door.

"Finished with your food, Henry?"

"Take it away, John."

"How're you feelin' today?"

"Never better." Plummer was a handsome man, and his smile was dazzling. Only thirty-one, but he'd had more than his share of women, and his charm had even won him many friends along the way.

"Are ya sorry, Hank?" Biedler wanted to know. "Sorry at all?"

Plummer took a last look at the gallows outside, then turned to face Biedler.

"I've had a good life, John."

Biedler took that to mean that the young man who was—or had been before his arrest—the sheriff of both Bannack—where they were at the moment—and Virginia City, was not sorry.

"Well," Biedler said, "it's good that you had a good life, Hank, 'cause it surely wasn't a very long one." *

"I haven't been hung yet, John," Plummer said.

Biedler picked up the tray and left the jail cell, locking it behind him. *But soon*, he thought, *very soon you will be.*

PLUMMER HAD BEEN born back east, in Connecticut, the son of a wealthy man. He'd grown into a well-educated, dapper, handsome, and intelligent man. He knew that he could do anything he put his mind to—except control his passion. He called it "passion," anyway, while others called it his "temper." Whatever it was, it first flared when he was marshal of Nevada City, California at twenty-four. He had come west to make his fortune and found himself a partner in a Nevada City bakery, but soon became the town's leading lawman. This did not, however, quell his instincts for other pleasures, such as gambling and women. It was both that had caused him to lose his position as marshal, and in fact while still officially marshal of the town, he had been caught with another man's wife and ended up shooting the man to death. After being found guilty not once but twice, friends had convinced the governor of California that he was ill and would die in prison if not pardoned. The governor complied with their request. Henry Plummet went free.

But rather than leave California, Plummer stayed. Indeed, he even opened another bakery in Nevada City, though he soon sold his interest with intentions of leaving. However, his infatuation with a whore caused him to return. He clubbed a man over the head in a whorehouse fight, but luckily the man did not die. Later, he was involved in the robbery of a Wells Fargo office, but there was not sufficient evidence to arrest him. Finally, he did manage to kill a man and was jailed, but bribed the jailer and escaped.

Finally, he left Nevada City and California and the bloody years of Henry Plummer's life truly began.

MUCH OF HENRY Plummet's bloody years were spent in three locations—Lewiston, Idaho, and Virginia City and Bannack, Montana.

He rode into Lewiston in late 1860 and quickly got a job dealing faro in one of the local saloons. It took only a few days for Plummer's gun to claim its first local victim.

Having been born in Connecticut, Plummer had an affected speech pattern that did not fit in with the Idaho miners. One of them thought it so funny he decided to tease the twenty-eight-year-old. Plummer did not take kindly to the miner's barbs and quickly produced his gun. He invited the miner out into the street, and there dispatched him with little or no trouble. The man did not even have time to lose his teasing smile before he was dead.

Several other incidents quickly convinced the people of Lewiston that Henry Plummer was equally adept with cards and guns, and further that he had an evil temper that should not be roused.

Meanwhile, Plummer began to realize that Lewiston was a boom town ripe for the plucking if a man was smart enough—and he felt that he was. Plummer formed a gang of bandits who robbed gold and payroll shipments and also killed and robbed miners in broad daylight. He never appeared at any of these jobs, though. On top of that, his men were loyal and would never give him up. One of the reasons for that was that if any of his men crossed him, he met a swift demise in the form of lead from Plummer's guns.

There was no law in Lewiston, so a vigilante group was formed to find these bandits and deal with them. Plummer himself was one of the first to join the band of vigilantes. That way he was on both sides of the law and could make sure none of his men were caught. Lewiston quickly became a death trap for anyone with money, and so it soon became a ghost town. Whether the mines began to peter out or Henry Plummer had simply driven everyone away, Lewiston died and Henry Plummer moved on to greener pastures.

Ultimately, he ended up in Bannack, Montana, where the gold fields were still ripe and the miners were, too. This was where Plummer would form his most successful and secret gang of thieves. They operated with a secret handshake and a code by which they would be able to identify each other. When two of them met, they would say, "I am innocent."

And so they became Henry Plummer's "Innocents."

2

In January of 1863 Jack Cleveland walked into Goodrich's Saloon in Bannack, to the utter surprise of Henry Plummer.

"You look surprised, Hank," Cleveland said.

"I thought you were dead, Jack," Plummer said, now recovered from his surprise.

Cleveland sat down opposite Plummer.

"You mean you left me for dead in Lewiston, when you pulled out."

"I left Lewiston for dead, Jack," Plummer said. "Not you."

Cleveland looked around the saloon, which was small and mostly empty that early in the afternoon.

"I hear you got a nice little setup here, Hank."

"I don't know what you mean."

Cleveland sat back. "Sure you do."

"Where'd you get your information?" Plummer asked. Somebody, he thought, needed to be dead.

"Never mind," Cleveland answered. "Let's just say I know who's 'Innocent' and who ain't."

Instead of denying everything, Plummer asked, "What do you want, Jack?"

"I want in."

"So you wanna join up—"

"No," Cleveland said, cutting Plummer off, "I don't want to join, Hank, I want a piece of the action."

Plummer's eyes narrowed. "How much of a piece?"

"Half."

Now it was Plummer's turn to sit back. His urge was to draw his gun and kill Cleveland on the spot. He didn't do that, though. For one thing, Cleveland had been smart and had walked in without a gun. Plummer would have to explain why he had gunned down an unarmed man.

"Not a chance."

"Hank—"

"What happens if I don't give you half?"

Cleveland smiled. He was the only man Plummer ever knew who wasn't afraid of him. That made them even, though.

"I'll take the whole thing, Hank," Cleveland said. "The Innocents will be mine."

"Not a chance, Jack," Plummer said again. "It wouldn't be healthy to try."

Cleveland pushed his chair back. If he'd been armed, Plummer would have shot him right there and then. The man stood up and stared down at him.

"I'll see you here tomorrow at this time," Cleveland said. "You can make up your mind then."

"My mind's made up, Jack, and one day ain't gonna change it," Plummer said. "Be wearin' a gun when you come in tomorrow."

"Oh, I'll be wearin' a gun," Cleveland said.

And he was.

FIVE SECONDS AFTER Jack Cleveland walked into Goodrich's Saloon the next day, he was on the floor leaking blood at an alarming rate. Plummer had stood and drawn his gun, cleanly beating Cleveland to it.

"Help me . . ." Cleveland pleaded, trying to staunch the flow of blood from his belly with both hands, but those who were in the saloon that day were too afraid of Plummer to make a move.

The same could not be said for Hank Crawford, though.

He came running into the saloon, saw what had happened, and immediately grabbed Cleveland to haul him off to the doctor.

When Crawford came out of the doctor's office, Plummer was waiting for him.

"So?" he asked.

"He's dead."

"Did he say anything before he died?" Plummer was wondering if Cleveland had given him up as the leader of the Innocents.

"About what?'

"His life? His friends? Anything."

"From what I can see, he had no friends. I'll take care of his burial myself."

Crawford walked off, convinced that Plummer was afraid Cleveland had told him something.

Plummer watched as Crawford walked off, wondering what the man knew.

From that moment on, Crawford and Plummer were on a collision course.

IN DUE TIME Hank Crawford became convinced that Henry Plummer was corrupt. He was eventually elected sheriff of Bannack, and it became his business to stop the rampage of the Innocents, which he thought he could do by stopping Henry Plummer.

PLUMMER SAT IN Goodrich's saloon with his two best men, Buck Stinson and Ned Ray.

"What are we gonna do, Henry?" Stinson asked. "That sheriff's askin' a lot of questions, gettin' folks all riled up."

"Cleveland told him somethin' before he died," Plummer said. "I'm sure of it."

"But he can't prove nothin'," Ray said.

"Not yet," Plummer said, "but somebody gave up our code to Cleveland, and that same somebody might give it to Crawford, too."

"So what do we do?" Stinson asked again.

"That's easy," Plummer said. "We take care of him."

3

Several assassination attempts on Sheriff Hank Crawford failed. In the attempt that came the closest to succeeding, a seemingly unarmed man braced Crawford and challenged him to "take off your guns and face me." Crawford complied. The man then pulled a gun out of hiding and tried to kill Crawford, but the sheriff was too quick for him and disarmed him. The man went to jail and never said whether or not it was Plummer who sent him.

Another time Crawford, who was a butcher by trade, as well as being the sheriff, had an appointment to buy some cattle. Plummer arranged to be there, lying in wait, but something unexpected had come up and Crawford sent an assistant in his place.

Plummer knew if he was going to get rid of Crawford he would have to do it himself, and forget about trying to be subtle about it.

Finally, his chance came. Word came to him that Crawford had stepped into a café for a piece of pie and was unarmed. Plummer rushed to the place with a double-barreled shotgun. It was finally the end, he thought, for Sheriff Crawford.

★

CRAWFORD SAT IN the café, waiting for his friend, Frank Ray. He and Ray were going to discuss a partnership deal over a cup of coffee, but Crawford figured adding a piece of pie to the picture wouldn't hurt.

Because he was still more butcher than lawman, he had gone to the café unarmed, so when Henry Plummer entered with his shotgun, Crawford thought he was dead for sure.

"Plummer!"

"Don't get up, Sheriff," Plummer said. He looked around. This was better than he could have hoped for. The café was empty except for Crawford. No witnesses. He had an extra gun tucked into his gunbelt, and after he blew a hole in the lawman he could drop the gun on the floor next to him and claim self-defense.

"You don't want to do this, Plummer," Crawford said. His eyes went to the kitchen door and he wondered how much of a chance he'd have if he made for it

"You don't leave me much choice, do you, Sheriff?" Plummer asked. "I know Cleveland talked to you."

Crawford wet his lips nervously. "Cleveland never said a word, Plummer. He died before he could."

"I wish I could believe that, Crawford," Plummer said. "I really wish I could."

But the crazed look in Plummer's eyes convinced Crawford that this was a lie. He was a dead man.

Plummer cocked both hammers on the shotgun, but before he could pull the trigger, someone fired a gun and a bullet struck his right arm. It went through cleanly, breaking a bone as it went. He was lucky that Frank Ray had fired at an angle, and the bullet had gone through and kept going.

Ray, walking down the street, had seen Plummer enter the

café and feared for his friend's safety. He felt he had no choice but to fire, but he also realized that his shot—while it might have saved Crawford's life—had not killed Plummer. Ray turned and ran, but the damage was done. Plummer's right arm was useless, and the shotgun sagged in his left hand.

Crawford wasted no time. He bolted from the table to the kitchen, burst into it and then out the back door. He was never seen in town again. He knew that sooner or later Plummer or one of his men would be successful in killing him, so he gave up his badge—left it behind on the kitchen floor, as a matter of fact—and returned home to Wisconsin to mind his own business and be nothing but a butcher for the rest of his life.

AFTER CRAWFORD BOLTED from town, the way was clear for Plummer—recovering from his wound and practicing gunplay with his left hand because his right was now useless—to run for and win the sheriff's job. No longer being secretive about it, Plummer was plainly the leader of the outlaw gang, because it was the gang itself—by virtue of their number, and their intimidations—who swung the election for him. However, the job didn't last long because, as happens with boomtowns, Bannack eventually became a ghost town and Plummer and his gang moved on to Virginia City, where the greed and power of the Innocents would reach new heights.

4

John X. Biedler looked across the table of the Helena, Montana café at his fellow Deputy U.S. Marshal Nathaniel Langford.

"You did the right thing, Nate," he said, "testifying against Plummer that way."

"Wasn't no way I was gonna let that man wear one of these," Langford said, fingering the badge on his chest. "I worked too hard to get mine. If he'd gotten one I woulda taken mine off then and there."

"Well, I don't blame you for that," Biedler said, "but this don't do much to stop him, does it?"

"He's sheriff of both Bannack and Virginia City," Langford said. "Only law they got down there."

"And he's picking both towns clean," Biedler said. "Ain't a stage that's safe from him and his men."

Langford cut into his apple pie and shoveled a forkful into his mouth, washed it down with coffee.

"Nothin' we can do unless we're sent in there, John," Langford said.

Biedler shook his head. "Everybody knows he's the leader of that gang, but nobody will do nothin' about it."

"Ain't our place," Langford said. "I did my part by keepin' him from gettin' a Marshal's badge. I track down those they send me after, John. I don't pick my own jobs. They send me after Plummer and I'll take him down, but not before."

"Hmm . . . " was all Biedler said.

"I know that look," Langford said. "You got somethin' on your mind."

"I'm thinkin' about the miners," Biedler said, "and miners' law. You know, it don't take much to turn a bunch of miners into a bunch of vigilantes."

"We're lawmen, John," Langford said. "We don't approve of vigilantes, remember?"

"Oh, I remember, Nate," Biedler said. "I remember real well."

"Yeah, well," Langford said, pushing the empty pie plate away from him. "I gotta go." He stood up and put on his hat. "You still got that look on your face."

And it stayed there for quite some time after Deputy Marshal Nathaniel Langford had gone.

5

No one knew how, but while Plummer was in Bannack word got out that a gold party was leaving Virginia City. Plummer had an office in Bannack and one in Virginia City. Two of his men, Dutch John Wagner and Steve Marshland, found him there and gave him the news.

"Sounds like they waited until I was away to try to sneak it out," Plummer said angrily. He had Virginia City under his thumb. It angered him that they would try to pull something like this. "You boys go and get that gold, and while you're at it, you kill 'em all. You hear me?"

"We hear you, Hank," Wagner said.

"Kill 'em all!"

WAGNER AND MARSHLAND moved to intercept the gold wagon, moving much faster on horseback than the heavily laden party was able to. They set up in some rocks and waited for the wagon to come by.

"You nervous?" Marshland asked.

"Why?" Wagner replied.

" 'Cause you're sweatin', that's why."

"So are you."

"Yeah, but I'm sweatin' from the heat," Marshland said with a laugh. "You look like you're sweatin' and shittin' your pants."

"Why don't you shuddup."

"You worried 'cause Hank only sent us two?"

"Who knows how many men are with that gold?" Wagner asked.

"Hey, Hank knows what he's doin'," Marshland said. "He sent his two best deputies, didn't he? Just relax."

"Yeah," Wagner muttered, "relax."

FINALLY, THE GOLD wagon came into view with several riders accompanying it.

"Don't miss," Steve Marshland said.

Unnerved, Dutch Wagner fired a shot and missed. He succeeded in warning the riders, and suddenly a tarp was thrown from the back of the wagon and more men with rifles appeared.

"Shit!" Marshland swore. "It's a trap."

He stood up and immediately a bullet took him down.

"I'm hit!" he cried.

A volley of shots followed, taking chunks out of the rocks all around them. Wagner tried firing back, but there were too many men. He stood up to go to Marshland's aid and a bullet punched into his shoulder, knocking him off balance. He made his way to Marshland, who had been hit in the leg. Together the two gunmen limped to their horses, mounted up, and rode off. They had gotten away, but the trap had accomplished its purpose.

They had been recognized.

ONCE WORD GOT out that the "gold wagon" had been hit by two of Henry Plummer's deputies, the miners immediately banded together.

"This is Plummer's work," one miner shouted.

"We've had enough," another said.

The miners converged on Bannack, two thousand of them filling the streets, seeking Plummer and his men. Luckily for Plummer he was in Virginia City at the time.

The miners then broke into packs and began to track down Plummer and his deputies. Two of them, George Brown and Red Yager, were captured near a place called Stinkingwater Valley. They were immediately hanged, even though they confessed to many robberies and murders and gave out the names of their fellow "deputies" as the guilty parties. When it was clear that they were still to be hanged, Yager shouted, "Plummer's the one you want! He's our leader."

Those were the last words he ever spoke—but they were enough.

PLUMMER'S INNOCENTS WERE all tracked down and captured or killed. Deputy Marshals were sent in to take over from the vigilantes, although in truth they simply assisted them.

And so Plummer ended up in his old jail. He was thirty-one years old and had killed fifteen men. His Innocents had killed hundreds. His bloody years were about to come to an end.

Out in the office, John Biedler looked as Nathaniel Langford entered.

"Come to watch him swing?" he asked. "He's got about ten minutes."

"I knew from the look on your face that day you were gonna do something," Langford said.

Biedler gave his friend an innocent look.

"You set him up," Langford said. "You knew he wouldn't be able to resist that gold shipment, and you made sure there were enough men there so that somebody would recognize them as his men."

"Those were all miners," Biedler reminded Langford, "not lawmen."

"I know who they were," Langford said. "Vigilantes would not be that organized, John. You did it, but you don't have to admit to it. I only wish I had thought of it. Bannack and Virginia City—and the miners—are finally free of Henry Plummer."

"Want to walk him to the gallows?"

"No," Langford said. "I'll just watch, along with everyone else."

BIEDLER STUCK THE key into the door lock and said to Henry Plummer, "Let's get going."

Plummer showed bravado and accompanied Biedler outside. He turned and looked back at the jail.

"I built that jail," he said.

"I know," Biedler said. "You built the gallows, too. Come on."

They walked to the scaffold, and the miners watched eagerly as Plummer preceded Biedler up the steps. When it came time to put his head through the noose, though, his bravado disappeared. He began to cry and plead for them not to kill him, saying that he had a wife back in Connecticut.

"Shoulda thought of that before, Henry," Biedler said as he sprung the trap door that dropped Henry Plummer to his death.

Ned Christie's Fort

TROY D. SMITH

Troy recently won the WWA Spur Award for Best Paper-back Novel with *Bound for the Promised Land* (iUniverse, 2000). He also wrote *Caleb's Price* (iUniverse, 2001). His short fiction has appeared on the Web on the Read the West site, and has also appeared in *Boot Hill* (Tor, 2002). Here he crafts a riveting story about the long siege of Native American Black Hat Ned Christie's fortlike home.

★

Ned Christie was cleaning his guns when Walkabout, Peek Above, and Bear Paw showed up. The guns were his favorites—a matched set of forty-fours that his father, Watt, had carried in the Civil War. Watt had given them to his young son when he'd returned from his service in the Confederate Army, more than twenty-seven years ago now. Ned, a better gunsmith than even his father, had later converted the cap-and-ball revolvers to cartridge weapons. He was almost finished cleaning the second one when his wife, Nancy, opened the door for his comrades. He reassembled and reloaded it as he spoke with them.

"More?" Ned said. It was as much a grunt as a word.

Peek Above nodded. "Rusk again, and five others."

Ned had lost count of how many posses had assaulted his home in the past few years. Dave Rusk, who had led the last several, was only the latest federal deputy to set his sites on the Cherokee outlaw.

"I'll be waiting for them."

"We'll stay," Walkabout said, although he did not need to utter the words. Ned's friends had always stayed when he needed them. It was one reason he was still alive.

Bear Paw looked out the window. "They'll be here before long," he said. The conversation was held in Cherokee. Every conversation Ned participated in nowadays was in Cherokee, even though he spoke perfect English. He had long ago sworn never again to speak the language of his persecutors.

They waited.

Ned saw the posse members crawling through the rocks long before they announced themselves.

"What do they expect to do with six men?" Bear Paw said, contemptuous. "How stupid."

Ned nodded sharply, and all four Cherokees took their positions at the window slits.

The women were not frightened. Two of his wife's friends had come by, bringing food for the besieged family—one of them had two young children with her.

"You women had best get ready to run," Ned said. "We'll cover you." He had placed the pistols in his belt and levered a shell into his Winchester.

"You may need help reloading," Nancy said. He shook his head.

"I don't want these children getting hurt. Not like my boy did. Get ready to go." She sighed in quiet agreement.

"This is Deputy Marshal Dave Rusk!" The posse's

leader called out. "You'd best surrender now, Christie! This time we're here to fight till it's all over. Till we're dead, if need be."

"If that's what you want," Ned said softly to himself. His only reply to Rusk, though, was the Cherokee death cry—a high-pitched warbling noise, strange to white men's ears, which seemed to bounce around and vibrate like the voice of a ghost.

After that, he let his rifle speak for him.

All four Cherokees unleashed a barrage of gunfire at the posse. The white men were careless, several of them half-raised from their cover in order to stare intently at the house when they should rather have been crouched behind rocks, or hugging the soil. They dropped quickly enough when the bullets began to bounce among them. One of them dropped backward, unnaturally limp; a strangled cry came from another.

The barrage continued, and as it did, the women and children scurried from the house and into the woods. The posse men, wounded numbers in tow, scrambled back through the rocks to regroup at a safer distance. All was quiet for awhile.

"What do you suppose they're up to, besides licking their wounds?" Bear Paw said.

Ned shook his head. How could he predict what a white lawman might be thinking? Little they had done since the whole mess began, five years earlier, had made any sense to him. All he could do, all he could ever do, was use his wiles to defend against them when they came again. He let his good left eye lose its focus for a moment, to see afresh the events which had led to the life he lived now. It was the life of a cornered animal—but he had not always lived in such a manner.

In 1887—only five years ago, though it seemed more like a previous lifetime —Ned Christie had been a member of the Cherokee National Council. He represented the Going Snake district, had done so for two years, and made a good living as a blacksmith. Ned was a member, like his father, of the Keetoowah Society—both a firm believer in, and a vocal spokesman for, Cherokee freedom. That freedom was threatened by the growing number of white settlers on tribal lands. Those so-called "peaceful settlers" were a greater threat, by far, than the outlaws and renegades who had wandered through the Indian Territory since Ned was a child. Ned, like most of his tribesmen, was wary of a situation developing similar to that which had cost his family their Carolina homeland in his father's youth—when Ned's grandmother had died on the Trail of Tears. Now many of those white intruders were calling for statehood, which was only half a step removed from once more stealing Indian lands.

Despite the volatile situation, Ned had led a peaceful life, with a respected position and all that his family needed to flourish. Strange, the changes that can be wrought on a man's life in a single night.

He had been in Tahlequah, twelve miles west of his home. A Senate session was to begin the next morning. He had accompanied his friend John Parris to one of their usual Tahlequah haunts—the home of Jennie Schell, who could always be counted on to provide all the liquor, women, or other entertainments a man could want. The two friends had gotten blind drunk early on and stumbled out into the night, as they had done many times before. They carried with them enough liquor to last awhile. Soon they were joined by their hell-raising friend Bub Trainor and a couple of others.

Ned remembered a party at the nearby Triplett house; he remembered dancing, and giggling girls, and the insistent voice of a fiddle which made a man's feet dance seemingly of their own accord, even when he could no longer feel them. He remembered walking, or rather stumbling, alone on the banks of Tahlequah Creek; he remembered sprawling himself into the luxuriant spring grass, the fiddle still calling from the distance. Then he remembered no more until morning, when he awoke and went back to his hotel room to prepare for the day's session.

One of his fellow Legislators, Daniel Redbird, had approached Ned as he walked out of the hotel. Redbird's face was twisted with worry, and he seemed surprised to see his friend.

"What's wrong with you?" Ned had asked him.

"Are you crazy?" Redbird responded, his voice barely above a whisper. "What do you think you're doing, walking around in broad daylight?"

"I'm on my way to the session. It's why we came here, you know."

Redbird grabbed him by the shirt and pulled him into an alley, pressing him against the wall.

"I got drunk, too," Ned said, "but at least I slept it off."

Redbird shook his head. "I'm not drunk. I wish I was, though. You don't know, do you? You haven't heard. It's a good thing I got to you in time."

"Heard? Heard what?"

"The Light Horse are looking for you. There'll be federal deputies, too, soon. You're wanted for murder."

"Murder? Of who?"

"A deputy United States marshal named Dan Maples. He was here to shut down Jennie Schell's illegal liquor operation, and someone ambushed and killed him late last night."

"What makes them think it was me?"

"Your friend John Parris told them, when they picked him up this morning for questioning. He said he was with you and saw you pull the trigger."

"That's crazy. I was asleep by the creek all night. I never saw any deputy. I don't even have a gun with me."

"Try explaining that to the federal courts."

"I guess I'll have to."

"You really are crazy," Redbird said. "Do you know how many deputies have been killed around here the past few years? Dozens. Judge Parker will have you swinging from a scaffold while you're still trying to tell him your name."

"This is crazy. This is wrong."

"It doesn't matter, Ned. Send a letter to Fort Smith—but don't go there. Don't go anywhere." Redbird's voice lowered another octave. "You're wanted, Ned—*dead or alive*."

Ned took a deep breath. "I'd better head out," he said.

Redbird squeezed his arm. "Good luck, Ned. Your friends will believe you—but the white men are not your friends."

Ned Christie left Tahlequah.

He never knew for sure whether Parris and some of his friends were involved in the killing and had used Ned as a scapegoat, or if Parris had simply panicked when the police singled him out. Maybe he'd thought that the whites would hang the first Indian they found, innocent or guilty, so he had just tossed out another Indian name for them to focus on, in desperation. Either way, Ned's old life was over thanks to Parris. Ned had known somehow, even then—deep in his heart—that it was not just a temporary change. He would never see that old life again.

Ned had gone to his home and started his preparations, even as he told his wife and son what had happened. He cleaned his forty-fours as he spoke to them. He placed guns and ammunition all around the house for easy access. He contacted his friends in the Keetoowah Society—they brought him supplies and volunteered to help.

And he sent a messenger to Fort Smith. In a letter, he asked Judge Parker—the "Hanging Judge" to grant him bail if he turned himself in, so he could be free to look for the real killer. Not surprisingly, Parker refused the request.

The attacks began shortly afterward.

"THEY'RE UP TO something now, all right," Walkabout said, jolting Ned back to the present. Sure enough, the lawmen were crawling through the brush—not presenting themselves as targets, only giving away the fact that they were on the move. They soon gathered behind the cover of a buckboard which sat near the boundary of the rocks and brush and the clearing which lay between them and the Christie house.

Their intentions became clear before long. They hurriedly stuffed dry brush into the bed of the wagon and set fire to it. Then the three of them—the others being either dead or too badly injured to participate, Ned assumed—started pushing the wagon across the clearing. It became apparent that Ned's assumption was wrong. The missing lawmen were in the rocks, and began to lay down covering fire for their comrades.

"They'll not burn this house," Ned said "Not like the other one."

The Cherokees poured gunfire at the blazing wagon, but it continued to move forward. Between rifle shots, Ned could hear the lawmen coughing from the smoke which obscured their destructive vehicle.

They were stubborn, all right. But Ned Christie knew that he was more stubborn by far.

The wagon crashed into the side of the Christie home—which was more a fortress now than a house—and simply broke apart. The scattered pieces, though still aflame, posed little threat. Due to both the thick smoke and their comrades' covering fire, the three deputies were able to scamper away to safety. One of them, though, had been prepared with an alternate weapon. He had tied several sticks of dynamite together into a bundle, forming a crude but very potent bomb. He paused in his flight to light the fuse and hurl the bomb at the house. It hit the wall hard—so hard that the fuse was dislodged from the dynamite, which fell harmlessly to the ground. The fuse burned itself out, as did the broken wagon, and the Cherokee defenders laughed loud and long. The deputies' faces, no doubt, burned as hot as the remnants of their broken plan.

Ned reloaded and settled in, awaiting the next attack.

THE OTHER FIRE, three years ago, had not been amusing. It had almost cost Ned Christie everything. Perhaps it had cost him his soul, for it killed the last vestiges of the amiable, hopeful man he had once been—the handsome man he had once been—and transformed him into something cold. Something ugly.

At that point, the deputies had been attacking his house periodically for two years, always with the same result. They were painfully aware that they were becoming a laughingstock. Ned, on the other hand, had become a hero to his people, and a relentless demon to his enemies—but no one, anywhere, was laughing at him.

The new marshal, Jacob Yoes, decided to send his very best man. Deputy Marshal Heck Thomas was already something of a legend when he came to work for Parker's court, for catching Sam Bass in Texas. One of his first assignments at his new post was Ned Christie. Thomas was determined to bring in the notorious Cherokee outlaw—in pieces, if need be—or know the reason why.

Thomas had a plan for getting past Christie's sentries. He and the four members of his posse slipped through under cover of darkness—individually, from five different directions. They rendezvoused just before dawn at a previously selected spot and prepared to creep toward the house. The Christies slept soundly inside, with no one to help them except the distant sentries.

Thomas's plan was undone by Ned's dogs, who detected the intruders and sent up a boisterous alarm. In no time, Ned Christie had taken a position in a loft window and begun firing his weapons with a speed and fury Thomas had not anticipated. Ned's wife and his son, James, reloaded his weapons as fast as he could empty them.

But Heck Thomas had not gained his reputation for nothing—he was a canny man. He took note of the gun shop beside Christie's home. Knowing it was the man's livelihood, Thomas guessed that the fugitive might rush out to protect its contents. While his men covered him, Thomas rushed to the side of the shop and quickly built a fire. It did not take long for the gun shop to become an inferno. It spread to the house beside it.

While Thomas ran back to his comrades, his guide took

a bullet that shattered his shoulder. Thomas knelt beside the man and bandaged the wound. While he was thus distracted, Ned's wife and son ran from their now burning home and toward the safety of the woods. Thomas, seeing the figures running in the mad light of the house fire, assumed it was Ned and fired at them. Within moments a bullet grazed the deputy's own head.

Ned, recognizing that his home was beyond saving, ran toward the woods which had swallowed up his family. Thomas had recovered from the shock of his own minor wound sufficiently to send a bullet at his quarry.

Ned felt his head explode just as he reached the safety of the brush. He felt himself falling but saw nothing except orange and red, fading rapidly to black. He felt rough arms grabbing him, pulling him. He tried to fight them but could neither gather strength to his arms nor direct them. He felt like he was drowning in blood and mucus.

The arms belonged to his friends, the very sentries Thomas had avoided. They'd heard the shots and rushed to the house as quickly as they could. They scooped up not only Ned, but also his teenaged son, James—when Thomas had fired half-blindly at Ned's running family, his bullet had punctured the boy's lung.

The Christies were spirited away. Thomas and his posse were too crippled by their own injuries to mount an effective pursuit.

James recovered, with relative speed considering the nature of his injury. Ned's wound was another story. The deputy's bullet had crashed into his temple and lodged in his head, blinding his right eye and destroying the structure of his nose.

Ned did not speak for a long time. When he did speak it was in Cherokee, to swear an oath never to utter another word of English—and never to be taken from his Rabbit Trap hills.

Ned sat alone while he recovered—beneath a wooden shelter built on a rocky hill not far from the ashes of his home. From these rocks, he could see for miles in every direction. He sat there, gun in hand, and watched, and waited for them to come back. Sometimes he turned his good eye on the ruins of his home. Sometimes he ran his fingers lightly over the ruins of his face. There was no fiddle music now, no cool grass, no giggling girls. There was Ned Christie, and his war, and the rocks.

The deputies did not return for a long time. If the great Heck Thomas had failed, many people said, it would take an army. Approaching with anything less seemed a waste of time.

When Ned recovered completely, he set about the task of rebuilding his house. This time his designs were different. This time he was not building with an eye to a comfortable home, he was constructing a fort. He put it on a different site, on the opposite side of the valley from his previous one—above a spring. The walls were two logs thick and filled in with sand. There were no windows, only gun slits on the top floor. He lined the inside walls with oak two-by-fours, bulletproofing them even further.

The peace was short-lived. Although Heck Thomas did not come back—not wanting to risk his men's lives in what he believed would be a futile assault—other deputies were willing. Chief among these was Dave Rusk, who had been a member of Thomas's posse on the night Christie's home had been burned. Rusk and his posse attacked the new fort only to be turned away; they prowled through the woods, hoping to run into the outlaw. Ned's old friend Bub Trainor often joined the white men's posse, acting as a guide for them. This betrayal stung Ned deeply.

Rusk had a side business. He'd opened a trading post in the Oaks community, twenty miles north of Tahlequah. Ned decided to let the irksome lawman have a taste of his own medicine. Let him know how it feels to be hunted, to have his home and family threatened. Ned and several companions rode to Oaks and burned down the store. They did not find Rusk, but they did tar and feather a Cherokee clerk they found working for him.

From that moment, every robbery or depredation against white settlers for miles around was blamed on Ned Christie and his gang. The reward for him was increased to a thousand dollars.

And now, once again, here was Rusk—hiding in the brush, trying desperately to regain his reputation by bringing down the Cherokee outlaw that the locals claimed was invincible. There were no more foolhardy attempts at burning or bombing; the posse merely lurked just out of sight, taking potshots at the house.

Ned and his friends did not waste ammunition, even though they had an abundant supply. They fired only often enough to discourage the lawmen from coming closer.

By nightfall, reinforcements arrived—Rusk had about thirty men at his disposal now. It did not matter. Their gunfire had no effect on the fort. Let them charge into the clearing, all thirty of them, and they would die to a man—they all knew it. By dawn they had quietly slipped away, leaving behind their spent shells, their bundle of dynamite with no fuse, and their dried blood on the rocks.

"They won't be back for awhile," Bear Paw said.

"They'll be back," said Ned.

"They won't be back today."

"No."

Walkabout, Peek Above, and Bear Paw stayed for a little while. They slept. Then they left, without words, only with nods and the low grunts of men who do not need words to express their solidarity.

BEAR PAW WAS present three weeks later when the posse returned. Bear Paw had two youths as companions this time, Charlie Soldierhair and Ned's favorite nephew, Arch Wolf.

Arch stepped out of the house at sunrise, water buckets in hand, headed for the spring. He had made it only a few steps when a voice called out in English for him to surrender. Arch tossed the buckets aside and raced back to the house, drawing his revolver as he ran. A hail of bullets followed him. By the time he was pulled into the house, he'd been hit in the arm and the leg.

Ned had already bounded up the stairs and taken up a position at a gun slit. "How's Little Arch?" he called down.

"He's bleeding bad," said Nancy.

"Damn them. I hope they don't murder James." Ned's son had been hunting and had taken the dogs. He was expected back later in the morning.

The shooting began in earnest, from both sides.

A lawman yelled out to the house. It was not Rusk this time, but someone Ned did not know—it didn't matter, they were all the same.

"This is it, Christie. This time we mean business. If you're not going to surrender, at least send out the women and children. We know you have some in there."

"Go with the children, Nancy," Ned called out. Their daughter Mary was in the house, with her infant child, and so was Nancy's little nephew Charley Grease. Charley was only seven years old.

Nancy nodded. She looked up to where her husband knelt, rifle in hand. "I'll. see you later," she said, "when they've gone away again."

"All right, then," he said. "It shouldn't take long."

"Maybe we should take Little Arch with us?" she said.

"No," Arch croaked. "I'm not going anywhere."

"He's safer here than he would be out there," Bear Paw said. Little Arch's wounds had been bound and the bleeding stopped. "If he goes out there, they'll put him in jail or hang him."

"They're coming out," Ned yelled toward the brush in Cherokee. He knew they'd have interpreters.

The women and children passed through the front door. At the last instant, little Charley pulled away from his aunt and ran toward the far inner wall of the house.

"Charley!" said Nancy. "Get out here!"

"No, I'm staying with the men! I'm a man!"

"Aw, we'll take care of him," said Charlie Soldierhair. "If it gets bad we'll stick him in the root cellar."

Charley Grease stayed with the men.

The shooting resumed.

After a few hours, flaming arrows were fired at the house. They had no effect on the sturdy walls and only burned themselves out:

"They sure do go to a lot of trouble for some poor Indians, don't they," Bear Paw said.

That afternoon, the cannon arrived. Nancy's eyes widened when she saw the lawmen setting it up, behind the cover of a large tree. She had been making fun of her captors before that—especially Rusk, who was present after all but was not in charge. Suddenly, it did not seem funny anymore.

"There's still a little child in there," she said, but they did not believe her.

The first blast from the cannon bounced harmlessly off the wall, leaving only a mark. Arch made his way upstairs and took up a weapon—the Cherokees concentrated their fire on the tree which shielded the cannon.

Little Charley was sent to the cellar.

By twilight, thirty-eight cannonballs had been fired at Christie's fort. Little damage had been done. The lawmen decided to double the powder charge—it was too much, and on the thirty-ninth shot the cannon exploded. The tree, by that time, had been shot to splinters by the Cherokee rifle fire.

James Christie was arrested when he tried to slip to the house with more ammunition.

When it got dark, two deputies were able to creep close enough to set dynamite charges around the house. Just before daylight, almost twenty-four hours after the attack had begun, the fuse was lit.

Ned Christie's fort was rocked to its foundations. One corner collapsed. A fire broke out and swiftly turned into a conflagration. A Cherokee interpreter made a final call for the outlaws to surrender.

Ned Christie answered with his death song. It wailed above the roar of the flames, and floated on the smoke, and echoed off the rocks. It vibrated in the bones of Nancy Christie.

The Cherokee warriors stood among the licking flames, the strangling smoke, and fired their weapons through the collapsed wall of the fort. Responding bullets thunked into the walls around them.

The burning roof collapsed. A timber struck Charlie Soldierhair and knocked him to the floor, setting his clothes ablaze. He rolled. Another section set Little Arch's hair on fire, and his head ignited like a torch. Bear Paw beat it out with his hat. Ned hoped that his wife's little nephew would be safe in the cellar—there had not been time to get him, and the lawmen would have shot anything that ran from the house anyhow.

"This is it," Ned cried out to his companions. "Run for the woods!"

They made their break, in separate directions. Charlie Soldierhair, horribly burned, stumbled only a few feet before he collapsed to the ground in agony. He was placed under arrest when the smoke cleared and the lawmen found him. Little Arch broke free but was captured later— he had lost all his hair in the fire. Bear Paw escaped in the smoke. The lawmen never even knew that he had been present.

Young Charley Grease was found burned to a crisp in the ruins of the collapsed house.

Ned Christie ran straight at his oppressors, firing his Winchester over and over again. He appeared from the smoke like a ghost, screaming a war cry; he was the spirit of his people made flesh, his blood a wet vestige of the suffering of generations.

He felt the bullets ripping through him. They jerked him. He felt the weight of his father's guns on his hips, pulling him down to the ground, into the ground, and he tightened his grip on his rifle.

He felt light, then, unburdened—and for a moment, he felt free.

Eight months later, James Christie was found shot dead, his body decapitated.

A quarter of a century later, a timid blacksmith came forward—near the end of his life—to say that he had witnessed Bub Trainor murdering Deputy Marshal Dan Maples that night in Tahlequah. He had long been afraid to admit it, fearing reprisals from Trainor's friends.

Ned Christie's body, before burial, was tied to the front door of his ruined fort and put on display in Fort Smith, for the entertainment of the public. Dan Maples's brother emptied a revolver into the corpse.

Grave Dancer

LORI VAN PELT

Lori is the only other author to also appear in *White Hats*, along with Rod Miller. Her choices have been unusual, which is why I chose to include her in both volumes. She picked as her White Hat lawyer Willis Van Devanter, who eventually became the first United States Supreme Court Justice from Wyoming. Here—while Tom Horn appears in the story—she actually tells about J. P. Julien, the man who invented the trapdoor mechanism used for the first time on the gallows used to hang Tom Horn.

Her work has appeared in *White Hats* (Berkley, 2002), *American West: Twenty New Stories from the Western Writers of America* (Forge, 2001), and the forthcoming *Hot Biscuits*. She has also published *Dreams and Schemers: Profiles from Carbon County, Wyoming's Past* (High Plains Press, 1999), a nonfiction collection; the title of which is fairly self explanatory. She lives with her husband in Wyoming.

★

The prisoner stepped onto the platform. His cowboy boots made dull thuds against the wood. All time stopped. A stifling silence overcame the spectators. Perhaps we all held our breath.

Tom Horn had, a full year before, been convicted of murdering young Willie Nickell. In a few short moments, he'd pay for the crime with his own life. He'd been a stock detective, someone ranchers paid to eliminate cattle rustlers. His could have been an upright profession, but Horn's sinister action reduced it to a despicable business.

On this late November morning of 1903, I stood near the gallows at the Laramie County Jail with my friend, J. P. Julien, one of Cheyenne's fine architects. He designed the special trapdoor mechanism for the gallows that would prevent another man from touching Horn. A perfect absolution of guilt for those about to commit a murder themselves, and an improvement over the usual method of several men standing in a circle and all pulling ropes at the same instant. With that method, no one knew whose tug sent the condemned to his death because all had the same opportunity. Julien's design eliminated the need for human contact. Death, when it came, would be as much of a surprise for the hangmen as for the hanged.

Horn took another step forward. This time his boot struck wood and rang hollow. Another sound, the sound of water dripping in precise increments, rose from beneath the platform. Julien took a deep breath. We waited.

Horn's death would ease the fears running rampant in the city about his possible escape from jail. Indeed, he had tried it once before and failed. Human helpers, it appeared, assisted even the damned. Suddenly Horn turned, shifting his accusing gaze to me.

I shivered and awoke with a start, soaked in sweat. My nightmare would come true today. Horn would die. Julien's mechanism would trigger the platform's release, dropping the condemned man to hell. And I would attend the execution, watching and waiting beside Julien. What had I gotten myself into?

I FIRST MET James Julien at the recent Halloween masquerade ball at Cheyenne's Keefe Hall. Laughter and the thrum of conversation filled the ballroom that evening. Many of the conversations revolved around the fate of prisoner Tom Horn, languishing in the county jail, and most of them were most uncomplimentary to the condemned man.

"Horn did it. He himself said so. Hang him and get 'er done," said one man, pouring himself a glass of punch.

"There's talk the governor will decide," said another. "Silly to involve Chatterton, if you ask me."

"Damn legal folderol," said the first man. "What a waste! The fellow's been put up all high and mighty by the county jail for a whole year. They should have hung him right after the trial and been done with it."

"Think he'll escape?"

"Well, there's a damn fine chance, ain't there? He tried it once. He's probably got some patsy on the inside who'll manage it for him. And we know he's got friends on the outside, that's for darn sure."

I moved closer, hoping to enter the conversation. But the men stopped talking, as if they suddenly realized no one here appeared as he was. They might have said too much in front of a costumed man—someone who could be anyone—who could turn against them. Someone who might be a Horn ally. That my costume disguised me as writer Edgar Allan Poe undoubtedly contributed to their uneasiness.

I turned from the punch bowl, intending to take a glass to my wife, Amy. Instead, I found myself face-to-face with William Shakespeare.

"Hello," I said. Shakespeare gruffly returned the greeting. From behind him, Amy, dressed as Poe's child love, Annabel Lee, spoke.

"Samuel, I'd like you to meet Mr. Julien. He's an architect. He tells me he has need of an assistant."

"Mr. Julien," I said, extending my hand. He extended his own, "Mr. Richards. Your wife tells me you've recently attended university."

"Please, call me Samuel." I explained my meager qualifications. Hiring on with an architect was a position I had dreamed of obtaining, and Julien's reputation preceded him. He had designed many of the Union Pacific Railroad depot buildings, and to my mind, Cheyenne's was exquisite. I had a feeling I could learn much from this man. "If I may inquire, what project are you working on?"

Julien's voice was deep but not loud. I strained to listen.

"Your timing could not be better, young man," he said. "I've embarked on a project of the utmost importance, and would need your help to continue with other projects while I'm preoccupied. Those projects involve some drafting work, and perhaps after a time, you could be moved more into designing. Would you be interested?"

I could not see his face, as he wore the mask of the Bard. But his tone sounded genuine.

"Yes, Mr. Julien. I'd be quite interested."

"Come tomorrow morning, promptly at eight. We'll talk about your duties then."

"Thank you, Mr. Julien."

He lifted his mask. "My name is James," he said, smiling and revealing a thin, hollow-cheeked, square-jawed countenance and bright blue eyes. "But most people call me Julien. Suit yourself."

I revealed my own face, certain my enthusiasm shone through my skin. My face was rounder, and I hoped my brown eyes conveyed as much intelligence as his did.

"A pleasure meeting you, Samuel," he said, departing and mixing in again with the other party-goers. He walked with a slight limp.

"Oh, Sam," Amy said. She had come to stand close to me and we embraced. "What a magical evening. I'm thrilled for you. Mama will be so pleased." She had not removed her youthful mask, but in the mystical green depths of her eyes I saw her delight.

"Thank you, darling," I said, returning her hug and then handing her a glassful of punch. Her mother, Mrs. Albert Alexander, known to friends as Elizabeth, and to me—her son-in-law—as Mrs. Alexander, would indeed be happy to learn I had finally found employment. Perhaps Amy and I could soon move into a home of our own and release her mother from the burden of keeping us. "Would you permit me this dance to celebrate?" I asked.

We swirled with the other dancers, moving to the lilting music of Cheyenne's mandolin club members. I held my delicate wife in my arms, happiness coursing through my body. We waltzed amidst other cloaked couples—a knight in shining armor held a damsel in distress, and Marie Antoinette bowed to a skeleton. Assorted ghosts and goblins and others dressed in costumes from the simple to ornate filled the floor.

Some of the dancers revealed their faces, seeking air and relief from their hot coverings and from what someone called "this tiresome charade." Some I recognized from their laughter and others from overheard snippets of conversation. Amidst the frivolity, I noticed another costume. The Grim Reaper, carrying his scythe, stood near the refreshments table. He played his part magnificently. He stood at his post for most of the evening. He never revealed his identity. He did not dance.

THE NEXT MORNING I walked to Julien's residence. I passed a livery stable. The reeking odor of burning flesh assaulted me. I ventured a peek inside the dark depths of the stable. The farrier fitted a shoe to a horse. Though I knew he'd dipped the heated metal into a bucket of water to cool it down before fitting it, the iron remained hot enough to burn the hoof. By the burn mark, the farrier could ensure the shoe would fit properly before he nailed it in place. The bay horse appeared undisturbed by the process. I could not say the same for myself. The bitter stench from the smoke made my eyes water. My lungs cried for clear air.

The farrier stood, waving the hot horseshoe in the air. "Mornin' to you," he said. I returned the wave and walked on, ever more appreciative of the opportunity to do work I enjoyed. I hoped that the acrid scent would dissipate before I entered Julien's office, and that the costumes I carried in a box to return to Mrs. Clark, the costumer, would not be sullied by the odor. I planned to return them to her that evening.

Once inside his comfortable home on the corner of Seventeenth and Reed streets, I relaxed. Julien greeted me warmly, and introduced me to another Cheyenne architect, William DuBois, who had dropped by to invite Julien to a luncheon.

Julien's wife, Sarah, served us coffee in the dining

room. After she departed, he explained my tasks. Sketching buildings was one of the most enjoyable assignments I'd had at the university, and Julien could put me to work promptly with similarly pleasing duties.

"And you? If I may, what is the project that you are working on?"

"Oh, Julien's gallows," said Mr. DuBois.

Julien winced. He stood with difficulty and held out his hand. "Thanks, Bill. We'll talk later. I'll plan on that luncheon Saturday." Thus curtly dismissed, Mr. DuBois excused himself and left.

I looked into my employer's eyes, confused. My inquisitive glance expressed my question with no need for words. Julien returned to his seat.

"I am to work on the gallows upon which Tom Horn will hang," he said steadily.

"Did you design them?"

"The gallows? No." He sat across the table from me. "Frankly, the idea came from another prisoner. A man incarcerated in the Colorado State Penitentiary in Canon City," he said. Julien tapped the fingers of his right hand against the table. The slow rhythmical movement regulated his words. "This is not the first time the design has been used here." The galloping sound of his fingers filled the silence.

"I see," I responded. "But what does this have to do with you, then?"

He resumed his unhurried explanation. "The Canon City man told Sheriff Kelly of the workings of the gallows prior to the execution of Charlie Miller here a decade or so ago. I merely refined the design with trapdoors by making a trigger mechanism."

I grimaced at his choice of words. In effect, he was

telling me he'd refined a mechanism to "pull the trigger" and kill condemned men.

"Then why did Mr. DuBois refer to it as your gallows?"

Julien cleared his throat. He explained that he had assisted Sheriff Kelly with erecting the gallows prior to Miller's execution. Because of that, some people had referred to the instrument of death as "Julien's gallows."

"A nasty, mistaken term. Should the mechanism operate properly, as in the past, there would be no need for my name to be associated with the gallows at all."

"But an architect designing a gallows?"

"You say that as if it's an unpleasant thing," he answered, I thought somewhat gruffly. Our conversation caused my stomach to quiver. "It is a design like any other."

I disagreed but could not bring myself to say the words aloud to my new employer. A gallows was not like any other thing. A gallows was a weapon. Shocked that a fine architect such as Julien would take it upon himself to design any part of a weapon when, in my mind, he was a builder, a creator of gathering places for people to live in and dance in and admire, I again spoke.

"You didn't build the whole thing?"

"No," he said. "I hope, by the use of the mechanism, to eliminate the need for any of the hangmen to touch the condemned. That way, no one man need feel responsible for killing another under such dire circumstances."

I stared at him. He stopped tapping the table with his fingers. How could he turn an object used for a morbid purpose into a good thing?

"Did it work?"

"For Miller?"

"Yes."

He pursed his lips. "Reasonably well."

I did not inquire as to his meaning. My imagination supplied numerous distasteful possibilities of its own.

"You are disappointed," he said quietly.

"Yes," I admitted.

"The sheriff has requested my assistance," he said. "I'll not go back on my word."

"I respect that," I said.

He nodded. "Samuel, I would not ask you to take upon yourself any duties you would find distasteful. Should you decide to work for me, I will not give you any task that I myself would not do. The decision is yours."

"I would be working on building designs?"

"Yes."

I took a deep breath. I needed the job. "Then I will stay." A relieved look swept his face of the taut lines that had covered it moments earlier. The rest of the day passed quickly and I accomplished the tasks set before me with ease. But our conversation haunted me.

Had it not been for that strange discussion, I would not have ventured into the realm of Carrie Caspar, spiritualist. But because she was located next door to Mrs. Clark's costume shop, I chanced a visit. Carrie Caspar's sign announced she appeared in Cheyenne for only a brief time, encouraging customers to take advantage of the "once-in-a-lifetime opportunity."

My savaged spirit needed comfort, and though I looked upon her field as nothing more than trickery, curiosity impelled me to enter the room she'd rented. At the very least, I might gain a laugh from the experience. And I felt in dire need of laughter that afternoon.

As soon as I entered the darkened room, Carrie appeared. She was a beautiful woman, dark-haired and dark-eyed, with skin the color of sanded oak. She was nothing like the hag I'd pictured in my mind. Her eyes bored into my own. I felt as if she knew all about me.

"What is it you have come to see Carrie about, dear sir?"

Her voice had a bell-like quality.

"Tell me my future," I said, keeping my words brisk. She nodded, motioning for me to sit across from her at a table covered with a heavy black cloth. At the center of the table was a clear glass ball resting on a stand. *Here we go*, I thought, wondering what unearthly topics she'd choose.

Her eyes narrowed. She reached across the table for my hand. She took it in her own and held it. My hand had cooled from the outside temperature. She held it for an uncomfortably long time. I found this woman extraordinarily beautiful. *I should be home with Amy,* I thought. *For goodness sake, what brought me here?*

Carrie's eyes popped open. She looked directly at me. "You will assist in the achievement of another's dream. I see dancing, a waltz, perhaps?" I smiled, recalling the masquerade ball. That wasn't difficult for her to discern. The ball was held last night, a fact she might have gleaned from the costumer next door. She closed her eyes again.

"I see bricks and stones and wood. A stream? And something tumbling, crashing. . . ." When she opened her eyes, she retained her hold on my hand. We peered at one another across the table. I feared pulling my gaze from hers. Gooseflesh tingled across my arms. She shivered.

She abruptly released my hand. "Do you feel that?"

I nodded, afraid to speak.

"You sparked something very deep. I feel chilled. Please go." She closed her eyes.

I left a small sum on the table and walked outside, trying to shrug off the strange feeling of dread that overcame me. I didn't succeed. Served me right for dabbling in fantasy.

When I arrived at the Alexander mansion, though, my young wife greeted me affectionately and dispelled my anxiety. At dinner, she recounted her day.

As we prepared to eat dessert, an apple pie, she brought me a brandy snifter. "You might enjoy this, dear Sam," she said.

"What's the occasion? My new position?"

Mrs. Alexander, dressed in her customary lace and finery, held her own brandy snifter aloft. "That is indeed worthy of honor," she said with asperity. I could tell from her tone she doubted I would ever make anything of myself.

Amy frowned. "Yes, it is, Mother, but I have even better news."

"What is it, Amy?"

She practically squealed with delight. "I've seen Dr. Johnston this morning."

"And he pronounced you in good health?"

Suddenly shy, she kneaded the tablecloth with long, slender fingers. "Yes," she said, "and—" She hesitated.

"Well, tell us," her mother urged.

"Samuel, you and I, well, we—" She stopped and looked at me. "We're to have a baby. I'm with child."

I placed my snifter on the table and rushed to hold her in my arms. I pulled her to me and kissed her full on the lips. "That's wonderful news, my darling."

Mrs. Alexander sipped her brandy. "Wonderful," she said in a clipped tone, indicating she herself was uncertain.

★

THE DAYS PASSED quickly. Julien found my sketches pleasing, and I had even gathered enough courage to show him a few of my original designs. His comments were encouraging. Despite myself, I had grown interested in his trigger mechanism. Governor Chatterton had not excused Horn. The execution was less than a week away. The townspeople talked of nothing else but Horn, his villainous deed, and his upcoming punishment.

The condemned man's fate and Julien's tool even entered conversations that occurred between my wife and I in the privacy of our bedroom. Amy and I often read aloud to each other before falling asleep. I liked to read the stories of Poe. Among my favorites of his works were "The Raven" and "Annabel Lee."

I began reciting "The Raven" from memory, arriving at the line, "Deep into the darkness peering," when Amy said, "Please stop, Samuel, stop."

"What is it, dear?"

She climbed into bed beside me and rolled to face the wall. "I do wish you were not so enamored of Mr. Poe. Could you read Shakespeare instead?"

"Certainly, Amy. I will read anything you like."

"Shakespeare didn't dally with death like Poe does," she said. "Poe finds the subject too impressive for my taste."

I picked up a volume of Shakespeare's work. Knowing she referred to the romances penned by the bard, I did not retort that Shakespeare consorted with death himself in works such as *Hamlet* and *Macbeth*. Even *Romeo and Juliet* flirted with death, but the argument would have been lost on my pretty wife. I began to read a sonnet, the first I came upon. "To me, fair friend," I intoned, "you never can be old. For as you were when first your eye I eyed, such seems your beauty still."

"Thank you, Samuel." She sighed heavily. "I suppose I'm not interested in reading tonight."

"What is the matter, love?"

She turned her face toward mine. "Oh, Samuel. I wish you'd leave this ghastly business with Mr. Julien behind."

Astonished, I said, "He pays me well, Amy. I thought you wanted me to have a job."

She frowned. "Yes, but I never dreamed you'd be involved in a man's death."

"I'm not."

"You are. Scarcely a moment passes when you don't mention something to do with Julien or his mechanism or the gallows. I rarely hear of your efforts with buildings."

I blinked. "I hadn't realized . . ." I began, but again she interrupted.

"I fear your preoccupation with death is harmful. Not for yourself only but for our child as well."

I touched her cheek with my palm. "But I'm working for those who live," I said gently. "I have been working on office buildings, and Julien likes my designs, so the chances for future work appear bright." She covered my hand with her own. I continued, "Julien's mechanism is a force for good, Amy. It will help the hangmen. It removes the necessity of the hangmen touching the condemned. By not touching the prisoner, they will feel less like murderers themselves." I remembered Julien's argument for that same good—a position I disagreed with—on the first day of my employment.

"The condemned? The prisoner? You can't even bring yourself to discuss the man as a human. And hangmen are murderers. What has happened to you, Samuel?"

"Hangmen are not murderers, Amy," I retorted. "They are doing the job society set upon them. And I'm doing my job as well." I found it difficult to keep my voice low. If I raised my voice, Mrs. Alexander in her bedroom next door would surely hear our argument.

"Well, Samuel, I disagree. Anyone who has any part in another's death is, to me, a murderer."

"And myself, then?"

She stared at me. "Decide for yourself."

"Its useless to argue. You'll never understand," I said, pulling the bedcovers tighter.

"Samuel, I pray daily for understanding. And I've been praying lately for God to understand you and not punish you for your part in this."

"You introduced me to Julien yourself."

"Yes, I did, but . . ." She shook her head. "Oooh," she said, for she could not argue with my logic. "Samuel, I cannot stand your erratic behavior."

Angered by her own unusual outburst, I said, "Perhaps you'd prefer I stay at a hotel. I could obtain lodging at the Inter Ocean until this business is concluded."

She did not speak for long moments.

"Amy?" I asked.

I heard her sigh deeply. "Yes, perhaps you should."

A gray overcast sky covered the city the next morning. Stunned by our disagreement, I had taken a room at the Inter Ocean before walking to work. The weather apparently dispirited Julien as well.

When I arrived, he said, "What if it doesn't work?"

"The mechanism will work," I assured him, surprised by his unexpected lack of confidence. The hairs prickled on the back of my neck at providing reassurance about an instrument of death.

"It's been pointless," he ranted. "A pointless effort that's cost me time and money and perhaps my career."

"No, Julien. Your work has not been pointless," I argued. "At the very least, the hangmen will feel better about their unpleasant duty. And perhaps this will better the city in some way." I paused. I did not know how. "Thank God the whole sordid affair will be finished tomorrow."

He looked at me as if I'd lost my senses. "Samuel," he said, "it will never be finished." The light of his blue eyes dimmed. He turned back to the window, watching the wind pluck brown leaves from the lone cottonwood as gray clouds obscured the sky.

We lunched at the Inter Ocean. The whistle of the noon train jarred me. Travelers scurrying to eat and return for the train's departure crowded the dining room. Conversation proved difficult amidst the sounds of dishes clattering and the steady hum of others talking. We didn't find speaking necessary that day. The plan was in place. Julien would test the gallows that evening. I agreed to assist.

I had vowed to find another job, to steer my mind away from death, as Amy wished. I had intended to tell him of my decision to find other employment while we ate, but I did not. I was drawn to Julien and his queer task like steel seeks a magnet. I could not bear to tell him on this day when he appeared so distraught.

A waiter dropped a plate. The white disk slid to the floor and then spun and bounced back and forth like a child's top. To the waiter's amazement—and our own—the plate did not break. He stooped to retrieve it and dropped another. That plate shattered. The waiter whispered a curse.

★

JULIEN TESTED HIS device through macabre rehearsal. For this final experiment, the sheriff and deputies at the jailhouse lent assistance. They used three fifty-pound bags of flour to approximate the weight of the condemned man. The noose was attached to the flour sacks. Two deputies, careful not to touch the trapdoors themselves, placed the sacks there, on the spot where Horn would meet his fate tomorrow. The wood creaked under the weight.

I heard the lonely sound of dripping water. Could Horn hear it, too? His cell was located on the second floor of the jailhouse, near the place where we congregated. A canvas curtain masked our presence, but surely the muffled sounds of human activity carried to the prisoner.

Julien, though he knew his mechanism functioned properly through the commencement of the annoying noise, appeared anxious. He would not be satisfied until the trap sprung and the flour sacks fell.

The weight of the filled sacks had released the plug on the water can located across a board from a counterbalance in the room beneath us. When the can dispersed enough water to make it weigh less than the counterbalance, the counterweight would drop, causing a rope to run through a pulley. The opposite end of the rope was attached to a hinged four-by-four beam supporting the trapdoors. When the counterweight dropped, the rope would tug the hinge, opening the trapdoors.

If the gallows malfunctioned, the only harm would be a little extra misery extended to the condemned. Since he was a killer himself, some folks argued that didn't matter. He'd get what he deserved for murdering that fourteen-year-old boy.

Yet I knew it would matter to Julien. He'd feel remorse.

Although his attention settled upon the hangmen, Julien didn't want to cause the prisoner extra pain.

We jumped when the trapdoors sprang. Flour dust rose from the dangling flour sacks. The squeaking sound of the doors swinging on their hinges accompanied the grainy white mist accumulating in the air. We did not speak but set to cleaning up our mess. I felt keenly aware of the living, breathing man doubtless considering his fate in the nearby cell. Horn had been trapped between life and death for the past many months. Tomorrow, the doors between would finally swing.

EXECUTION DAY DAWNED gray and dreary. A howling wind added to my unease. A few moments before eleven o'clock in the morning, Tom Horn's muffled footsteps sounded on the platform. Already the proceedings differed from my nightmare. Horn's hands and feet were bound. One of the men who had assisted with our test the night before placed the noose about his neck and covered his face with a black hood.

Julien stood beside me. His expression was unreadable. Numerous spectators filled the room. I recognized the farrier and a few others.

Charlie and Frank Irwin, friends of Horn's, launched into a loud rendition of "Life's Railway to Heaven," at the doomed man's request. Following the musical interlude, stifling silence ensued.

Despite Julien's good intentions, despite his worry over the feelings of the hangmen, a human factor interceded this day. Horn, with feet bound and head cloaked, could not step onto the trapdoors himself. Two men, Sheriff Ed

Smalley and T. Joe Cahill, lifted the prisoner to his proper position, then stepped back abruptly.

"What's the matter," Horn said, "getting nervous I might tip over?"

Julien bit his lip. His skin drew taut against his face like the canvas of a tent sucked inside out by the wind. His plan had failed. He had not intended men to intervene.

Water dripped for thirty-one seconds. Everyone started when the trapdoors sprang. Horn fell. His head and shoulders dangled within our view. His body turned away from spectators as if taking this death journey was a private matter. Seventeen minutes later, the killer was pronounced dead of strangulation.

Julien whispered, "Deep into that darkness peering, long I stood there wondering, fearing. . . ." His voice cracked.

I finished Poe's verse, saying softly, "Doubting, dreaming dreams no mortal ever dared to dream before."

"IT IS DONE," Sheriff Smalley proclaimed to the noisy crowd gathered outside the jail. Julien and I stood among them, having left the building together. Reporters clamored for more details. To my mind, the sheriff said all that was necessary, but he patiently answered their questions, providing all the grisly particulars.

"On Julien's gallows?" one shouted.

The sheriff nodded, sealing Julien's fate. This single incident was so morbid that his connection with it doomed his magnificent building designs to obscurity.

I saw the pained look appear before Julien could reset his face into a more pleasant expression. What he had most hoped to avoid had come to pass. His name would be forever linked with executioners' tools.

"I have failed," he said to me, a somber expression casting an ashen color over his face. "I have done no more than dance on the grave of a condemned man, a fact for which I will be always remembered."

"Julien," I said, touching his arm. He pulled away from me and disappeared into the crowd. Despondent, I pushed through the crowd and emerged in the street. Julien was nowhere to be seen.

A touch on my own arm startled me. I whirled, discovering the tearful visage of my wife.

"Amy! What are you doing here? You'll catch a chill."

"Waiting for you, of course, Samuel. I couldn't let you suffer through this alone."

I took her elbow and steered her through the dispersing crowd. Echoing the sheriff's words spoken only moments before, I said quietly, "It is done."

Amy pressed her lips together and nodded. She did not speak. We walked together in silence, the flat sound of our footsteps marking time. By unspoken agreement we turned toward Ferguson Street, where her mother lived. Amy put her arm in my own. We walked the rest of the way alone. The sun had broken through the clouds with enough warmth to heat the wrought-iron gate and melt an icicle clinging to its spikes. The icicle dripped with measured precision, methodically elongating its own form and saturating a pile of dirty snow below.

★

Author's Note: *Speak the name "Julien" in Wyoming, and it's likely listeners will first remember him in connection with* the gallows. But Julien, a Civil War veteran, arrived in Cheyenne, Wyoming following the war and for a few years was the only architect and contractor in the city. He built Cheyenne's first Union Pacific station and others along the railroad route east to Omaha and served as a consulting architect on the Wyoming State Capitol. Julien's version of the gallows was used for the Laramie County executions of Charlie Miller and Tom Horn, and for nine other male inmates at the Wyoming State Penitentiary during the years 1912 through 1933.

Julien Horn (who was hanged for the murder of Willie Nickell), his wife, Sarah, and architect William DuBois, as well as Dr. George Johnston, the Irwin Brothers, Governor Fenimore Chatterton, Sheriff Ed Smalley, and T. Joe Cahill, were all real persons living in Cheyenne during the time of this fictional story. Other characters, with the exception of Poe and Shakespeare, are fictional.

Readers interested in a detailed description of the gallows should read Larry R. Brown's "Just Ice," *True West*, June 1997. For more information on Tom Horn, consult Chip Carlson's book, Tom Horn: "Killing men is my specialty . . ." (Cheyenne: Beartooth Corral, 1991). The Wyoming State Archives also houses some information on both Horn and Julien.